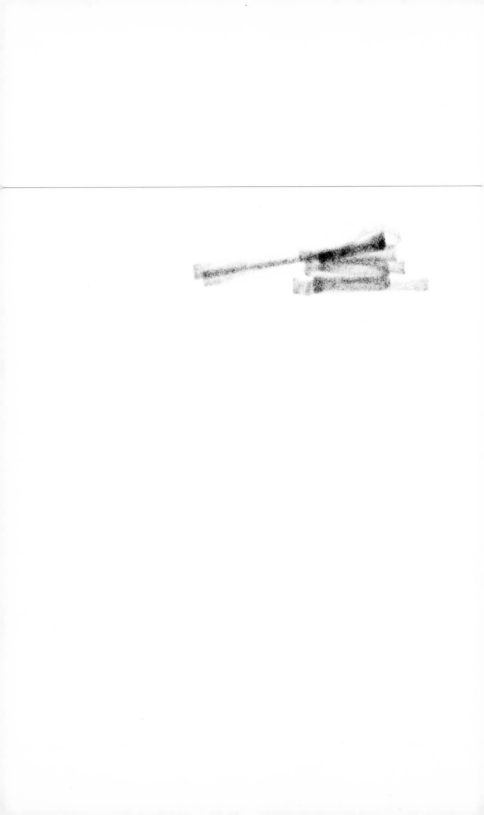

A FAMILY AFFAIR

This Large Print Book carries the
Seal of Approval of N.A.V.H.

A FAMILY AFFAIR

FERN MICHAELS

WHEELER PUBLISHING
A part of Gale, Cengage Learning

GALE
CENGAGE Learning·

Farmington Hills, Mich • San Francisco • New York • Waterville, Maine
Meriden, Conn • Mason, Ohio • Chicago

GALE
CENGAGE Learning®

LIBRARY OF CONGRESS CATALOGING-IN-PUBLICATION DATA

Michaels, Fern.
  A family affair / Fern Michaels. — Large print edition.
    pages cm (Wheeler publishing large print hardcover)
    ISBN 978-1-4104-6658-7 (hardcover) — ISBN 1-4104-6658-2 (hardcover)
    1. Dancers—Fiction. 2. Princes—Fiction. 3. Families—Fiction. 4. Life change events—Fiction. 5. Large type books. I. Title.
PS3563.I27F357 2014
813'.54—dc23   2014010068

Published in 2014 by arrangement with St. Martin's Press, LLC

Printed in the United States of America
1 2 3 4 5 6 7 18 17 16 15 14

A FAMILY AFFAIR

■ ■ ■ ■

PART ONE

■ ■ ■ ■

CHAPTER 1

The klieg lights seem extra-bright, way too hot. Two minutes to go. Please, God, let me get off this stage in one piece. The headdress seems heavier than usual. Eighty seconds. Kick high. Twirl. Smile. Sixty seconds. Kick. Twirl. Smile. Show those teeth. Forget the sweat dripping into your eyes. You know the routine. You can do it blindfolded. I'm burning up. Thirty seconds. Hold it together. You can do this. Ten seconds. One last kick. Follow, Connie. Then you can collapse.

The music reached a tumultuous crescendo, and she was off the stage, the Vegas crowd enthusiastically shouting their approval of the chorus line's performance. Her long legs were so wobbly, she could barely stand. Connie reached for her.

"Trish, you okay? Your timing was off, but I don't think anyone else noticed. God, girl, what's wrong? Here, let me take your headdress. Trish, you're burning up! Girls, come

9

here. Something's wrong with Trish!"

The chorus line swarmed around Trish just as the floor gofer, a young guy named Ernie, tried to fight his way through the scantily clad women. He was waving a folded note at Trish and fought to be heard above the clamoring voices surrounding her.

"That guy who's been here every night this week asked me to give you this." He thrust out the hand holding the note. "It's a note asking you to have a drink with him, and that's a thousand-dollar bill folded inside it. A thousand-dollar bill! Do you know how rare those are? The guy is a *prince.* That means he's royalty!" Ernie screamed, his freckles lighting up like mini Christmas lights.

"Prince, king, who the hell cares? Get out of here, Ernie," Connie shouted. "Can't you see that something is wrong with Trish?"

Trish sucked in her breath as she felt a cool cloth being run over her face and neck. It felt wonderful. Because Trisha Holiday was a kind and caring person, she struggled to speak. "Give it back, Ernie, and tell him, 'Thank you but no thanks.'"

"But it's a thousand-dollar bill, Trish! Are you sure?"

"She's sure. Now, get out of this room. We need to get changed," someone shouted,

10

menace ringing in her voice.

Ernie ran for the door, his spiked hair moving in his own breeze.

"I'm okay, girls. Just help me get out of this costume. Guess I got that flu bug that some of you had. Seriously, I'm okay. I'm going to go home to bed. I'll drink lots of juice and take some aspirin. That's what you all said you did."

"You're running a high fever, and you're flushed," someone shouted.

Someone else held out an aspirin bottle. A third chorus girl handed Trish a glass of water. She gulped at the little white pills as she peeled off her heavy costume. Someone took it from her hands and hung it up alongside her headdress. She struggled to pull on an oversize sweatshirt over her head, but in the end she needed help. Sweatpants followed. She felt someone slipping her sneakers on her feet, and someone else tied them. A puffy down jacket was placed around her shoulders. Her purse was thrust into her hands.

Time to go home to her cozy apartment. "Thanks, girls. I'm okay now. Tell Nathan I don't think I'll be at work tomorrow. God, he's going to fire me! He gave me such a hard time when I asked for a week off to go home to help see my sister through her divorce. I need this job."

"Don't worry about it, Trish. We'll threaten a walkout if he pulls something like that," Connie said. Trish heard murmurs of agreement backing Connie up. They were a great bunch of girls, and she loved every one of them.

"I think you should get a room here at the casino," Connie said. "Or I'll drive you home."

Trish shrugged into the down jacket. Somebody else pulled up the zipper. "Like I can afford to stay here! Get real, Connie! I can make it home on my own. I feel better now that I'm out of that heavy costume. Thanks for the offer, though. I'll see you when I see you."

Trish was out of the dressing room and walking on wobbly legs. She was burning up and chilly at the same time, and she wasn't even outside yet. Thank God she had a nearby parking space. She crossed her fingers that her old Honda Civic would start up and not fail her. Then she crossed her fingers again that the heater would work. It was all she could do to pull open the heavy stage door, but she managed to do so by pulling with both hands, using her shoulder to hold it in place. As she stepped outside, the door slammed shut as a blast of arctic air assaulted her.

Trish could see her car and the expanse of asphalt she had to traverse to get to it. She could do it. She was aware of a small group of people to her right. God, what if she got mugged? She almost laughed at the prospect. She had forty-six dollars in her purse and a single credit card that had nothing left on it. She stepped forward and felt the wind buffeting her as she struggled to get to her car.

She was less than two feet from her Honda when her knees buckled and she collapsed to the ground. Fortunately, the thick, puffy jacket helped to break her fall. She heard voices, felt herself being picked up, and heard someone say something in a language she didn't understand.

Strangely enough, she felt safe in the arms holding her. She was being carried. *Somewhere? Hospital? Back to the casino?* The conversation surrounding her sounded agitated by then. The people were arguing — she could tell that by the tone, even though she could not understand the words they said. One voice, a male voice, was higher. It was a nice voice. A concerned voice. A voice of authority.

Trish struggled to open her eyes, but they felt like they had lead weights on them. She looked up into the handsomest face she'd ever seen in her life. "Please don't hurt me," she whispered. She wondered if the handsome man had heard what she had said. Or did she just think she had said those words aloud?

"I would never hurt you, Trisha Holiday."

They were in an elevator, and the voices were still jabbering in that strange language. They, whoever they were, weren't going to hurt her. At that moment, she didn't care what happened next. All she wanted was a warm bed, with warm blankets wrapped tightly around her, so she could sleep. Sleep. Until her fever broke. Beyond that, she just didn't make herself care.

Prince Malik Mohammed kept up a running conversation with his security detail. "Is the doctor standing by? Is the room ready for this young lady?"

"Yes and yes, Prince, but this is a very foolhardy thing you are doing. Your father would not approve. The years you have spent here have you acting like an American. You cannot do this."

"Enough, Rashid. Remember *your* place. We *are* doing it. Does that mean you or one of the others, including Dr. Amir, is going to notify my father?"

"I did not say that, Prince. Did I tell your

father of your many college escapades? No, I did not. I am loyal only to you, as you know full well. But this is different. These Americans can view this as a kidnapping. Do not be foolish is what I am telling you."

"There is no more room for discussion. Ah, there you are, Amir. We have a patient for you." Prince Malik watched as Rashid, his longtime security guard/confidant/boyhood friend, gently lowered Trisha Holiday onto a king-size bed. They withdrew to a sitting room outside the bedroom while the doctor examined his new patient.

"We should never have come here, Malik." Long years of friendship allowed Rashid to talk to Prince Malik informally. He became the subservient security guard only when others in their party or strangers were around.

"Why not, Rashid? I've been here in America for seven long years, studying, with no breaks. I finished my studies as you did. I am now a Ph.D., as you are. I hold two master's degrees, as you do. I've done everything my father has asked of me. This is my reward before returning home next week. I earned this vacation. You like it, too. Admit it! All the music, the noise, the bells and whistles. This is a fun place. You know as well as I do that when I return home, I

15

will once again be under my father's thumb. Can't you cut me some slack until then?"

Rashid was a tall man with the physique of a bodybuilder. He worked out on a regular basis, as did Prince Malik. Suddenly, he laughed and slapped Malik on the back. "Want a beer?"

"Sure."

"You need to notify the young lady's superior or her friends. When they find her car still in the parking lot, things will start to pop. And your name is the first one that will be mentioned. You sent the young lady a thousand-dollar bill in a note. That will not go unnoticed."

"Which she returned, Rashid. I have to say, I did not expect that. I can't believe she would turn down money. I checked out the pay scale for her type of work, and the dancers are not paid much money. I think she might be *the one*, Rashid. I've watched her every night this week. Seven long years, and I finally found a woman I think I might like, and how do I find her? Sick."

"That should work in your favor, Malik. She'll be grateful to you for being there to help her. Who knows how long she might have lain out there in the cold if we weren't there? Yes, I think she will be grateful."

"I don't want her to be grateful to me. I

want her to like me for who I am. We were just there at the right time. Anyone would have done the same thing."

"No, they would have taken her to the hospital. Or they would have called nine-one-one."

"We have the entire twenty-first floor. We have a doctor and two nurses on call twenty-four/seven. It was much easier and better for her to bring her here. She's being seen to as we speak. I don't even know where the hospital is around here. I didn't want to call attention to myself by calling nine-one-one. Miss Holiday is in good hands — the best hands. Amir is a skilled physician. Aside from treating us for colds, all he has done since coming here seven years ago is to keep up on the latest medical journals and tour various hospitals and observe.

"Go into the office and make the necessary calls. Tell anyone who needs to speak to me to come up here. If they want to send some of their people to watch over Miss Holiday, that will be fine. I'm sure when she wakes up, she will speak for herself."

Malik jumped up and walked over to the bedroom door, straining to hear something, anything, that was going on behind the closed doors. Was Rashid right? Was it a mistake to come to Las Vegas from Califor-

17

nia, where he'd lived for seven years? Yes and no, he decided. He'd attended the University of California, Berkeley and loved every minute of it. He had made friends, blended into college life. He'd studied hard to make his father proud of him. Academics came easy to him, and he hadn't had to struggle at all. He'd breezed through the seven years and earned three degrees in the bargain. He loved American baseball and football. Loved wearing tattered blue jeans and a baseball cap. He loved hot dogs with the works, pizza with everything on it, pounding beers with his friends. And he'd given back in the only way he knew how — he'd tutored friends for free on his off time.

Though he'd dated, he had had no serious relationships. Rashid said he was looking for the impossible dream when it came to women. All he knew was that until this week, when he'd dragged Rashid to the casino to watch the same show every night, he hadn't met the right one. One of the dancers caught his eye the first night, and she had smiled at him. And in that split second in time, he was, as his American friends were wont to say, a goner. But it took him till tonight to get up the nerve to send a note backstage. He knew now that sending the thousand-dollar bill with the note had been the wrong thing to do. Trisha Holiday's sending it back proved to him that he was right. She was the one. He knew it in his gut, in his heart, and in his mind. And woe to him when his father found out. Back in Dubai, the woman his father had chosen for him waited. His balled fist slammed into his open palm. He could never marry someone he didn't love. And yet what hope did he have that he could defy his father? None.

The bedroom door opened. Amir, his doctor since birth, smiled at him. "Relax, Malik. Miss Holiday has the flu. She has a high fever. I've given her some shots and set up an IV drip. She's dehydrated. She's asleep now. I feel confident when I say I think her fever will break by tomorrow. Today, actually. She'll be uncomfortable for a few days, but she'll recover.

"You cannot stay here. It is not seemly. You need to go to your own suite, and I will update you. I sent a text to Carpas to hire two round-the-clock female nurses. He returned my text, saying they are on the way. I will wait here until they arrive, then return to my own suite. Tomorrow promises to be a busy day. It's late. Get some sleep.

"You are to be commended, Malik. Without a doubt, you saved that woman's life.

She could have lain out there in the freezing cold and died before someone came along."

Malik shuffled from one foot to the other. "How soon are you going to notify my father? Not that I care, mind you," he said defiantly.

Amir laughed. "Rest easy, Malik, I am not going to be a . . . What is it the Americans say in those old movies I like to watch? Ah, yes, a stool pigeon."

"That's a relief. I'd really hate to have to have Rashid kill you for ratting me out." It was said jokingly, but Dr. Amir blanched, until Malik laughed and slapped him on the back before leaving the suite to go to his own quarters.

Trisha Holiday slept off and on for seventy-two hours. When she woke, she drank broth, juice, and sucked small amounts of apple sauce from a spoon. While she didn't know it at the time, she had lost nine pounds. She also did not know that she had had a steady stream of visitors: the entire chorus line, her immediate boss, as well as the owner of the casino. When she was told about all those who had visited, she smiled wanly and drifted back off to sleep.

It was Malik himself who shopped for her,

buying nightgowns that were pretty but not sexy, a hairbrush, and other things that a salesgirl had told him a lady who had been sick would need. He took a lot of good-natured ribbing from his staff, especially Rashid. He simply didn't care. All he cared about was seeing and talking to the person whose life, he was convinced, he had saved.

On the fourth day, precisely at noon, Malik was escorted into Trisha Holiday's room to be formally introduced to the patient by her physician. For the first time in his life he was tongue-tied as he stood at the side of the bed and offered his hand. Her clasp was weak and dry, but she smiled.

"The doctor told me you are the one who brought me here. Thank you. How can I repay you?"

"No payment is necessary, Miss Holiday. I'm glad to see that you are feeling better. Are you eating? Is there anything I can get for you?"

"I'm not very hungry, but thank you very much. Are you really a prince?"

Malik laughed. "I am. Is that okay with you?"

"I've never met a prince before. What do princes do? Here in America, that is."

"They go to school, and in their spare time, they save damsels in distress." He laughed again, showing off what Trisha thought were the most beautiful teeth she'd ever seen. The rest of him was pretty much okay, too. Then she remembered being carried by a handsome man.

"Are you the person who carried me here? I remember that. I thought you were the handsomest man I'd ever seen." She blushed a bright pink at her words.

"Obviously, you were delirious, young lady," Amir said, smiling broadly. "This rascal does not need to have his ego inflated."

She thinks I'm handsome. He grinned, once again showing his pearly whites. "You look tired, Miss Holiday. I'll come back and visit later. I think I'm going to try my luck with the slot machines downstairs. Would you like me to play for you?"

"That's not allowed. Employees cannot gamble. We have to sign contracts," Trisha said before her eyes closed, and she was asleep again.

"It's cold out, Malik. Wear a warm coat. I don't want to treat you, too, because unlike Miss Holiday, you are a terrible patient."

Malik flipped the physician the bird and whistled for Rashid, who was on his cell phone. "I'll be staying here in the casino, Amir, so I don't need a coat."

Malik turned to motion to Rashid. "Come

22

on, Rashid. Let's go spend some of my father's money. I am feeling lucky today."

"It's your sister on the phone, and she's complaining again about your being here while she's stuck in the palace with nothing to do."

Malik waved his hand at his old friend, dismissing his sister's complaints, and waltzed out of the suite, knowing full well Rashid would cut the call short and follow him.

"Your sister is a pain in the neck. Why don't you marry her off and be done with it?" Rashid grumbled when he caught up to Malik.

"Because no one will have her. Even my father knows that. She's destined to be what here in America they call an old maid. She's too bossy and outspoken, and all she does is shop and spend my father's money. Her thinking is too modern, and that's why my father keeps her close to the palace. He never knows what she'll do next. But you already know this, so why am I wasting my time telling you yet again?"

"Sounds kind of like you, Malik," Rashid taunted in a good-natured way.

"I have kept a strict accounting of my personal expenditures since coming to America. As you know, I have never defied my father, like Soraya does day after day."

Rashid made a funny noise in his throat. "What do you call what you are doing now, what I am aiding and abetting you with?"

Malik laughed, a sound of genuine mirth. "Helping a damsel in distress. Even my coldhearted father would never turn his back on someone who needed help."

The elevator door opened, and both men stepped out to the melody of the chiming and buzzing slot machines. Across the room, a roar went up when a little round grandmother with rosy cheeks shouted for the world to hear that she had just won two hundred dollars. Malik laughed out loud, as did Rashid.

"What will it be, Rashid? Poker, roulette, or the slots?"

Rashid pretended to think. Malik knew that Rashid would choose the slots, while he himself would hit the poker table, to play the game he'd learned during his first year of college.

The two separated, but Rashid was always positioned so that he could see Malik from his location at the slot machine. They both played intensely, winning some and losing some. They stopped for lunch, after which they went back into the casino. They were about to separate again when Rashid's cell phone rang. Malik was about to walk over to the poker table when he turned around to see his friend and bodyguard gingerly lower himself onto one of the seats by a slot machine. He was listening, not talking. Malik knew that something was wrong. His first thought was that something bad had happened to Trisha Holiday. He hadn't had a second thought when Rashid handed the cell phone to him. It could only be his pesky sister, railing yet again. He rolled his eyes at Rashid but reached for the phone.

"You need to give it up already, sister. If you call again today, I will order your hair to be cut and leave you bald. What do you mean, I should shut up? Don't you ever dare tell me to shut up."

Rashid was making such strange faces that Malik blinked and bellowed, "What?" so loud, playing customers stood up to see who was affecting their concentration at the gaming tables. Malik lowered his voice. "All right, I'm listening. Talk to me."

Rashid's movements were those of an old man when he got up from his seat at the slot machine. Gently, he guided Malik to the chair and pushed him down. He stepped back, never taking his eyes off his friend as he waited for Malik to end the call with his sister.

Their world as they had known it in America for the past seven and a half years had come to an end. In a matter of hours, that life would be nothing more than a memory.

Malik ended the call and looked up at his friend. "Arrange for our departure, Rashid. Such a tragic accident. My father was a young, vital man, an experienced equestrian. To be thrown from his horse and to die instantly is something I cannot comprehend."

"Do not torture yourself, Malik. You need to tell me now, what is my position? With you taking over for your father, you will require more security than I can give you. Come. We must tell the others, calls have to be made, and things have to be put into place."

Rashid held out his hand to pull Malik to his feet. "I know you were not, are not, prepared for your new role, but life has just . . . How do you say it here in America? Ah, yes, thrown you the biggest curveball of your life. You are up to it, Malik."

"You will be my closest adviser, my second in command. Your education now is the same as mine. We will run our country together to make my father proud. Can you see yourself as my second in command? If you say no, I will kill you, Rashid."

It was clearly meant as a joke, and both men knew it. Rashid simply nodded, his eyes wet as he threw his arm around Malik's shoulders.

On the twenty-first floor, the commotion was that of a beehive in motion. Aides, guards, secretaries were scurrying about, packing, gathering up belongings. Both men stood just inside the doorway and waited.

Casmir, one of the aides, bowed low, the commotion stopped, and the suite grew silent. "The plane will be ready in two hours."

As one, the entourage expressed their sympathy. Malik accepted his people's condolences, smiled weakly, and retreated to his room. He needed to *think.* He wanted to cry, to wail, when he saw the white *kandura,* his official robe, draped on his king-size bed, along with the *ghutra* and the *agal,* or black band. Nestled next to the headdress and robe was a pair of new sandals. He looked down at his blue jeans, his Golden Bears T-shirt, and the Dodgers baseball cap clutched in his hand. The jeans and T-shirt were his favorites, washed a thousand times so that they fit him like a second skin. His Nikes were worn and battered. He kicked them off.

Sheik Malik bin Al Mohammed sat down on the edge of the bed. He dropped his head into his hands and cried. Not for the loss of his father — because he had never been close to his father — but for the loss of the life he'd come to love there in America. When he left that hotel in Las Vegas, he would be wearing his traditional garb. He would no longer be Malik, the student with his three American advanced degrees. He had to step into his father's sandals.

Malik's thoughts whirled and twirled as he recalled one of his professors, an older man, one he truly liked and respected, telling him that one's life was whatever one made of it. Everyone in life had choices, he'd gone on to say. He wished that he had carried that particular conversation further. He wished he had explained to the professor about his life in Dubai and what was expected of him.

How was he supposed to make those choices when, from birth, he'd known exactly what his future held? And he had accepted it, but in his thinking, he was certain that his father would live to be a very old man, and he wouldn't have to take his place until he himself was advanced in age.

He thought about Trisha Holiday, who

was only one door away. He felt his heart start to flutter in his chest.

Malik's thoughts turned back in time to when he and Rashid were small boys in the palace, playing games, laughing and hollering as they chased each other the way children do. And then his school years, Rashid always at his side into his teen years, his shy glances at young ladies. He thought of his sister, Soraya, who was even more of a prisoner than he had been. He was starting to understand how she felt, why she rebelled against the law and order of their father. He made a mental promise to himself to be kind and compassionate to his sister when he returned home.

Malik's hand reached out to touch the long white robe and the head scarf. How he dreaded putting them on. As children, he and Rashid had sneaked into his father's room to try on the robes and play in them when his father was away. Back then, it was all a great game. In their naive world, they'd waved scepters about and beheaded their less-than-royal subjects. How stupid they had been. Like he would ever behead anyone. Even barbarians didn't behead anyone these days.

Malik sat on the edge of the bed until he lost all track of time. The knock on the door startled him.

"Enter."

Rashid, dressed in his own white robe, stepped into the room. "It's time, Your Highness."

Malik looked down at the gold watch on his wrist. "So it is. Give me a few minutes, Rashid."

"Will you be saying good-bye to our guest?"

"Of course."

Rashid backed out of the room and closed the door behind him.

In the blink of an eye, Malik stripped down and donned the *kandura,* then the *ghutra.* When he had the *ghutra* settled firmly on his dark head, he slipped the black *agal* around to hold the scarf in place. He looked down at his feet; the *kandura* was longer than Rashid's, a sign of his importance. How strange that he didn't feel important. He slipped into the new sandals, not liking the way they felt on his feet. Seven years of wearing sneakers and Brooks Brothers tasseled loafers had not prepared him for the feeling.

Malik looked around the room for his duffel bag. He spotted it on the chair by the writing desk. He gathered up his jeans, his T-shirt, and his Nikes. His hands, when he touched his American clothes, were almost reverent. Maybe one day, he and Rashid would play a game in the palace and wear *these* clothes. A dream. He wondered if dreams ever came true. No, those dreams were gone forever.

Malik squared his shoulders, looked at himself in the mirror, and winced. With long, purposeful strides, he crossed the room and opened the door. Waiting for him in the main sitting area was his full entourage. They bowed, as did he.

"Come, Rashid. I must say good-bye to our guest, and then we can be on our way. I trust everything has been taken care of."

"Yes, Your Highness," Rashid said solemnly as he led the way to Trisha Holiday's room.

He knocked and waited at the door until one of the nurses opened it. He stepped aside, and Malik strode past him and crossed the room to stand at the side of the bed. Rashid motioned for the two nurses to follow him to the sitting area so that Malik could have a private moment with the patient.

Trish was propped up in a nest of pillows, freshly bathed, powdered, and weary to the point where she was dozing off. Her eyes

31

snapped open when she felt Malik's presence.

"Prince! Good afternoon. It is afternoon, isn't it?"

Malik didn't bother to correct her. "Yes, it is afternoon. I trust you are feeling better."

"I am, Prince, just a little weak. Thanks to you and your people. I feel almost like royalty with all the care I'm getting. If I were home in my apartment, I would be heating up canned chicken soup and sleeping on the sofa, watching some awful television."

Malik smiled. "I came to say good-bye and to tell you that there is a . . . family affair I must see to. You can stay here as long as you like. Everything has been paid for. Instructions have been given. Your job will still be waiting for you when you have fully recovered. I also wanted to tell you I am sorry we met under such circumstances. I would have liked to have had that drink with you after the show."

"I'm sorry, too. Perhaps we'll meet again someday, if you return and I'm still dancing. Hopefully, I will still be dancing, unless my legs give out." Trisha was babbling and didn't know why. Suddenly, she felt as if she had just lost her oldest and dearest friend. Her eyes burned. She felt her hand in his, and then she felt his lips on her hand.

He let it go and stepped back.

"Good-bye, Miss Holiday."

"Good-bye sounds so formal, Prince. See, just my luck, I meet a prince, then . . ."

"He turned into a frog?" Malik laughed.

Trisha smiled. "In a manner of speaking," she said, pointing to his clothing. "Ya know, a plaid belt or maybe one studded with rhinestones would dress up that outfit. You should think about it."

Malik laughed again, the sound booming throughout the room. He turned, waved, and was gone.

Tears rolled down Trisha's face with the sound of the closing door.

"What's so funny?" Rashid asked in the elevator.

Malik stopped laughing long enough to tell Rashid what Trisha had said. "When we get back home, the first thing I want you to do is find me two belts, one plaid and one studded with rhinestones. That's an order, Rashid."

"Consider it done, Your Highness." Rashid turned his head so Malik couldn't see the laughter in his eyes.

Thirty-five minutes later, they were at McCarran International Airport. Ten minutes after that, they were airborne. Their next stop: Al Maktoum International Airport in Dubai.

CHAPTER 2

Trisha gathered up the remnants of the Christmas wrappings. She looked at the three beautifully wrapped presents sitting on her cocktail table, pleased that they had come out so pretty. One for her sister, Emma, one for her niece, Melissa, and one for her best friend, Connie. A cardboard FedEx mailer sat on the floor, along with a FedEx airbill. Tomorrow she would mail it on her way to work. Connie's gift would have to wait until the Christmas party in two weeks. She was ahead of herself this year. Normally, she was a last-minute Christmas shopper, but while she was recovering from the flu, she'd had too much free time on her hands. So she'd shopped over the weekend, and she was done earlier than she had ever been.

In three more days, she could return to work. Actually, she felt well enough to return immediately, but she had to obey the doctor's orders and take his release slip with her when she reported to work in three days. Nathan, her boss, was a stickler when it came to the girls' health. Dancing was strenuous, as well as exhausting. So, for the next three days, she had nothing much to do except cook some nourishing food, watch television, and take a walk every day. Her mind raced as to how many more ways she could serve the leftover Thanksgiving turkey she'd cooked for several friends a few days ago. She'd already made hash, patties, a salad; all that was left was to cook the carcass and freeze the soup.

After Trish disposed of the scraps from her Christmas wrappings, she got out her soup pot and the vegetables and spices she would need to make the soup. She was rummaging in the cabinets for containers to store the soup in when the bell to her town house sang its three-note song. *Connie?* She looked at her watch. *No, not Connie.* It was too early in the morning for a visit. She shrugged as she made her way to the front door. She looked through the peephole before she opened the door. She eyed the dead bolt and the security chain, something she had installed herself the day she moved into the town house. A FedEx driver was standing in front of the door. By stretching her neck, she could see the truck sitting in front of her building. Safe to open the door. She did.

"You need to sign for this, ma'am."

Trish reached for the clipboard and signed her name with a wild flourish. She thanked the driver, then closed and locked the door. She hefted the slim envelope, wondering who could have sent her something by FedEx. *Emma?* No, it was an international airbill. Her heart kicked up a beat as she made her way to the wheat-colored sofa in her living room. *The prince?* Her hand started to shake as she ripped at the tiny piece of cardboard that would open the mailer. Another envelope was nestled inside, with a heavy gold seal on the front and a circle of gold wax underneath. *Impressive,* she thought.

What could be inside? Why would someone be sending her something like this? *The prince? An early Christmas present? An invitation? To what? Open it, Trish!* Instead of opening the heavy seal, Trish leaned back into the softness of the wheat-colored sofa and closed her eyes. She'd lost count of the number of times she'd thought about Prince Malik. She thought about his kind, dark eyes, his generosity, his easy laughter, the way he'd had his people take care of her.

How many times had she played the scene over and over in her mind, wondering if she hadn't been sick that night, whether she would have accepted the thousand-dollar bill and had a drink with the prince? She'd finally answered herself. She would not have accepted the money, but she might have had a ginger ale with him after the show. She had a rule, and that was never to drink with customers. Most of the girls were just like her. Some were mothers with kids at home with babysitters, and the only thing they wanted after the show was to go home. While she wasn't married and didn't have kids, she was just like them. All she wanted after a night's work was to go home, take a hot bubble bath, and crawl into bed.

Trish opened her eyes and stared down at the cream-colored envelope. She tapped it against her knee as she wished someone was here with her when she opened it. Finally, she couldn't stand the suspense a second longer. She picked at the wax seal with a fingernail. Inside was an exquisitely worded invitation inviting her to Dubai three days from then to celebrate Dubai's national holiday, aptly named National Day. A private jet would be waiting for her at McCarran International Airport if she accepted the invitation. She read the invitation several times, till she had it committed to memory. She was about to slide the heavy card back into the envelope when she realized there was a folded note still in the envelope. She unfolded it with shaky hands. A personal note from the prince, but he wasn't a prince anymore. He was a sheik. She smiled when she read the note.

Hello, Miss Holiday.
    Greetings from Dubai.
    I hope you are well and fully recovered from your ordeal. In the spirit of the holiday season, I would be honored if you would accept my invitation to join my sister and me to celebrate National Day, our national holiday. If you are agreeable, please call the number at the bottom, and I will have arrangements set in place. Be mindful there is an eleven-hour time difference. My sister and I look forward to entertaining you and showing you our beautiful country.

It was signed simply "Malik," with no title in front of his name.
    What to do? What to do? What to do?
    Three days! Could she be ready in three days? What to pack? Did she have the right clothes for a trip to Dubai? She'd packed

away all her summer clothing months ago. She didn't have anything fancy. What to do? What to do? What to do?

Trish walked out to the kitchen, looked at the turkey carcass and all the things she had ready in preparation for making turkey soup. Without thinking, she scooped up the remains of the bird and tossed them into a trash bag. The vegetables were returned to the refrigerator; the soup pot and spices were returned to the cabinet. She wasn't making soup that day. She reached for the trash bag and raced out to the Dumpster in the parking lot. She tossed in the bag, then ran back into the house. It was freezing cold. Dubai was hot and dry. She thought she could feel the sun warming her bones.

Back in the living room, she picked up the phone to call her sister, Emma, but the call went straight to voice mail. She then called Connie, who lived in the same gated community she lived in. Connie's sleepy voice came across the wire.

"Oh, Connie, I'm sorry for waking you, but I have to talk to you. *Now!* Can I come over? I made some cinnamon buns earlier. I'll bring them with me. Please, Connie, I have to talk with you."

"Bring the coffee, too," Connie grumbled good-naturedly.

Ten minutes later, Trish was sitting at Connie's dining-room table. She watched as Connie read the engraved invitation and the personal note.

"You're going, right?" Connie said, her eyes wide as saucers.

"I don't know. Should I? I want to. I don't have the right clothes. It's seven degrees outside. Dubai is hot and dry. I've heard stories about women who go to places like Dubai and are never seen again. I tried calling my sister, but the call went to voice mail. For sure, Nathan will fire me if I take off for a few weeks.

"Think about it, Connie. When will I ever get a chance to do something like this again? It just fell into my lap, so to speak. I read up on Dubai when I got back home after being sick, and it's a modern city. It has the seventh largest shopping mall in the world. It has the highest building in the world. I can't remember how many feet high, but it is the highest. They're in the middle of building an airport that will be the biggest in the world when it's finished, and they have some fancy-dancy hotel that cost over six hundred fifty million to build. I think everyone who lives there is a millionaire. Oh, I'm so confused. Why me? Why did he pick me?"

41

"Maybe because you're pretty, not full of yourself, you did return his thousand dollars, and in the end, he had his people take care of you when you were so sick. Maybe he's like the Chinese. You save a life, then . . . whatever that saying is. Maybe, Trish, the guy fell in love with you. Did you ever think of that? You have stars in your eyes when you talk about him. I rest my case."

"Nathan . . . I've taken so much time off already. My sister is not going to approve."

"When you get there, sign in at the American embassy. If they don't have an embassy, then go to the American consulate. I doubt Nathan will fire you. I don't know for sure, but I've heard via Ernie, who seems to know just about everything, that the prince had a talk with Nathan, as did one of the owners of the casino. That means to me that you are golden as far as he is concerned, and no matter how much time you take off, your job will be waiting for you.

"Your sister? Well, she'll get over it. You'll never get another chance like this. I can guarantee that. Sometimes, Trish, you have to reach for the brass ring. As to clothes, I think we girls can outfit you so that you won't be a disgrace to the prince. But you said he's not a prince, but a sheik. That's even better. I'll make some calls. But first, you have to decide if you really want to go or not."

"I do! I do!"

"Then let's get this show on the road, no pun intended. First, hair, nails, pedicure. You have a passport, so that's no problem. I think you should get a light spray tan so you glisten. Highlights in your hair. The works, Trish! Clean out your bank account if you have to. This is a once-in-a-lifetime gift that's been given to you."

"Okay, okay, okay. I don't have any fancy luggage. Do I need fancy luggage, Connie?"

"We'll work on that. So are you going to call and accept?"

"You betcha. Okay, I'm going home to make my appointments. Thanks, Connie. You can call me on my cell, okay?" At the door, Trish turned. "You're sure this is the right thing to do?"

"Yes, I'm sure, and I'm jealous. All the girls will be jealous, but in a good way. You know that. Get going. But leave the cinnamon buns."

Trish laughed as she slipped into her jacket. "Nathan would skin you alive if he saw you eating all those buns."

"I'll do an extra half hour on the treadmill. *Go!*"

■ ■ ■ ■

Trish walked down the portable stairs of the private Gulfstream belonging to Sheik Malik bin Al Mohammed. It was hot and dry, not to mention breezy. She could see a Mercedes stretch limo with the flag of Dubai whipping from the front of the vehicle. The door was opened by a man in a long white robe. Out stepped one of the most beautiful women Trish had ever seen, dressed in Western clothes. She smiled at Trish and held out her hand. "Welcome to Dubai, Miss Holiday. I'm Soraya, Malik's sister. He wishes me to apologize to you for not being here personally to welcome you to Dubai, but he had to go to Abu Dhabi early this morning. However, he will return in time to dine with us this evening."

Soraya had the same warm, caring eyes as her brother. The same welcoming smile and, Trish suspected, the same sense of humor. "Thank you. Please, call me Trish."

"Then you must call me Soraya. Did you have a good trip? Was everything satisfactory?"

Trish found it hard not to stare at the beautiful young woman welcoming her to Dubai. The outfit she wore had to have cost more than Trish earned in a year. Chanel, if she wasn't mistaken. Her jewelry looked to be priceless and probably was. She was as beautiful as her brother Malik was handsome. They had the same warm dark eyes, the same tawny skin, the same wonderful smile. She felt dowdy in comparison.

"Absolutely. It was marvelous. The food was wonderful. I enjoyed the special tea and the rice cakes. I need to learn how to make both. I slept a lot, so the trip went faster than I thought it would. I also read up on your country. I can't wait to see it all, so I can tell my friends all about it."

Soraya stepped aside so that Trish could slide into the limo. It was as plush as the Gulfstream. Glasses of sparkling water filled with ice cubes waited for her on a little shelf. Soraya motioned to her to drink it.

"One must drink a lot of water here."

When both women were settled, Soraya started to talk. "Malik has appointed me as your tour guide. I love showing off Dubai. In return, I would ask that you tell me everything there is to tell me about America. Malik shared the experiences of his school years with me, but I want a woman's perspective. My dream has always been to travel to America, but my father would not allow it. I cried for days when Malik left.

My father paid no attention. I was to study here, and that was the end of it. Malik has promised me that I can make the trip soon. I am not sure whether he is placating me or not, but I can be relentless when it comes to things like that." She laughed, the same musical sound as her brother's laughter.

"Can't your mother intercede?"

"I have no mother. She died giving birth to me. Malik and I grew up motherless. Having a mother was something we both missed sorely. That is not to say my father ignored us, but it is not the same as having a mother. My mother was very beautiful. It has been said that we both look like her. My father was neither handsome nor beautiful. He had swarthy looks, and his face was heavily pockmarked. He used to say that he could not believe my mother chose him to marry when she came of age when he was so ugly. He referred to himself as ugly at all times. When he would tell us those stories when we were little children, we thought of them as fairy tales. He said he could never marry again, because he could not replace such perfection as my mother. Do you have parents, Trish?"

"I did, of course, but they died from carbon-monoxide poisoning. I was away for a weekend sleepover at a friend's when it happened. I have a divorced sister who lives with her fourteen-year-old daughter, my only niece, in Princeton, New Jersey. I miss my parents and think of them every day. My sister took over my care until I was old enough to go it alone and be on my own. We're very close, even though she lives at one end of the country and I live on the other end. We talk daily and try to see each other at least twice a year, sometimes three times, depending, of course, on our finances. Air travel across the country is expensive.

"Soraya, can we stop at the consulate so I can register? My sister made me promise I would do that."

"It has already been taken care of, Trish. Malik filed the papers the day you said you would accept his invitation. I had one of the servants place the papers in your suite. You, of course, can call the consulate yourself when you feel like it and speak to your people. We can even stop by if that will make you feel more comfortable when we do our tour. Malik wants you to see *every-thing.*"

"I'm beyond excited," Trish gushed. "Between us girls, I wasn't sure if I should come or not. My friends encouraged me. It seems like I should be doing something for your brother, instead of the other way around. I don't know if he told you this or not, but if he hadn't found me when he did, I would have died out in the cold. I will never be able to repay him for saving my life. And yet, here I am. It isn't quite computing in my head."

"That's Malik for you. He's a wonderful person, even if he is my brother." This last comment was said with a wink of the eye. Trish laughed.

"It is not much farther, Trish. I know you must be tired. Air travel is wearying. Perhaps you would like to take a swim or a nap. It's the heat of the day, and you aren't used to our weather here yet. Tell me, what is it like to be a dancer? How is it you decided to do this?"

"It's exhausting, but I love it. I always wanted to be in show business. Ideally, I wanted to be a movie star, but I simply wasn't good enough. I have always loved to dance and took lessons all my life. Las Vegas was the closest I could come to fulfilling my dream. All the girls in the chorus are friends. We're like our own little family. I can't imagine doing anything else, but I do work part-time sometimes when I need extra money for something or other that is not in my budget."

Soraya leaned forward. "Budget? What is that?"

Trish laughed. "Living within your means, not spending money recklessly. I have a mortgage payment, and my car is old. I paid that off, and now I have to get a new one. That's going to be a huge bill, so I'll be working weekends again. Normal household bills. I had to budget rather harshly because I needed to buy a new bed. It took me ten months to save up for it, and I had to work in a department store weekends. I did that because as an employee, I got thirty percent off anything I bought in the store. I guess you don't live on a budget."

"No. I must try that. Malik lived like that when he was going to school. He did not call it a budget, though. He just said he lived like the other students. He had a ledger with a list of his expenditures. It made my father crazy that Malik wore jeans with holes in the knees and sneakers that looked like they were soaked in mud. He bought food in a store and listed in great detail strange goods. My father would have to look it up to see what he was buying. My father's eyes almost popped out of his head when he saw that Malik had bought something called a rattletrap. He asked me what that was, and I did not know. It's a car, but we only

49

figured it out when he called Malik to ask. He paid three hundred American dollars for it. My father was appalled."

Trish burst out laughing. "Sounds just like my car. A lot of college kids drive rattletraps. I'm sure your brother just wanted to be like his friends, so he would, as the saying goes, blend in and not be different."

"But Malik drove it himself! He had to learn how to do that. Rashid was supposed to drive him wherever he wanted to go, but Malik would not hear of it. My poor father was beside himself. He simply did not understand or refused to understand. In the end, he thought Malik was becoming too Americanized. They had sharp words, with Malik threatening to stay and not return. Then my father had his accident. If that had not happened, I think Malik would have stayed in your country."

Trish thought Soraya was too chatty. It almost seemed like she had a list of things she wanted to talk about and was in a rush to get them all out. Things her brother wanted her to speak of. Why? On the other hand, Soraya was young, and maybe she just liked to chatter to another female near her own age. Though Trish thought she was perhaps five or six years older than the young woman sitting next to her.

"We're home. This is the palace, Trish."

She was there! At a palace! Trish strained to see through the heavily tinted windows but was unsuccessful. In a minute, she'd be outside. Then, a few minutes after that, she'd be inside the palace. A real palace.

Oh my God! I'm actually in Dubai.

CHAPTER 3

And then Trish stepped into another world.
She felt like a tourist must feel when visiting Las Vegas for the first time. She needed
sunglasses to ward off the glare from all the
gold she was seeing. It appeared that everything was trimmed in gold, coated in gold,
or *was* gold. She knew she was gawking like
a rube, but she couldn't help it. She wondered if she was supposed to say something.
Like, "How beautiful," or maybe, "I never
dreamed I would see something so opulent,
so unbelievable." *So decadent. So tacky.* In
Las Vegas, at least you knew it was make-
believe, a place to have fun and games, with
all the gilt and noise.

And then she said something so stupid,
she couldn't believe the words had actually
come out of her mouth. "Who polishes all
this gold?"

Soraya stopped in her tracks, her expression puzzled by the fact that a guest should

ask such a question. "I have to admit, I don't know. I would imagine the servants. If it's important for you to know, I can find out."

Trish flushed a rosy pink. She shook her head and mumbled something as she followed her host to an elevator whose interior was as big as her living room back in Las Vegas. Inside, there was seating for four with satin-tasseled, gold-covered chairs. Ankle-deep carpeting. Art hung on the walls. In an elevator no less. Absolutely mind-boggling. She hoped she would be allowed to take pictures, because she knew her friends and her sister would never believe it when she tried to describe the incredible wealth she was seeing.

The operator was dressed in a *kubaya,* and he pressed a button the moment the doors slid soundlessly shut. Evidently, royalty didn't press buttons on their own. What did royalty do to pass the time? Did they do anything for themselves? How had Malik survived in California for seven years on his own? How had he blended in with the other students? She wondered if she would ever find the answers to her many questions. Then again, maybe questions were out of bounds, off-limits. She made a mental note to play things by ear.

The elevator stopped, and the doors slid open. Soraya stepped aside to allow Trish to go out first. The servant bowed, his face expressionless.

"This is your suite, Trish. You will have three servants, Zahra, Nada, and Ara. They will see to all your needs and tell you how things are done. Later, we will introduce you to Mustafa, who will be your bodyguard. Samir will be your personal driver. Hasim is your backup driver and bodyguard in case neither Mustafa nor Samir is unavailable."

"Six servants! Oh, Soraya, I don't require all that. I'm used to taking care of myself." *Crap, another verbal screwup,* according to the expression on Soraya's face.

"But who will draw your bath? Who will turn down your bed? Who will fetch you your early morning coffee? My brother ordered all this. One does not argue . . . ever, with Malik. His words are law."

Trish felt like a schoolgirl caught doing something she wasn't supposed to be doing. She forced a smile she didn't quite feel, and said, "I guess I am just not used to so much attention. I'm sorry if I misspoke."

"It is of no importance. Do not fret."

The heat on her face made her uncomfortable. Easy to say not to fret. She *was* fretting. Big-time.

A small lady, whom Soraya introduced as Nada, motioned to Trish to follow her. Gawking again — she simply couldn't help it — Trish followed the little lady through the suite of rooms. Silks and brocades, the furniture trimmed in gold, patches of ankle-deep carpeting, overhead fans, though the suite was cool. There was obviously air-conditioning coming from somewhere, because she could feel cool air swirling around her ankles. Everything was so magnificent, it took her breath away. She whirled and twirled as she tried to take it all in. She could fit her entire town house into the sitting room. She got dizzy trying to count the number of chairs and what appeared to be love seats.

Was she supposed to entertain people here? She was about to blurt out the question, but instead bit down on her lip and followed Nada to her bedroom. She gasped aloud as she stared at the biggest bed she'd ever seen in her life. She almost asked where they got the sheets and coverlet but thought better of it. A dozen people could sleep in the bed, which had a small ladder one used to get into it. Maybe it wasn't a ladder but a set of steps. *God, what if I fall out?* Wisely, she didn't voice that thought, either.

More chairs, more settees, priceless art on the walls. At least she assumed it was priceless art. Certainly not pictures bought at Target, like the ones in her town house back in Vegas. It was almost impossible to comprehend. Such wealth. Such decadence. If this was a guest suite, she could not help but wonder what Malik's and Soraya's suites looked like. She couldn't begin to imagine.

She was shown the bathroom and, once again, gasped aloud. It appeared to be gold from top to bottom, with gorgeous tile and ceramic work throughout. Like the sitting room, her whole town house could be fitted into the magnificent bathroom. There was a settee covered in scarlet silk, two chairs covered in gold silk. The walls were glass and mirrors, so that she could see her reflection a dozen different ways. The vanity was long and wide and held pots, jars, and ornate containers of God only knew what. A blow-dryer and a curling iron were set into niches in the wall, the plugs unseen. Luscious, healthy-looking green plants were nestled next to what she thought was the biggest bathtub in the world. She gave up trying to count the jets that she could see. Marble steps, padded with what looked like gold rubber strips, had to be climbed to a place where another set of steps descended into the tub. Again, she almost blurted out a question, how much water did it take to fill the tub? Dubai was the desert. Where did the water come from?

Damn. What is wrong with me? Why was she being so critical? She needed to kick back and just enjoy her vacation instead of picking it apart. If she kept this up, her hosts would send her packing before she could catch her breath. Trish turned to face the two women.

"It's all so beautiful. I've never seen anything so gorgeous, so splendid. It takes my breath away."

"Wonderful. Malik will be so pleased that you like everything. He worries when we have guests. He wants to be a good host, as do I. I will leave you now. One of the servants will come for you for dinner, which is served at eight o'clock. Tonight dinner is not formal. Malik knows you will be tired, so he suggested casual clothing. Wear anything you feel comfortable in. There are many books and magazines in your sitting room. Nada will show you how our television works. There is also a stereo system, with all your American music. Malik is addicted to it, so he has all the latest tunes. If you care to swim, Nada will take you to the

57

pool. It is very private, and no one will be in it but you. If you wish something to eat, Nada will have Zahra fetch you whatever you want. I will leave you now."

Trish wasn't sure what she should do, shake hands, shrug, smile. The hell with that. She was a hugger, always had been. Her arms went out, and she clasped Soraya to her and almost drowned in the heady scent of her perfume. Screwup or not, she didn't care.

"We hug where I come from. It's a show of thanks and affection."

Soraya giggled. "I like it. Malik told me of this. He said men slap each other on the back and shake hands, and women hug and kiss cheeks. Rest now. You must be tired after your long flight. Nap if you feel like it."

Trish wasn't sure what she wanted to do, other than be alone with her thoughts and try to figure out how she was going to handle all the opulence that surrounded her.

She turned to Nada and said, "I'm sure you have something else you would rather be doing. I think I'll just walk out to the garden and sit there for a little while. I'll be fine. Tell me what it is I need to do if I need you."

Trish was stunned when she saw Nada's

eyes fill with tears. Shit. Now what did I say? she thought. She found out quick enough.

"But I am here to serve you. I can run your bath and turn down your bed for a nap. Would you like something to drink? I will fetch it. *It is my job.*"

Ah, therein lies the rub, Trish thought. If Nada retreated to . . . wherever, others in the palace would think she, Trish, did not like the servant. *So much to learn.* "I don't want a bath right now. Later, before dinner. I don't wish a nap, because if I nap now, I won't be able to sleep tonight. I would just like to sit in the garden for a while and rest. Perhaps you could fetch me some coffee."

Nada's face lit with a smile. A task to be performed. "But of course, Miss Trisha. I will do that immediately. Sheik Malik said we are to serve you American coffee. He has it shipped here from Hawaii for himself."

"Your English is flawless. Where did you learn it?"

"Here in the palace school. It is mandatory. We have many American guests here who do not speak Arabic. It is a pleasant language."

A pleasant language. That was a new one on her. She needed to start a diary so she

59

didn't forget a moment of this visit.

Trish kicked off her shoes and walked barefoot through the doors and out into the garden, which could only be described as an oasis. She heard trickling water and smelled scents she'd never smelled before. She almost laughed out loud when she saw the Adirondack chairs scattered about the garden, with gaily painted wooden tables also strewn about. There was grass and a wild profusion of colored flowers everywhere. Trees whose names she didn't know, with glossy, shiny leaves. Little paths with colored stones that led to somewhere, probably to more chairs and little tables. The chairs had tufted cushions and looked comfortable. Hometown America. Sort of. Kind of.

Trish sat down on one of the chairs and hooked her big toe onto a footstool to draw it nearer. She realized she still had her purse on her shoulder. If ever there was a cigarette moment, this was that moment. She didn't smoke a lot and didn't consider herself a smoker, but at that moment she found herself wanting a cigarette. Malik smoked, because she had smelled it on him the night he picked her up off the ground. And the suite she had stayed in smelled of cigarette smoke, so his entourage smoked, too. Did women in Dubai smoke? She had no idea. Obviously, someone smoked, because there were gold-rimmed ashtrays on all the little tables. She fired up a cigarette and almost immediately felt the tension leave her shoulders.

Trish turned when she saw Nada out of the corner of her eye, pushing a little table on wheels with a full coffee service and several plates with cold domes sitting on top of them.

"It is what we serve with tea in the afternoons. Sweets. Shall I pour your coffee, madam?"

Trish nodded as she continued to smoke. Coffee and a cigarette. It was as American as you could get. She thanked Nada and reached for the cup. She sipped at the fragrant brew. Even back in the States, she didn't think she'd ever tasted coffee this good.

"Just ring the little bell on the tray if you wish anything else, madam. Before I leave, would you like me to bring the cell phone Sheik Malik left for you? He said yours will not work here and that you need a special one. He thought you might want to call your family or perhaps some friends from your home."

"Yes, thank you very much. I would like

to call home."

"One moment. I will fetch it, madam."

Moments later, Trish was holding a cell phone that looked like any other cell phone. She clicked it on and pressed the country code for the United States and dialed the number. A moment later, she heard her sister's voice. Trish squealed out a greeting, hardly stopping to breathe as she proceeded to describe the palace and the garden she was sitting in that very minute.

She stopped for a moment to listen to her sister and responded, "No, no, I haven't see him yet. I will tonight at dinner. Dinner is at eight, and it's casual. Casual here might mean something different from what we consider casual back home. Yes, I am registered at the consulate. They did it for me." She listened some more, then signed off, saying she wanted to call Connie. "Love you, sis. I'll bring you a present from Dubai. Give Missy a hug for me."

Trish pressed in the digits of Connie's number. She quickly calculated the time difference, knowing that Connie was about ready for the second show of the evening. When her friend answered, she could hear all the backstage chatter. She momentarily felt homesick. She started to babble as soon as she heard Connie's voice.

When she finally wound down long enough to catch her breath, she heard Connie say, "C'mon, cut to the chase and tell us the good stuff. What did *he* say? What did *he* do? Is *he* still as handsome as you thought? Did *he* kiss you yet?"

"I haven't seen him yet. Oh, Connie, I'm so overwhelmed. I've asked the most stupid questions. I feel like a hick. You would, too, if you could see this place. I don't belong here. This is not . . . I could never get used to this kind of living."

"Trish, you're just visiting. It's a vacation of a lifetime. Can't you just roll with it and enjoy it for what it is, a vacation of a lifetime?"

"At the moment, I have no other choice. It's all so new. I just can't imagine all this wealth. It's mind-bending, to say the least. I'll call you tomorrow and let you know how it goes when I meet up with Malik. I have to figure out what to wear. What do you think *casual* means over here, Connie?"

"Casual is whatever you want it to be. Wear the white piqué sundress. It will show off that wonderful spray tan you paid good money for. Wear your cross on the chain. This is no time to deny your faith. Are you listening to me, Trish?"

"I am. I'm wearing it now, but it's not

noticeable under my shirt. You know I never take it off. My mother gave it to me on my tenth birthday. The white sandals with the inch heel, right?"

"Absolutely. You'll look like a million bucks, kiddo. No matter what they wear, you won't be overdressed or underdressed. You're a nervous wreck, aren't you, Trish? I can hear it in your voice. Relax and just go with the flow."

"Easy for you to say. God, Connie, why do you think he invited me here? I know you said he likes me, but he's half a world away. There's no way we could have a long-distance relationship and make it work. Remember, he's not a prince anymore. He's the sheik. Just because Malik helped me when I was sick doesn't explain this . . . this vacation. There has to be an ulterior motive somewhere. I just can't figure out what it is."

"You'll figure it out. Gotta go, Trish. Showtime. We just got the final call."

"Love you. Tell everyone I miss them. I'll bring presents for everyone, all the way from Dubai."

The moment the connection was broken, Trish closed her eyes. Suddenly, she felt lost and all alone. The words *ulterior motive* kept ricocheting around and around inside her head. She poured more coffee and fired up another cigarette. She needed to think.

An hour later her thoughts were no different. She was tired of smoking cigarettes she didn't want, tired of drinking the excellent coffee. She needed to move about. A walk through the garden, sniffing the fragrant flowers, might help. She realized she was still in her bare feet. The mossy, spongy grass felt good beneath her feet. Such a simple pleasure in this land of unbelievable wealth.

Trish let her thoughts go to Malik and how she'd been attracted to him from the moment he lifted her in his arms. She remembered how safe she felt there. She thought then about all his visits to her sickroom, the inane conversations. She remembered how her heartbeat quickened at the look in his eyes, how happy she felt when he smiled at her. All the dreams she'd had of Malik. Sweet, wonderful dreams. She'd cried when he told her he was leaving to return to Dubai, knowing she'd never see him again. She'd cried into her pillow so no one would know how she felt.

When Trish finished her tour of the garden and was back on the Adirondack chair, she ignored the cigarettes and coffee. She leaned back and closed her eyes. She shifted her thoughts to her sister back in New Jersey and her friends in Las Vegas. For some crazy reason, she thought about Ernie and how shocked he was when she told him to return the thousand dollars to Malik. A smile tugged at the corner of her lips.

Trish looked down at her watch. Hours to go till it was time to meet up with the man who had literally saved her life. Hours till she set eyes on Sheik Malik bin Al Mohammed.

Just hours.

CHAPTER 4

Trish looked down at her watch for what she was sure was the hundredth time. The time hadn't changed much since the last time she looked, not even a minute ago. The little gold circle on her wrist said the time was 7:31 p.m. Dubai time. She had been awake now for close to thirty hours and was starting to feel it.

The soak in the massive tub had almost put her to sleep. The heady scent of the bath salts had soothed all her senses. The bathroom smelled wonderful! She smelled wonderful! The world smelled wonderful!

Trish could see her reflection in all the mirrors lining the walls. While a tad creepy, it allowed her to see every part of her body. She whirled and twirled. The white piqué sundress the girls back home had helped her choose was, in her eyes, perfect. At home, in the summer, she could go anywhere in it. To a summer party, out to dinner, on a movie date, out for a walk in the park . . . with someone. The gold chain and cross around her neck, the last gift from her mother, sparkled in the overhead lighting. She hadn't applied much makeup; the spray tan had done its job. A little mascara, a little eyeliner, some lipstick, and that was it. What she would do when the spray tan faded, she had no idea. Maybe the spray tan was a bad idea. Too late to worry about that.

Trish looked down at her white sandals. She'd paid way too much for them, but the girls had goaded her with the "once-in-a-lifetime vacation and throw caution to the winds" argument. And they did match the dress perfectly.

Trish paced because she didn't want to sit down and wrinkle her dress. She walked around the suite of rooms and was on her ninth lap when she decided to go outside and smoke a cigarette. She nixed the second half of that idea almost immediately as she didn't want to smell like cigarette smoke. Instead, she peered at herself in one of the mirrors on her last lap to stare at her hair and the earrings one of the girls had loaned her. Real diamonds, but only half a carat each. Still, they were diamonds. Her hair, now, that was another story altogether. Fortunately, she and her sister had been blessed with natural curly hair, thanks to their father. What that meant was that she could style her hair just about any way she wanted to, and it would stay in place. The only thing she had to do was highlight it from time to time, something she'd done the day before coming to the Arabian Peninsula.

The next thing she knew, she was out in the garden, taking deep breaths in an attempt to calm her nerves. She wondered if Malik was as nervous as she was. Probably not. Men played it cool and didn't get emotional the way women did.

Fifteen minutes to go.

Trish walked up and down the little stone paths. She stopped often to smell the flowers and finally ended up picking a vibrant scarlet flower she'd never seen before. She stuck it in her hair, over her ear, then giggled. Soraya would probably frown. Malik would probably grin. Damn, she could hardly wait to see him. That first moment, she knew in her heart, in her mind, in her gut, would tell her why she was there. That first one-second look would say it all. The girls back in Vegas had agreed when she told them that. Just one second, and she would know her destiny.

Her adrenaline was at an all-time high.

She knew when she crashed, it would be for twenty-four hours. Then she'd miss out on a whole day of her vacation. Was there an alarm clock in her bedroom? She couldn't remember seeing one. Maybe she would need to tell Nada to wake her in the morning. Jet lag was awful, just awful.

Ten minutes. Trish continued to walk in the garden.

Five minutes.

Three minutes.

Trish headed back into the suite and walked to the huge sitting room. She just stood there, her eyes glued to her watch.

Two minutes.

One minute.

Trish almost jumped out of her skin when she heard the knock on the door.

Nada appeared out of nowhere and opened the door. A tiny little lady wearing a pale yellow gown of some sort smiled and motioned for Trish to follow her.

Nada whispered to Trish as she swept by. "You look ravishing, Miss Holiday."

Startled, Trish swung around and hugged her new maid. "Thank you for saying that. I was worried I might . . ."

"You look perfect. Enjoy your dinner."

Like that was really going to happen. She wouldn't be able to eat a bite of food. She was absolutely sure of it.

"Where are we going?" Trish asked nervously after they had walked for over five minutes, up one hall and down another, then around a few corners.

"To Sheik Malik's apartments. He wanted dinner to be informal this evening. Normally, dinner is served in the dining room. Tomorrow or the next day, Nada will show it to you. My name is Lily, Miss Holiday. I am Princess Soraya's personal maid."

Trish wondered if Malik had maids or male stewards.

"Ah, here we are. Do not be nervous, Miss Holiday. I can feel you shaking as you stand next to me. The sheik and the princess are wonderful people. They will put you at ease. I am going to knock on the door now, then leave you. Have an enjoyable dinner and a pleasant evening."

Trish didn't trust herself to speak. She had to concentrate on putting one foot in front of the other, then opening the door. Which she did.

And there he was, striding toward her with his arms outstretched, his sister behind him. He was dressed in creased khakis, loafers, and a white button-down shirt with the sleeves rolled to mid-arm. Trish locked her gaze on him as he did with her. This was

71

the second she'd been waiting for from the moment she received the invitation to come to Dubai. She didn't know what Malik was seeing in her eyes, but she knew what she was seeing in his. She smiled from ear to ear, her knees turning to rubber as she stepped into his arms, his grasp tight.

Patricia Holiday, also known as Trisha or Trish, had just met her destiny.

Malik released her, stepped back, and looked at her with such burning intensity, Trish was mesmerized. "It is so good to see you again, Trish. I am so happy, as is my sister, that you agreed to accept my invitation to visit us here in Dubai. I hope everything is to your satisfaction."

"Oh, it is. It is. It was so kind of you to invite me. I can't wait to see your world."

"Come, come. We must sit and talk. You must tell me how things are back in Las Vegas, the city that never sleeps and has no clocks."

Trish didn't realize until that moment that Malik was holding her hand. It felt cool and dry, whereas hers felt like a hot rock. He squeezed her hand just before he motioned for her to sit in one of the deep, comfortable chairs in a small seating arrangement.

"It's different in here," Trish blurted as she looked around.

There was no gold or gilt here. What she was seeing could pass for a bachelor pad back in the States. Or an elevated dorm room. The room they were sitting in had the same kind of comfortable furniture she had back in Vegas. There were ordinary carpets on the floor, cone-shaped floor lamps, end tables with pictures of young American guys, probably friends from college. Green plants dotted the corners and looked healthy and lush. Huge pictures of the ocean, with giant waves crashing on shorelines, hung on the walls. Plantation shutters, a product of the South, covered the windows. Paddle fans hung from the ceiling and whirred softly. Bookshelves lined the far wall and were crammed with books of every size and description. A humongous television that looked to be at least a hundred inches was directly across from the seating area, along with a stereo system.

Beyond the sitting room was a small kitchen with stainless-steel appliances and four stools resting under the counter. Beyond the immediate kitchen was a bit of a dining room with a round table holding a bowl of fruit and four chairs with padded covers. Cozy. A carryover from Malik's days in the States, which he wasn't ready to let go of. Trish felt sad that in this mind-boggling building of gold and wealth, this little area was Malik's personal oasis. There was no need to see the bedroom or bath. She could envision them with her eyes closed.

Malik laughed, his eyes lighting with mirth. "I rather thought you would like it. My sister thinks it is horrible. She said she could never live in such . . . I believe the word she used was *squalor.*"

"Stop it, Malik. He loves to tease. What I said was, it was much too small for me. As long as he can drink his American beer and toast hot dogs, my brother is happy. Rashid, too. Both of them are incorrigible."

Trish winked at Malik. "I love hot dogs with the works and good cold beer. I swig from the bottle, do you?"

Malik burst out laughing, then couldn't stop at the expression on his sister's face. "I told you she would love dinner this evening! I'm making it myself. By 'the works,' I assume you mean chili, sauerkraut, onions, mustard, and ketchup?"

Trish was giggling now, too. "That's the only way to eat them. Especially at the ballpark. I hope you have bibs! I dribble."

Malik continued to laugh, slapping his thigh over and over. "I do, too. I just use a dish towel."

"That'll work for me." Trish continued to giggle. "What's your feeling about ramen noodles?"

"Ate them three times a week with my friends. We bought them by the case. That way we had more money to spend on beer."

"You are hopeless, Malik. Our father must be turning over in his grave at the way you turned out. What is Trish going to think?"

Without any prompting, Trish spoke up. "I like it. Everyone I know acts like Malik. It's like meeting my friends all over again. I guess you don't like hot dogs or beer, huh?"

"You know what, Trish? She does. She just won't admit it. She's as stubborn as a mule. The last time I made them, she ate three of them and drank two bottles of beer. I had to carry her to her quarters."

In spite of herself, Soraya laughed. "Sadly, what he says is true. Our problem is that Malik treats me to these American things, but he will not allow me to go there to visit. Nor would my father. It is a very sore point with me. He says I am too young to travel by myself. And yet he went with an entourage of his own. Tell me that is fair!"

Always outspoken on anything concerning women's issues especially, Trish sat straight up in her chair and looked at Malik. "That is not fair. Why were you able to go, and

75

she can't? Is it because she's a woman?" The edge in her voice had crept in without her even knowing it. She tried to backpedal by smiling.

"I said I would think about it, sister. I didn't say no. Many plans have to be put into place."

"Baloney! That's his favorite word, more fitting than some he uses. That's like telling a child you'll think about giving them ice cream next week if you don't forget to order it. I want an answer sooner rather than later."

Malik threw his hands in the air. "No wonder my father banished you to the other side of the palace. All you do is nag and whine. And you're doing it in front of our guest. Shame on you, Soraya."

"Get off it, Malik. See? His sayings have rubbed off on me. I think with what I've learned from him, I could handle myself in America. Don't you agree, Trish?"

"Well . . ."

"I think this might be a good time for me to start grilling our hot dogs," Malik said, getting up. He winked at Trish as he rounded the corner.

"He just wants to show off that new range he bought. It's a Jenn-Air and grills and does everything but eat the food for you.

My brother, the chef!"

So, even here in Dubai, half a world away from her home, things were, to a certain extent, no different. Brothers and sisters argued and baited one another just like brothers and sisters all over the world.

Trish and Soraya made casual conversation while Malik bustled about his mini kitchen. "He is so proud of this . . . this apartment. He spends more time here than in his own quarters. He says he can think better here," she whispered. "And he had this up and working in less than ten days. He is so proud of that Jenn-Air cooking range."

Trish winked at Soraya. "You sound a tad jealous. Would you like a place like this yourself? You know, someplace to run off to where you could think or run naked through the rooms, do something silly or unexpected?"

Soraya whispered again. "How did you know?"

"Because I'm a girl, and you're a girl. That's what we do back home. We all need that sanctuary we can go to from time to time."

"Do you have one?" Soraya asked, curiosity ringing in her voice.

"See, that's the good thing. I don't need

one, because I live alone in my town house. I can do whatever I want, whenever I want. There is no one watching me, hovering about me, telling me what to do and when to do it. I'm my own person. I'm independent. No one pays my bills but me. I am in control of me."

"And you like that . . . that independence?"

"Well, yeah," Trish drawled.

"Okay, dinner is served," Malik called from the kitchen. "Everything is on the counter. Help yourself."

"This is just like a barbecue back home," Trish observed, giggling as she speared a hot dog and put it on a steamed bun. Thank God the ice was broken and they were just like three old friends, sitting around, eating, and enjoying each other's company.

Soraya continued to bait her brother. "Show Trish what's in that icebox you have."

Malik leapt off the stool he was sitting on and opened the freezer-side door of the refrigerator to reveal stacks and stacks of Sabrett hot dogs. On the shelves of the freezer door were what looked like hundreds of packages of hot-dog rolls. He showed it all off proudly as he grinned from ear to ear.

"Now, show her the refrigerator side," Soraya chortled as she bit into her hot dog.

Malik opened the other door to reveal shelves of Budweiser beer, condiments, and a small bowl with apples that were shriveled and angry-looking.

"I thought Muslims didn't drink," Trish said.

"They don't. We don't. Only in here can I do that. It's like the Jewish guys I went to school with. Their parents, they said, kept a kosher house, but they ate pork and bacon on the outside. At home they kept the dairy away from the meat. It's the same thing here." He laughed, that delightful sound Trish loved.

"If you say so."

"I say so. How do you like your hot dog?"

"Best I ever ate. Cooked just right."

For the next hour, they laughed and enjoyed each other's company. "Okay, I cooked. You girls can clean up."

"I think this is where I say good night and leave you two to yourselves," Soraya said, sliding off her stool.

Trish was already off her stool and gathering up the paper plates and napkins. She had wondered when Soraya would leave them alone or if she would. She now had her answer.

"Let's take a walk in the palace garden,"

79

Malik said to Trish. "I'd like to show you how we grow things here in the desert. You look tired, Trish. Would you rather go back to your suite?"

"It's just the jet lag. I would love a walk in the garden. I love the evening air." She would love anything, she wanted to say, as long as she was seeing or doing it with Malik.

Ten minutes into the walk, with Malik holding her hand and explaining the palace's horticulture, Trish leaned against a stout trellis and tried to keep from falling asleep on her feet. She closed her eyes and felt her knees start to buckle. Once again, she felt strong arms reach for her and pick her up. Her eyelids felt like they were lead weights. She forced them open a crack and murmured, "You have the most beautiful eyes, and I love your smile."

Malik cradled her in his arms and smiled down at her. "We really have to stop meeting like this, or people are going to start talking about us."

"Hmm, yes, but I feel safe here with you."

"I will always keep you safe, Trish Holiday."

Trish murmured something else. Malik had to lean down to hear what she was saying. He thought she said, "It takes forty-eight hours to digest a hot dog." The silly grin he was feeling stayed with him.

Within forty-two seconds, the palace grapevine was twittering and chittering about the sheik carrying the American houseguest from his *cave* to her suite. Thirty seconds after that, the chittering and twittering confirmed that the sheik returned to his *cave* with a silly smile on his face.

The smile wasn't just silly, but it was sappy, as Malik returned to his cave to finish the cleanup. He popped two bottles of Budweiser and carried them to his sitting room, where he waited for Rashid's knock.

"Come in, Rashid!"

"Like old times, eh, Malik?" Rashid said, sitting down and propping his feet on the coffee table. "So, how did it go?"

Malik turned so that he was facing his old friend. "She's the one, Rashid."

"Does she know she's the one?"

"I think so. I guess you heard the palace grapevine?"

"That's why I'm here. What happened?"

"Jet lag. She leaned back against the trellis, closed her eyes, and that was it. I caught her just in time. Kismet! She said I had a beautiful smile and beautiful eyes. She said she felt safe with me. Yes, she's the one! Tell me your thoughts, my friend."

81

"My thoughts are, I am happy for you, Malik. Now what?"

"I have to make a plan. I don't want to scare her off. This life is strange to her. I want to show her everything, so I'm going to need you to step into my shoes, cover for me at meetings and do my job, while I do that. Will you do that for me? By the way, did you know it takes forty-eight hours to digest a hot dog?"

The stupid look on Rashid's face caused Malik to laugh out loud. "No, I didn't know that. Of course I will do whatever you want, but only if you assure me that Soraya won't be breathing down my neck every minute of the day. If you can guarantee that, I'll step into your shoes."

"Done! Want another beer?"

"You know it! How'd she like your cave?"

"She loved it. As much as I do, and as much as you do, but you won't admit it."

"The palace is buzzing tonight," Rashid said.

The old friends laughed and clapped one another on the back.

"Life is good, Rashid. Let's hope it stays that way." Malik twisted the caps off the beer bottles and raised his. "To happiness!"

"To happiness."

CHAPTER 5

The days leading up to the end of Trish's vacation passed in a whirlwind. There were times when she barely had time to catch her breath, with all there was to see and do. Malik was the perfect host. Soraya was just as perfect when Malik would have to disappear for several hours at a time "to attend to palace business," as he put it.

The only regret Trish had was that the romantic part of the vacation, which she longed for, had simply not happened. There had been no kisses and no sex, something she was sure would have happened by now. It was hard not to throw herself at Malik and ask him what was wrong with her that he didn't at least want to hold her in his arms and kiss her. If nothing else, at least on the cheek.

It was close to midnight, and Trish was getting ready for bed. Malik had seen her to her door. He squeezed her hand and wished her a good night's sleep. She wanted to scream at him. *How can I have a good night's sleep when all I do is dream of you?* But she'd said no such thing. She bit down on her lip and somehow willed herself to force a smile she was far from feeling.

Two days to go, and she would be headed back to the States with bags of new clothes Soraya had insisted on buying for her. Jewelry Malik had insisted on buying for her. Trinkets and souvenirs she had purchased with her own money for her sister, her niece, and her friends. Just proof that she had been here. A once-in-a-lifetime vacation that hadn't begun to live up to her expectations.

She was in bed, nestled between silk sheets that were changed every single day. She leaned back into the nest of pillows and called her friend Connie. She started to babble, almost immediately complaining about Malik's behavior. "Either there is something wrong with me or he's gay. I've done everything but throw myself at him, and he just smiles at me. I just give up. Two days to go, then I'm homeward bound. You have any advice for me, Connie?"

"We've skirted around this for almost two weeks now. Are you in love with Malik, Trish?"

"No. Yes. Oh, Connie, I don't know. The customs here are so different from ours. For all I know, he might have a woman stashed somewhere, and he's just being nice to me because . . . I don't know why. None of this makes sense. Why bring me all the way across the world just to be nice to me? I guess I hoped . . . I read the signs wrong. That just makes me a foolish woman. I wanted so badly to talk to Soraya, and while we are friends, Malik is off-limits in our conversations unless she brings up his name. I would never dare ask Rashid anything about Malik. Women over here have their place, and you stay in that place unless you are invited out of said place. I tried talking to my sister the other day, but she has her own problems, and she never approved of my coming here to begin with."

"Well, you have two more days, Trish. What's on your agenda for those two days?"

"I don't have a clue. Malik and I meet for breakfast, and he outlines a plan for the day. We dine here at the palace in the evening, and usually, Soraya or Rashid joins us. It's all very formal. After dinner, Malik and I take a walk in the garden. There are many gardens here, each one more beautiful than the previous one. He holds my hand. That's it. *He holds my hand.* Are you telling me you have no advice for me?"

"I guess I don't, Trish. What do the two of you talk about?"

"Everything and nothing. Malik's time in the States. His cave, where he goes to unwind and relax. He talked at great length about his father's passing. He wasn't ready 'to step into his father's sandals,' as he put it. He thought he would have at least another thirty years of being a prince before he became a sheik. He said his father sent him to school in the States so he would learn business, because the oil is running out here and it yields only a six to eight percent return.

"He needs to run this country commercially, and I guess he's pretty good at it, to his own dismay. Everyone over here is concerned about the country's prospects when the oil runs out. He said that Dubai would be doomed if his father hadn't seen the handwriting on the wall earlier and put plans into motion for the country. Now he has to follow through on those plans."

"It sounds like he has a lot on his plate," Connie observed.

"He does. Soraya told me several days ago, just in passing, that Malik did not want to step into his father's sandals, but he had no other choice. Here's the kicker, Connie.

Soraya would love the job, but since she's a woman, that can't be. The only way, according to Soraya, a woman could step in is if she was married to the sheik and he passed away. Only then could a woman, the wife, step in. I don't know if that's carved in stone or something Soraya just thinks could happen. Sometimes, to be perfectly frank, she's a little ditzy. Can you imagine a life dedicated to shopping, massages, manicures, pedicures, facials, and having teas? That's her whole life.

"Soraya can be a bit of a spitfire, though. She refuses to marry any one of the men her father picked for her. Malik says she's going to be an old maid if she doesn't make up her mind soon. The flip side to that is there is no chance she can find a man, because she is not free to pick one and goes nowhere where she could find one. Secretly, I think she has a thing for Rashid."

"Sounds like palace intrigue to me. I miss you, Trish. The girls and I can't wait to see you again. Let's get together the moment you get back."

"Okay. Guess it's time to go to sleep. Did I tell you they use pure silk sheets here, and they get changed every day? It's hard not to get used to some things."

Connie laughed as they said good night.

Trish curled up and tried to settle herself. Was she in love? How could she not love the kind, considerate, handsome man who had held her in his arms twice? A tear rolled down her cheek. She brushed it away, but then more tears flowed. In less than forty-eight hours, she would be on her way home.

Since sleep was out of the question, Trish got up, put on a robe and slippers, and walked out to her own garden, where she sat down and smoked a cigarette. Then she smoked another, and still another, all the while crying and sniffling. She wished she had a strong drink, maybe two drinks. Anything to take away the pain she was feeling.

Trish sat for a long time, the tears trickling down her cheeks. When she couldn't stand sitting any longer, she got up and paced up and down the little paths until finally she thought maybe she could sleep.

She didn't see the many eyes that watched her, and she had no idea that the palace grapevine operated in the dead of night. Within minutes, Sheik Malik bin Al Mohammed was wakened and apprised that his guest was crying in the garden and smoking cigarettes. She had been doing so for hours, he was told.

Alarmed at this strange news, Malik called

in Rashid, then his sister, to demand an answer to his guest's distress. Both Rashid and Soraya stared at Malik as if he had sprouted a second head, saying they had no clue as to what was wrong.

Unsettled at being awakened in the middle of the night, Soraya fixed her gaze on her brother and opined, "Perhaps it is you, my brother, that has upset our guest."

"Me! Don't be ridiculous. If that is the best you can come up with, go back to bed. Rashid?"

Rashid shrugged. "Women are strange creatures. How many times have we discussed this? Too many to count. Maybe she was crying with happiness. It is possible. Women do cry when they are happy. Your sister herself told me this."

"And you believe my sister!" There was such outrage in Malik's voice that Rashid cringed.

Rashid shrugged. "There is a way to find out, Malik. You simply ask her in the morning, when you meet for breakfast. Of course, she might not like your asking, knowing that people are and have been spying on her. You don't know a lot about women, do you?" Rashid said.

"About as much as you do, obviously. Women cry. I understand that. I just don't know the why of it. We have treated her like a princess. We showered her with gifts. We have seen to everything. What did we miss? Well? What did we miss?"

"Look, this is just a wild guess on my part, Malik, but maybe it's *you*. Maybe she expected you to . . . I don't know . . . be more amorous, more like American men. She is an American, you know."

"What are you saying? I have too much respect for Trish to . . . to . . ."

"Yes," Rashid drawled.

"You know what I'm saying. Do you really think she thinks I should . . ."

"Like I'm suddenly an authority on women? I don't know, Malik. Maybe she was expecting you to sweep her off her feet, declare undying love, like in American films. It is a possibility, and it's the only one I can think of."

Malik sat down on the edge of his bed. "Rashid, I can't kiss her, have sex with her, not that I don't dream of that night and day, because I have to be true to my faith. Only if we are betrothed can I kiss her."

"Aha! You know that. I know that. But does Miss Holiday know that? Of course she doesn't. She's American. She thinks you aren't interested in her in a romantic sense. See, Malik? Now it all makes sense. She thinks she isn't good enough for you. Otherwise, you would have made a . . . What's the saying? A move on her . . . by now."

"Is that possible, Rashid?" Malik asked, misery ringing in his voice.

Flushed with this newfound knowledge of women, Rashid beamed and said, "It's the only thing that makes sense. Once you eliminate the impossible, whatever remains, no matter how improbable, must be the truth. Therefore, it must be true."

"Then that makes me stupid, Rashid."

"Yes, my friend, it does."

"So, what do I do now?"

Rashid threw his hands in the air. "What do you want me to do? Draw you a diagram? Figure it out. I'm going back to bed. Remember this, though. You have only two more days. Actually, less than two days. Good night, Malik."

The moment the door closed behind Rashid, Malik got dressed and beelined to his cave, where he popped a bottle of Budweiser and sat down to contemplate his next move. All those years of study, all the academics, and here he sat, looking like a fool.

He was a fool. He now had less than forty-eight hours to make a decision. Why had he thought that miraculously something would come to him to help him along? Was it his intention to wait till the eleventh hour to declare his intentions? How stupid was that? Where did that kind of thinking come from? Rashid was right: He knew less than nothing about women, and he had no one to ask. Just blunder along and hope for the best. Well, obviously, that wasn't going to be good enough. . . . Correct that thought. . . . It wasn't good enough for Trish Holiday.

He loved her. Had loved her the minute he set eyes on her. Had been waiting for her to give him a sign, a clue, that she felt the same way. She'd told him that she loved his eyes, his smile, that she felt safe with him. Wasn't the man supposed to make the first move? But they were of different faiths. How could he expect her to know or understand what he was thinking if he didn't tell her? The playing field had to be level; only then did the game start.

Not that any of this was a game, though in a way it was. He'd thought that by inviting her here, she'd know he cared about her. So, he screwed up there. He'd waited too long to tell her how he felt.

Malik popped another Budweiser, then another and a third and a fourth. When he consumed the fifth bottle, he stopped. By the time he had the bottles lined up like soldiers, he had a good buzz on. And with the buzz came clarity of a sort. He looked at his watch: 4:55 a.m. He squared his shoulders, looked around for his baseball cap, and jammed it on his head. He left his cave and strode down the hall, then down another hall, around two corners, until he got to Trish's suite. He didn't bother knocking. Why should he? He owned the joint. He knew eyes were on him, but he didn't care. He walked toward the bedroom, and here he did knock. He waited until he saw the light go on, then opened the door.

Trish sat up in bed, a look of alarm on her face. "What's wrong?" she managed to gasp.

"Everything is wrong! I did everything wrong! I'm sorry! Will you marry me?"

Will you marry me? Four of the most beautiful words Trish had ever heard in her life. She tried to make her tongue work. It refused. So she nodded and leapt out of bed and into Malik's arms.

"Since you said yes, I can kiss you now." And he did, until they were both so light-headed, they had to hold on to one another to stay on their feet.

Trish found her tongue. "What took you so long to ask me? I would have said yes on the first day."

"You would have?" Malik said in stunned surprise.

"Uh-huh. Kiss me again. I liked it."

When they broke apart the second time, Trish said, "I thought there was something wrong with me, that I had bad breath, I smelled, that I wasn't good enough for you. I thought a hundred different things. How many beers did you have?"

"Five!" Malik said proudly. "I needed them for courage. I'm not supposed to be in here without a chaperone."

"I won't tell anyone."

"Everyone already knows, trust me. I'm going to leave you now. I'll see you at breakfast."

"Are you going to kiss me again?"

Malik looked at the bed. "No!"

Trish laughed. She waved good-bye and absolutely loved the silly grin she saw on Malik's face. She wondered how she looked to the eyes that were watching her, not that she cared. When the door closed, she turned around and hopped up on her bed and did a jig among the tangled silk sheets. *Oh my God, I am getting married!*

CHAPTER 6

Promptly at five minutes to seven, Trish and her shadow made their way to the dining room, where Malik was waiting for her, a silly grin on his face. Trish knew her grin was just as silly. He held her chair, the silly grin still on his face.

"I'm not sure I can eat. I didn't go back to sleep. I couldn't wait to get here this morning. I am sooo happy," Trish babbled.

It was all Malik could do not to sweep her up and run from the room. There was so much he wanted to say, so much he wanted to do for this woman sitting across from him. First, he wanted to get up on his feet and shout to the palace that he was in love, but that would have been stupid. Everyone in the palace already knew.

Instead of going back to bed, he had gone to Rashid's room and woken him for a second time to inform him about what he had done.

Rashid had grumbled good-naturedly but had got up and sat down on a settee alongside his old friend. "Now what?"

"Now you plan my wedding, Rashid. I have things to do. Maybe Soraya will give you some advice. She loves telling people what to do. Don't we have wedding planners here at the palace? You know, like that crazy movie we saw back in the States."

Rashid rubbed the sleep from his eyes. "Let me make sure I have this right. You want *me* to plan *your* wedding. Me, who knows as much as you know about things like this. I have no idea if we have a wedding planner here at the palace. I'm thinking we don't, or at some time or other, we probably would have heard about it. No member of the royalty has gotten married in this palace that I know of. Your sister, after all, kept rejecting all the prospective husbands your father presented to her. Anyway, I think women are supposed to do things like that. Soraya has nothing to do, so let her have a go at it."

"I trust you, Rashid. Find a wedding planner and work with him or her. I want my wedding to be perfect. Besides, when Trish goes back to the States, I am going to allow Soraya to go with her. It will just be long enough for Trish to do what she has to do

96

before she moves here permanently. That just leaves you, Rashid. I know you'll do a good job. Nothing tacky, now. But I want it a mix of our way and Trish's way. A wedding to remember. Perhaps two ceremonies, one Muslim and one Christian. Check that out. I feel so much better now that I know our wedding is in your capable hands."

Those capable hands flew in the air. "I quit. Wedding planning is not in my job description, Malik."

Malik laughed. "You can't quit. You are bound to me for life. We both know that. Two ceremonies, the private one and the palace one. Do a really good job and don't bother me with details. I have a honeymoon to plan. Do it for me, Rashid. I promise to have Trish bring you back a planeload of White Castle burgers."

"You cannot bribe me, Malik." Rashid's tone belied his words and made it clear that he could be bribed that easily.

"I just did. We both know you would cut off your arm for those burgers. Like me with the hot dogs, which take forty-eight hours to digest. I wouldn't go back to sleep if I were you. You have a busy day, starting right now."

"I need a date, Malik! When do you want to get married? I could be wrong, but doesn't the bride-to-be have some input here?"

"The sooner the better, but at least a month from now. Trish will need two to three weeks back in the States. She is as anxious to get married as I am, so don't worry about that. Soraya will need that much time, too. See how perfectly this is working out, Rashid? I'm killing two birds with one stone, and my sister and her incessant pestering will be done with. She will come back here joyfully and, I hope, a changed young woman."

"Well, that's not going to happen. You're a fool if you think so," Rashid said sourly.

"Carry on, Rashid. I have to meet my prospective bride for breakfast. By the way, my next project after getting married, palace business, and seeing to my sister is going to be finding you a wife. I think that's your problem."

Rashid dropped his head in his hands and pretended to sulk as Malik left his suite of rooms. The moment the door closed behind him, Rashid's clenched fist shot into the air.

The palace buzzed and hummed as the two lovebirds finished their breakfast just as Soraya entered the dining room, late as usual. She eyed her brother, sparks shooting in his direction. "And I have to find out this wondrous news from a servant!"

"I didn't want to wake you, sister. Had you been on time for breakfast, you would have known sooner. Spending less time in front of a mirror would do it, Soraya."

Soraya ignored her brother. She bent over to hug her soon-to-be sister-in-law and murmured all the right words about how happy she was to welcome her into their lives. Trish hugged her back.

"I have a surprise for you, Soraya. I am going to allow you to go to the States with Trish when she returns to settle her affairs. You will return with her. Let's make sure we both understand that."

"Of course! Of course! Truly, I can go? Oh, you are the best brother in the whole world. No chaperones, though. Just Trish and me. I want to experience this all on my own. Say yes, Malik. Please, no chaperones, just Trish."

Malik looked at Trish, and she bobbed her head up and down. Since Malik could deny his bride-to-be nothing, he agreed.

Soraya was off her chair in a nanosecond. She did her best to smother her brother with kisses and hugs. "Oh, I am too excited to eat. I must pack." She was almost out of the dining room when she ran back. "Who is planning the wedding?"

"Rashid." Malik hated the sound of his sister's laughter as she ran from the room.

Trish burst out laughing. "Are you having second thoughts about your wedding planner?" Trish giggled.

"Not one little bit. Well, perhaps a little. All right, a lot. But Rashid will not fail us. I think I can guarantee it will be a wedding to remember. Come. Let's go to the garden. It's been too long since I kissed you."

Trish needed no urging. She bolted from the chair and reached for Malik's hand. She couldn't wait to feel his lips on hers.

Life certainly was wonderful.

In between earth-shattering kisses, the ecstatic couple talked of what married life would be like, living in the palace, how many children they wanted, how they would be raised, and what Trish's role would be until the children came along. Many more kisses later, Malik got down to what he called "the serious stuff."

The serious stuff turned into a one-way discussion of money, lots of money, way too much money for Trish to comprehend. "I spoke to my advisers early this morning to bring them up to date, not that they weren't already up to date. I've spoken to them several times since my father's passing, and they told me the only record they have of a marriage here in the palace was that of my father many years ago and how the situation was resolved with my mother's parents. So, we must abide by that ruling.

"On our wedding day, you will receive five million dollars. It will be deposited in banks in Switzerland or perhaps Liechtenstein. Possibly the Antilles. The account will be solely in your name. My advisers will hold meetings with you, and you will tell them how you want your money invested. That is my wedding gift to you. Then there is a rule in place that every year we stay married, on the anniversary of our wedding day, another five million dollars will be deposited into your account. In addition to that, for every child born of our union, five million more will be deposited.

"No one will ever be able to touch that money but you. Also, you will have an account here at the palace, where you will have access to as much money as you need to use for whatever you want. We also have credit cards and accounts at all the souks. All you have to do is sign your name."

Trish's eyes popped wide. "No! I am not marrying you for your money. I can't accept that. The palace account, yes, but nothing else, Malik."

"It's not negotiable, Trish. It's how it is done here. Are we going to fight?" he teased.

"No, Malik, I have no wish to fight with you. Life is too short. I just want you to know that I am not marrying you for your wealth. I'd live in a tent in the desert with you if it came down to that. I never once thought . . . What in the world am I to do with all that money?"

Malik nodded, as though he had known all along what she would say. "I need to speak of two more things. You won't like hearing them, either, and I don't like to speak of them myself, but it must be done. One, you must learn to speak Arabic. Not fluently, but enough so that you can greet and carry on a conversation of sorts with our people. And we ask, note I said *ask*, that you read the Koran. In turn, I will read your Bible. Will you agree to this?"

Trish didn't miss a beat. "Absolutely."

"That brings me to the last thing on my list of things to discuss. In the event of my death, you will step into my sandals. Only a wife can do this, not my sister, and she fully understands this. If there are children, boys specifically, even if young, they wear the sandals, so to speak, with trusted advisers until they come of age.

"In the event we divorce, you get to keep

102

all your monies, but you must leave the kingdom and never return. There will be many papers for you to sign. I myself went through all this when I left for America. I signed until I thought my fingers would fall off. It is our way, and we can change nothing. We agree now, speak of it now, and then we never have to speak of it again."

Trish turned thoughtful. "Should we divorce, who gets the children, assuming we have children?"

Malik knew this question would come up. "The children would stay here. You would have my promise that they would be tutored in both faiths. When they came of age, they could seek you out on their own. This is written in stone, Trish. I cannot change it even if I wanted to. In the event we have no children by the fifth year of our marriage, you will leave Dubai voluntarily. I will remain. And then, like my father, never marry again."

"Would I be allowed to see the children if we were divorced?"

"Unfortunately, the answer is no. We will not divorce, Trish. That is a promise I make to you from my heart. I'm sure we will have as many children as we want. But not right away. We need to spend our first year together. I know this is like a blow to the gut, but it all needed to be said. I know you agree now, but when you are back in the States, you might want to change your mind. I hope that doesn't happen."

"It won't happen, Malik, because I love you. We'll make this work for us. I don't see any other way. Don't look so somber. It wasn't that much of a punch to the gut. I more or less thought it would be something like that. I'm marrying you with my eyes wide open. So, now kiss me, and let's seal our fate."

Trish looked deeply into Malik's eyes and saw only love and honesty. "All right, I agree. But, Malik, what if we have no children?"

Malik burst out laughing. "I don't see that happening, do you, Trish? I see us with a large family to love. Let's start off with two girls who look like you and two boys who look like me."

Trish smiled because she knew Malik expected her to smile, but the smile didn't reach her eyes. She hadn't liked this conversation, had known in some way it was coming, but, still, she didn't like it. *Two too many negatives. Please, God, don't let this be a mistake on my part.*

Trish looked down at her watch. Just minutes until it was time to leave for the airport for her return to the States. Compared to the way Soraya was dressed, she felt like a bag lady. She wore comfortable sandals, linen capris, and a loose-fitting top the color of a misty mountain. Soraya was dressed in one of her many Chanel suits with high heels. Everything about her screamed designer and wealth. She herself had only the one piece of luggage, whereas Soraya had three huge suitcases and two trunks. Where she was going to store these things in Trish's small town house was a mystery to her.

She'd tried to explain discreetly that her friends and she herself did not *dress up* every day. She'd also tried to explain that appointments for facials, massages, manicures, and pedicures had to be made in advance and couldn't be done daily. If Soraya heard her, it was not evident in her manner. In her gut, she knew Soraya was going to be disappointed in the lifestyle back in Vegas. Then again, maybe not. Malik had taken life in the States in stride and had made it work for him. But by the same token, he had committed to living the college life and wanted to blend in, to be part of it. This was just a vacation for Soraya.

In the end, Trish had shrugged it off. What would be would be.

Trish was in the grand center hallway, sitting on a settee and waiting for Soraya, who had returned to her suite to change her shoes one more time, and Malik. She felt sad that she was leaving and yet anxious to return to the life she'd had before coming to Dubai. The plan was that Malik would go to the airport with them, see them off, then go on to Abu Dhabi for meetings.

Trish looked at her watch again. Time was suddenly so precious. She wished she could wave her arm and stop time, but that wasn't possible. She had to fight the tears that were burning her eyes.

Then she saw him striding toward her, and her heart melted. This was only the second time she had seen Malik in his official white robe, the *kandura,* and with the white scarf, called a *ghutra,* on his head, complete with the *agal,* the black band to hold the scarf in place. When she'd seen him the first time, she had been sick and hadn't really taken it all in. He looked truly regal, imposing as well as important. The first time he had simply been the man who saved her life. Trish felt her heart fluttering in her chest. She blinked as he drew closer, then burst out laughing when she saw the rhinestone belt around his waist. Somehow, she knew in her gut the stones weren't rhinestones at all but diamonds. How this man tried to please her. She loved him so much, her hair hurt. She said so, and he laughed.

"What do you think, Trish? Will I make a statement when I walk into my meeting with all the sheiks and emirs?"

Trish laughed. "Within seconds, you will have them all begging to find out where you got such a . . . conversation piece. On you it looks . . . splendiferous."

"I miss you already, and you haven't even left yet. Please hurry back, and please do not break my heart and change your mind."

"You silly man, as if that could ever happen. Never!" Trish said vehemently. "Where is Soraya?"

"Probably changing her clothes for the tenth time. She wants to look perfect for you, so you aren't ashamed of her."

"Good grief! Tell me that was a joke, Malik."

"No joke. Listen to me, Trish. As soon as she gets all her junk in your place, I want you to burn it and buy her a pair of blue jeans, sneakers, and get her a Berkeley Golden Bears T-shirt. Will you do this for me? If you can't burn her things, when she isn't looking, give them away. She's going to make a fool of herself with her highfalutin sense of fashion, and I don't want to see her hurt. I want her American experience to be genuine."

Trish's eyes popped wide. "Are you serious?"

"Never more serious, dear one."

Trish swallowed hard. "Well, perhaps there is a better way, less drastic, more . . . gentle."

"Well, if there is, I'm sure you'll find it. Ah, here comes the fashion plate now. One can only guess how much that outfit cost."

Soraya rushed up to them on her high heels. She took one look at Trish and almost cried. "I am overdressed!"

"What was your first clue, sister? You are going on a plane ride, a long plane ride. The idea is to be comfortable. You are not going to a movie premiere, where you have to outdo everyone else," Malik snapped.

Soraya eyed Trish's casual clothing and bleated, "I will change. Oh, I can't change. I have no clothing like Trish's. What shall I do?"

"What you always do, cry, whine, and wring your hands," Malik said. "There is no time. Come. We must leave, or we will be late. The plane will be burning fuel, and I do not like to see waste." He turned to Trish. "Our city is sixty percent under construction, and traffic is slow, as you have seen since your arrival. My other plane is also sitting on the tarmac, burning fuel."

Wringing her hands and blinking away tears, Soraya followed her brother and Trish out to the waiting limousine, where Rashid stood at the open door. He was to accompany Malik as his next in command to Abu Dhabi.

"What is your problem, little sister?" Rashid asked.

"My brother tells me I am an embarrassment. I am dressed all wrong for a long plane ride. No one told me. Someone should have told me." Tears spilled down her cheeks.

Rashid looked at Malik's stern face and wisely kept silent, even though he thought Soraya looked quite beautiful. He shrugged as he held the door of the limousine for the two women to get in. He tried not to look at Soraya's gorgeous legs. What was wrong with him? Why, all of a sudden, was he looking at Malik's baby sister in such a way? Later, he would try to sort out his thoughts. Much, much later.

They were driving through the city known as the City of Gold, making small talk about nothing as they made their way to Al Maktoum International Airport. Trish's thoughts were everywhere but on the trip. She was trying to count the moments she still had with Malik. All she could do was stare across at him and smile. He looked, she thought, as sad as she felt.

Their driver was an expert at weaving in and out of the congestion, and Rashid remarked that they were making good time.

"Good time" meant she was that much closer to leaving Malik. Trish's stomach turned into a hard knot. Her tongue felt thick in her mouth. Her eyes were burning unbearably. Who knew that love could be so painful?

Time moved at the speed of light then. In a heartbeat, the limousine was crossing the tarmac, where two private planes waited, both burning fuel. The limousine stopped; Malik and Rashid were out in a nanosecond, followed by Trish and Soraya. They were herded toward the portable steps leading up to the plane.

Malik stepped back, bowed slightly, reached for Trish's hands, then kissed them both. They were in public, and in public, there were no displays of passion.

Tears trickled down Trish's cheeks. She whispered, "I'll be back before you know it."

Malik nodded. "I'll be waiting here, at this

exact spot, for you." He kissed his sister on the cheek. He looked her in the eyes and said, "Do not bring dishonor to our family. Do you understand, little sister?"

Soraya nodded before she ran up the steps behind Trish. At the doorway, both women waved. One sad, one happy.

Below the stairs, two men stood waving, both sad.

Settled inside the plane, Trish looked at Soraya and said, "And now your adventure begins."

"I can hardly wait. I will not embarrass you again, Trish. I promise."

Trish nodded as she leaned back in the comfortable seat and closed her eyes. She promised herself to think of nothing else but Malik on the flight home. Try as she might, the tears came and rolled down her cheeks.

Soraya reached for Trish's hand. "The time will go quickly, and before you know it, you will be back here, looking forward to your wedding. My brother loves you more than life itself. He told me this himself. Why, I do not know, because he never tells me things such as that. Maybe he thinks I am finally grown up, and I understand now. Tell me, what did you think of him in his robe?"

Trish sniffled. "I thought he looked quite

handsome. Dashing, actually. He could be a movie star. Like the actor in *Lawrence of Arabia.* I loved that movie. I must learn Arabic. Is it hard?"

"About as hard as it was for me to learn English. Do not worry. I will help you. Soon we will be sisters. I have longed forever to have a sister or other siblings."

"I'm honored to have you as a sister, Soraya."

And then they were airborne. Soraya clapped her hands in glee. "I'm finally going to America. Finally!"

CHAPTER 7

As Trish unbuckled her seat belt, she looked over at Soraya. "We're home! Malik said that he arranged for a car to take us to my place and that customs was taken care of. Are you ready for your big adventure in America?"

"I am so ready, Trish. I can't wait to step off this plane and experience everything my brother did when he first got here."

"It's going to be a bit different. Malik was in California and was going to school. It's a whole different atmosphere. This is Las Vegas, and there is no other place in the world like Vegas. Did you sleep well?"

"Actually, I did. What time is it? I forgot to set my watch."

"Almost midnight. The witching hour. This is the time of night when Vegas really comes alive. Not that we're going to be seeing it tonight. We're going home to bed. Tomorrow is a new day. I hope you aren't disappointed."

"It's the holiday season. How could I be disappointed? I've never experienced your holiday. I'm looking forward to it. You must call Malik now to tell him we arrived safely. He will be pacing in his cave like an expecting father. Put him out of his misery so we can get on with it."

Trish already had the phone in her hand and was pressing in the digits. She wasn't the least surprised when Malik picked up on the first ring. "Is it a boy or a girl?" she teased, then explained what Soraya had said.

"I miss you. I love you so much, my teeth hurt," Malik said.

Trish laughed. "That's my line. We're on the ground now. They're loading your sister's things into the car. I guess they'll deliver the trunks later, as they won't fit in the car. I've never seen your sister so happy. Don't worry. I'll take good care of her." They made small talk and finally hung up when the driver opened the door for her and Soraya. Soraya got in first, then Trish.

Homeward bound.

"It's cold," Soraya said. "I know this is your winter. I've never seen snow except in the movies. I will have to buy appropriate clothes."

"Why waste the money, Soraya? We're

pretty much the same size. You can wear mine. Even though I slept on the plane, I'm tired."

"Yes, but I am too excited to sleep. I wish it were daytime so I could see everything."

Trish yawned. "Tomorrow is another day. I just want to take a shower and go to bed."

Soraya chattered and giggled the whole way to the town house. She was still chattering when they climbed the steps to the front door. Trish stepped back when she saw and smelled the fragrant evergreen wreath hanging on her front door. Connie. That was so like her. She'd come over, hung the wreath, turned up the heat, and probably changed the sheets on the beds and stocked the refrigerator. A true friend, if ever there was one.

Trish opened the door. "Welcome to my home, Soraya." She reached up and turned on the foyer light. Even from where she was standing, she could see the twinkling Christmas tree in the living room. Not only was there a tree, but there were beautifully wrapped packages underneath it, too. The girls. Tears formed in Trish's eyes. Such good friends.

"Oh, it smells . . . delicious, just like the wreath on the door. It's a real tree!" Soraya squealed. "Did your maid do all this, Trish?"

"Stop right there! There is *no* maid. My friends did all this to welcome me home. From here on in, you fend for yourself, and that means you carry your own bags to your room and you unpack yourself. You run your own bath or take a shower. You fix your own food, and you clean up after yourself."

"Yes, yes, I get it. Just like Malik did. He knows how to do laundry. He knows how to cook and drive a car. I'm going to do everything just the way he did. Do you have any root beer?"

"I doubt it, but check in the refrigerator. I'm going to have a glass of wine and look at my Christmas tree for a bit. I wish Malik were here to see it. Make yourself at home. Your room is at the top of the stairs, on the right."

"I'll take pictures and send them to Malik right now. He's not sleeping. This is too good not to share with him. Besides, it will do him good to be jealous of me for a change." Soraya laughed as she snapped picture after picture.

At least she's actually doing something for herself, Trish thought as she poured herself a glass of wine and carried it into the living room. She kicked off her shoes and flopped down on the couch. Her eyes misted over as she stared at the fragrant balsam tree as memories of her childhood flooded through her. First thing in the morning, she had to call her sister.

The holiday season. The most glorious time of the year, especially in Vegas.

Half a world away, Malik stared at the pictures he was seeing. He smiled as he remembered many Christmases with his friends when he lived in the States. He adored the picture of Trish smiling as she held her glass of wine aloft for Soraya's benefit, the colored lights on the Christmas tree beside her. He didn't know for sure, but he rather thought the tree was a real one, the kind that smelled up the whole place. He wished he were there.

The first few days after returning to Vegas were busy ones for Trish, but she managed to make time for shopping with Soraya for more suitable clothes, especially jeans, sneakers, sweatshirts, and outerwear. While Trish was busy getting her affairs in order, her friends took Soraya to lunch or sightseeing. They enthralled her with Vegas lore, including lurid tales of Bugsy Siegel and the founding of Las Vegas, and the stories of their lives, and Soraya ate it up whole. Her eyes sparkled and her step was jaunty as she geared up for the Christmas party at the casino and her first night in the audience. It would be Trish's last night of work. The only reason she'd agreed to dance at all was that Soraya wanted to see her in the chorus line, to see the woman her brother fell in love with from the audience.

Trish loved the peace and quiet she was experiencing at the moment. Connie had stopped by earlier to, as she put it, "take the girl off your hands for a few hours." They were going to do lunch and a little Christmas shopping.

Trish reached for her cell phone to call Emma, then glanced at her watch, mindful that she was three hours behind. Something about her sister's voice on the phone had bothered her when she had called on her return to the States. Time to find out how big sis really was. She pressed the number one on her speed dial. Her sister picked up after two rings.

"Emmie, it's me. How's it going? Can you talk?"

"Yes, the office is empty. I was just doing some cold calling. I don't know why I bother. No one wants to buy a house or even rent one during the Christmas season. It's a way to kill time, I guess. I did get one lady who said to call her after the New Year.

With the economy the way it is, I'm not hopeful. What's shaking in Vegas?"

"Same old, same old. Is anything wrong, Em? You didn't sound like yourself when we spoke the other day."

"Everything is as good as it's going to get. Except for Melissa. She doesn't want to live with me anymore. Says I'm way too strict. I can't give her a fifty-dollar-a-week allowance, so she wants to live with her father and his new trophy wife. Because she's already fourteen, a judge will listen to her and go with her choice. Jeff had his attorney send me a letter saying we could do this the easy way or the hard way, meaning he'll take me to court to get full custody. I'm just going to let her go with him. I don't have the stomach for another court fight. That means child support stops, and he'll undoubtedly find a way to stop the spousal support, too. Sooner rather than later."

"Why didn't you tell me that the other day, Em?"

"And ruin your homecoming? Why would I do that? This is my problem, not yours. According to Missy, her father left the firm he was working for and is now working for some big international one, and all he does is travel to the Middle East. She thinks Saudi Arabia and Abu Dhabi sound romantic. That's another reason I didn't want to tell her about you and Malik. She brags to all her friends about how important her father is.

"Selling real estate in a down market is not romantic. That leaves the trophy wife, who is just eight years older than Missy, on her own. He wants Missy to keep her eye on his new wife. Missy adores her. They shop till they drop, do girl things, putz and putter around. According to Missy, I am a Neanderthal, square, don't know where it's at, and a nag at the same time."

"Oh, God, Em, I am so sorry. What about Christmas?"

"Jeff is taking his wife and Missy to Hawaii. I didn't fight that, either. No point. I've become active in several support groups, and we have plans for Christmas, just like your friends there. That's so none of us are alone. We do our little lunches, tree trimmings, secret Santa gifts. You know how it goes. Listen, enough about me. Tell me stuff, little sister."

So she did. Trish thought her sister sounded genuinely happy for her. I wish you would come back with me for my wedding, Em. Will you at least think about it?"

"I can't, Trish, as much as I would like to. I have to be here for Missy in case she wants to come back. Once a mother, always a mother. If Jeff found out, he'd make my life miserable. I hope you understand why I didn't tell either one of them about your going to Dubai and now about getting married to a sheik. Somehow or other, Jeff would make that work for him and destroy you in the bargain. I don't know who he is anymore. He's driven by power and money.

"Here's another thing. Some of the women in my various support groups all got screwed the way I did with the same lawyer Jeff used. Those same guys all belong to this new international group that Jeff is heading up. I overheard Missy on the phone with one of her friends talking about her father. Okay, okay, I was eavesdropping. Sometimes you have to do that with teenagers. Anyway, she was bragging about how her father was going to be a billionaire very soon. Not a millionaire but a billionaire, and he was going to buy her a Porsche as soon as she got her driver's license. Missy never even mastered riding a bicycle. Look, let's talk about something else."

"Just promise me you won't be alone for Christmas, Em."

"I promise, Trish. By the way, your gifts arrived. I put them in the closet. I haven't put up a tree. Maybe a little artificial one

121

since Missy won't be here."

"How are you fixed for money?"

"I'm making it. Hey, I'm the big sister here. I have a little cushion. I never spent any of the money from the sale of Mom and Dad's house, and I still have my share of the insurance. I know you never spent yours, either. I just couldn't. Knowing it's there if I need it is good. I'm sure the economy will pick up next year, and if it doesn't, I registered with the modeling agency I used to work for. My feet look the same, and so does my hair, so maybe something will come through with that. I'm sorry I ever let Jeff talk me into giving all that up when we got married."

"You gave it up for me. Don't put all the blame on Jeff, Em. You wanted to be there for me when I needed a mother the most. I will be forever grateful to you for stepping in when . . . after . . . you know. I also know Jeff didn't want me living with you, but you held tight. I love you for that, Em. After I'm married, I'll be in a position to help you out." She told her about the financial arrangements and giggled at her sister's reaction.

"Trish, that is so awesome. My God, what will you do with all that money?"

"I can't wrap my mind around it all yet.

I'll think of something. Right now, though, I'm just about broke. I'm going to rent my town house to one of the girls in the line. I don't want to give it up. I worked too hard to get it, did without too much to just give it up. You taught me that, Em. Always keep something in reserve. Like you with your inheritance and me with mine. You just never know what tomorrow will bring."

On the other end of the phone, Emma sighed. "In a million years I never thought Jeff would push me to the curb. I'm still trying to figure out how I could have been so stupid. There had to have been clues, and I missed every single one of them. My friends all say the same thing. None of us saw it coming. Out with the old, in with the new. The guys are all sporting young, as in *very* young, trophy wives who spend their days shopping and lunching at the country club."

"Don't be so hard on yourself, Em. You were being a wife, taking care of me, and raising a daughter. You did it all right. Jeff is the one who screwed it up. 'What goes around comes around.' You always used to say that to me. Then you'd finish it up with, 'Karma is a bitch.' "

Emma laughed. "I have to go, Trish, and at least pretend I'm working. There are at least two dozen divorcees standing in line for this crappy job if I bomb at it. Why does every woman who gets divorced think the only path to take is in real estate?"

It was Trish's turn to laugh. "I have no clue, Em. Love you. I'll call again in a day or so."

Trish sat for a long time after she disconnected the call. She'd never really liked Emma's husband, because he had always made her feel like a charity case and resented having had to feed her, clothe her, and put a roof over her head. *Bastard.* The thing that bothered her the most was Missy turning on her mother. In a way, she understood that teenagers thought only of themselves and keeping up with their peer group. She could see how the promise of a Porsche would tempt any young person. A trip to Hawaii for Christmas. Well, that was just the cherry on top. A young stepmother who spent all her time shopping and lunching, right down a teenager's alley. Poor Em.

Right then, at that precise moment in time, Trish Holiday came to the understanding that money was at the root of all evil.

Trish went back to her computer search. She was trying to make arrangements for her wedding gift to Malik. Her intention was to find his old rattletrap of a car, buy it from whoever had it, and ship it to Dubai. Soraya had provided her a list with the names of Malik's old roommates and friends who had sent condolences when their father died. Malik had asked her personally, as the only female in the family, to take care of it, and she had. There were nine names on the list.

She started with the first one, Malik's closest friend, Zack Molton. She dialed the number, waited until the phone was picked up, then identified herself and said what she wanted. He sounded nice, asked about Malik and how he was doing. Trish volunteered just enough information without giving anything away about Malik's private life.

"Well, let's see. Malik just called me and asked me to get rid of all his stuff. I didn't see him again after he left for his visit to Vegas. He got the news of his father's passing and left from there. We've spoken only once since he left. He called to thank me. Then I got a really nice letter — we all did — from the family. You probably don't know this, but us guys had a tree planted at Berkeley with his father's name on a plaque. We sent Malik a picture of it. When it comes right down to it, what do you do for a guy who has it all and is a sheik in the bargain? A tree sounded right to all of us. It will be there forever.

"But back to your problem. I gave the car to Duke Richards. I think he said he was going to give it to his nephew, who had just gotten his learner's permit. If you hold on a minute, I'll call Duke on my other line and see if the kid still has it."

Trish said she would wait and hold on.

Five minutes later, Zack was back on the line. "Okay, I'm back. Duke said his nephew sold it for seventy dollars to a friend because it kept dying out on him. He's going to track down the other kid and call me back. Malik sure did love that car. How are you going to get it to Dubai if we can locate it?"

"I don't know. I didn't get beyond trying to locate it. Do you have any ideas?"

Zack laughed. "This just might be your lucky day, Miss Holiday. Someone in our group has someone in their family who works at the port. I just don't remember offhand who it is. I'll check with the others and see what we can do. It's called networking. Even though our group is scattered all over the country these days, we stay in touch. Anything for Malik. I'd give anything to see his face if you can pull this off."

"I'll send you a picture," Trish promised. "Call me. Doesn't matter what time it is. I see that this is a Virginia number, so I'm three hours behind you. Thanks for your help, Zack."

Trish dusted her hands dramatically. She didn't know how she knew, but she just knew she was going to find the rattletrap and somehow get it to Dubai in time for the wedding. Now that the car was being taken care of, Trish let her thoughts go to her sister and what she could do for her. How sad she must be that her daughter chose her husband over her. Ex-husband. She wondered what, if anything, she could do about that.

She'd make it a family affair.

CHAPTER 8

Trish rolled over in bed, then rolled back. She sniffed. The scent of fresh-brewed coffee was wafting about her. Soraya making coffee! Unbelievable! Still, the young woman had taken to life here in the States like a duck takes to water. She knew how to work the washer, the dryer, the dishwasher, and the microwave and was proud of her accomplishments. She even made toast and cut up fruit in the morning. She said she loved doing it, and Trish believed her.

It was the day Soraya had been waiting for since their return. A week had gone by without a trip to the casino because Trish had had too many things to do. But today was the start of the first Christmas show, and she was going to dance, with Soraya front and center in the audience. Malik had told her last night, in his last call of the day, that his sister had called him a dozen times to thank him for allowing her to come to the States and then to regale him with all she'd done since her arrival.

A soft knock sounded on Trish's bedroom door. "Come in."

"I thought you might like coffee in bed today. I'll join you if that's all right."

"How sweet of you to do that. Is it drinkable?" Trish joked.

Soraya laughed. "Malik told me how to make it. One scoop for each cup and one for the pot. He said I couldn't go wrong if I did it that way. I tested it. Tell me what you think," she said anxiously.

Trish sipped the fragrant brew. "Excellent! I couldn't have made it better."

"What are we doing today? I can't wait for this evening. You have to help me choose something to wear that is appropriate for this evening. I have no wish to embarrass you. Is it dress up, or is it casual? Plus, it's cold out. I saw on your little television in the kitchen that it is twelve degrees outside."

"Casual is always good. The night I met Malik, he was wearing jeans and a cable-knit sweater. That white cashmere sweater you bought the other day and the black wool slacks will be perfect, if you're comfortable wearing them. Easy on the jewelry. There are people out and about who scout around, then rob you. Security is excellent, but you still have to be careful."

"I understand. So, how much progress have you made on Malik's car? He will go over the moon when he sees it. Did I say that right?"

"You did, and I hope you're right. The last call I had was to tell me they think the car is in a junkyard. They're working on getting it out. Zack said he would call me today if they were successful. He wanted to know if I wanted it *fixed*. The whole point of getting the car is so it's drivable, so I said yes. That means I'm going to have to scrounge up money from somewhere. I'll get paid to dance tonight, but it won't be all that much. I'm about tapped out. I still have gifts to buy for the girls and other odds and ends."

"How much do you need, Trish? I have lots of money. Just tell me what you need."

"No, sweetie, it doesn't work that way. This is a gift from me to Malik, so I have to pay for it. I have a little nest egg I can tap. Don't worry about it, and don't you dare tell Malik. This is one of those girl secrets I told you about. Girl secrets are not to be shared. Agreed?"

"You have my word. Tell me this. Will it pay to have the rattletrap fixed?"

"Lord, Soraya, I have no idea. If it's in the junkyard, that has to mean something serious is wrong with it. Maybe it even needs a new engine. That could run into some serious money. I'll know more when Zack calls me. He did say that Toby knew how to work on cars. I don't even know who Toby is."

"Tobias Little. He was number seven on the list of names. I remember Malik telling me that he worked on all the guys' cars at one time or another. He said he liked to tinker with cars. If I remember correctly, Tobias lives in California. Does that help?" Soraya asked anxiously.

"If that's where the junkyard is, and he cuts us a deal on labor and parts, it will work."

"I will cross my fingers that it all works out for you. So what are we going to do today?"

"Sadie said she is coming by for you at eleven. She said you agreed to babysit her little girl for a few hours. After that, we have to get ready to go to work. I'm going to finish packing up my personal things and moving them to the attic and basement. My friend who is taking over the town house has her own things. I'm just going to be doing boring stuff. Some online banking and a trip to the post office.

"Soraya, do you know anything about American lawyers and how they work with the emirates? Does Malik deal with them, or is it the council who does that?"

"All the time. We have hosted many dinners for American lawyers. They handle the private-sector business for the emirates. All the sheiks and emirs deal with them. I did hear Malik say once that those men are getting rich off the emirates, but that is all I know. Why are you asking me this?"

Trish waited a few moments before she spoke. "Can you handle another girl secret?"

"I absolutely can," Soraya said, jumping on the bed and sitting Indian style. "Tell me."

"You won't speak of this to your brother?"

"I can keep a secret, Trish. I will not speak to my brother of what you confide in me."

Trish set her coffee cup down on the nightstand and told her about her sister and what she'd said the night before. "My sister is struggling to survive, and her ex-husband is getting rich, supposedly from dealings in Saudi Arabia and Abu Dhabi. I want to find out how all that works. Jeff, my former brother-in-law, doesn't know that I'm marrying Malik. I want to keep it that way. He's already enticed my niece away from my sister with promises of money and all that goes with it."

"That is so terrible. When I was your

niece's age, I would have done anything to have a mother who cared about me. My father used to make up stories about what my mother would have done had she lived to see me grow up. At the time, I didn't know that the stories were made up. He would have tears in his eyes, so perhaps that's why I thought they were true. He told me my mother would sing me lullabies as I fell asleep, that she would shower me with kisses all day long, that she would dress me like a princess. He said she would never be far from my side, and always, always, she would smile when she looked at me. That she would hold my hand tight in hers.

"I loved those stories. To this day, I still think of them as I fall asleep. How wonderful to have someone you love wrap you in their arms, then look in your eyes and tell you how much they love you. I feel sad for your niece because I know from what you say, her father or the new wife will not do this for her. I hope she realizes her mistake before it is too late. But my father also told me that a mother's love never wavers no matter what goes awry. Was it like that with your mother, Trish?"

Trish felt her throat close up. She struggled to clear it. "Pretty much just as you describe it. For my sister, too, and I know she thinks of our parents every day, just as I do. My sister is very much like our mother."

"And I think you will be, too, when you become a mother. All right, I must now get showered and dressed. Eleven o'clock will be here before you know it. Is there anything I can do before I leave?"

"Nope. I'm good. Thanks for bringing the coffee. It hit the spot. I'll see you downstairs. Did the weatherman say anything about snow?"

"Just flurries, whatever that is," Soraya called over her shoulder.

"Soraya, wait a minute. If there's time, do you want to go pick out a Christmas tree this afternoon? If we're running tight, we can do it tomorrow. I want you to have the experience of picking out a tree. We'll put this one on the other side of the fireplace. You can never have too many Christmas trees. At least that's what my mother used to say. Emma used to have one in every room in her house when she first got married. And I think I'm going to take you up to Lake Tahoe this weekend and teach you how to ski. Would you like that?"

Soraya raced back in the room. "Oh, yes to everything. Thank you. I can't wait to tell Malik. He knows how to ski, but he said he spent more time on his bum than he did on his feet. I have pictures!" she said triumphantly.

The two women hugged each other before Soraya ran off again. How nice it was to make someone so happy. If only she could get Emma's ex-husband out of her mind. What he was doing to her sister and her niece was taking the edge off her own happiness.

Their cheeks rosy with the cold and brisk wind, Trish and Soraya struggled to carry the Christmas tree up the steps to the little porch of Trish's town house. Trish ran inside to get a bucket of water. They managed to prop the tree in the bucket, getting it to lean against the railing. Trish then cut the netting, and the branches spread out like eager hands.

"By tonight, when we get home, we can bring it inside, and then tomorrow we can decorate it. The house will smell wonderful. At this time of year, I always let cinnamon sticks simmer in boiling water. My sister always did the same thing. It takes me back to the time when I was little and still believed in Santa Claus."

"Look at my hands! I just love this smell.

Palm trees don't smell," Soraya said, giggling.

"We cut this close, Soraya. We have to hustle now to make sure we're not late. We have time. Just don't dawdle around, okay?"

"Okay, okay," Soraya said as she ran inside and headed for the steps, dropping her jacket on the floor.

Trish clapped her hands and whistled between her teeth, an ear-shattering sound. Soraya stopped in her tracks when Trish pointed to the jacket on the floor.

"Sorry!" Soraya ran down the stairs, picked up the jacket, and hung it on the clothes tree in the small foyer. "It won't happen again, I promise."

Trish smiled as she headed for the kitchen to wash the pine sap off her hands. She then called Malik and shared the events of the afternoon with him.

"Does the tree really smell?" he asked.

"Divinely. We'll bring it in tonight, when we get home, set it up, let the branches fall out more, and decorate it tomorrow. I'll send pictures. I have to go now. I love you more than life itself."

"I love you more!" Malik said.

"Impossible!" Trish laughed as she broke the connection. She galloped up the steps and headed for her shower.

Her mind galloped as fast as her feet when she tried to remember where she'd stored all the Christmas decorations. Especially the ones that had belonged to her mother. Emma had said it was only fair to share them, so when they had split them up, she kept the childish ones she'd made in school and Trish kept hers. Little balls with painted macaroni glued to them, small sleds made out of Popsicle sticks, then painted with their names on them and the date. There was also a pomander ball made with a real orange, which was petrified now. She clearly remembered sticking the cloves in the sweet-smelling orange. Last year it had still given off a scent. She always cried when she hung those treasures on her tree. Emma said she did, too. But, Emma said, Jeff had always made her hang her treasures in the back of the tree because they were so tacky and interfered with his designer tree and his designer ornaments.

At that moment in the shower, with her hair full of shampoo, Trish decided she didn't just dislike Jeff Davis, but she hated him, and she didn't care if the transplanted Mississippian had been named after the Jefferson Davis who had been the U.S. secretary of war, a United States senator from Mississippi, and finally, the president of the Confederate States of America. She hadn't, for even one minute, really believed the story he told everyone about being a descendant of the famous Southern secessionist, though she had often wondered what kind of person would brag about being the however many times great-grandson of a traitor to the United States of America. She wasn't sure if Emma believed it or not. Back at that point in time, perhaps. Today, not a chance.

For some reason, Trish's heart felt lighter now that she had owned up to hating her sister's ex-husband. Later, when she had more free time, she was going to think long and hard about Jeff and how she could play a role in meting out his just deserts. She was going to think really, really hard.

Ninety minutes later, Trish parked her car, and the two women got out just as Trish's cell phone rang. She motioned for Soraya to get back in the car, out of the cold and wind.

"Zack, thanks for calling me back. What do you know?" Trish listened, her face clouding over, then lighting up. "That's great. Yes, yes, I can afford that. Four days to get it in shape, a day to drive it to the port and get it on board. Three weeks till it gets to Dubai. That's perfect." She listened again. "How much will that cost?"

She listened again. "Okay, I can make that happen. I can send a check tomorrow by overnight mail. Color? Oh, I hadn't thought of that. What do you guys think? Okay, black. You're sure? Will you please tell your friends thank you for me? I will be sure to send pictures to you. Also, tell them I appreciate the free labor and that you're just making me pay for the parts. This was so kind of you, Zack. Thank you again."

"What? What? Tell me!" Soraya cried.

"Someone got it out of the junkyard. They put a new engine in it and a new starter. He said it purrs like a kitten. They got a break somewhere on tires, because the others were bald. They're going to repaint it black and put a racing stripe on it. Someone else patched up the leather seats, and they look like new. And they're throwing in the floor mats, which are almost new. They said the shopping at the junkyard was fabulous. Tobias will drive the car to the port and see that it gets put on board properly. All Malik's friends chipped in for the shipping as their wedding present to Malik. How great is that?"

"I don't think anything could be more perfect. I am so jealous of Malik and the friendships he made here. He is so loyal to them. And it appears they are to him, too. He spoke of doing something for all of them, but then he didn't say anything else to me. I hope he follows through. I didn't mean that the way it sounds. I mean I hope whatever he does will be wonderful. Such friendship deserves to be rewarded."

"That is such a load off my mind. I was so worried we couldn't pull it off, and yet we did. Zack was right. It's all about net-working. Come along, my dear sister-to-be, so I can welcome you to the world I lived in for lo these many years."

Soraya took a deep breath, then expelled it. "I'm ready, Trish!"

Backstage it was bedlam, with the girls chattering, Nathan grumbling, parts of costumes missing, doubles of others.

"Didn't anyone check the Christmas costumes before today? Ernie! That was your job! What's going on here?" Nathan whirled around when a page handed him a pink slip. His face turned red with anger. "She can't do this to me! She can't! It's too late. Showtime is in thirty minutes. Where in the hell am I going to get an angel at this point? Ernie!" he bellowed.

"Just stay here, Soraya. Try not to get in the way. I have to get dressed and put on my stage makeup," Trish said.

"Okay." Soraya tried to inch her way to a wall where nothing was going on.

Nathan, a bear of a man with a roar to match, spotted Soraya. His eyes narrowed. "Who are you?"

Soraya licked at her lips. "A friend of Trish's. I won't get in the way, I promise."

"Ernie! Trixie was in a car accident. She's okay, but she's been taken to the hospital just to be sure. That means we're short an angel. Young woman, how would you like to be a stand-in angel tonight?" Nathan didn't bother waiting for a response but roared at Ernie again to get the angel costume, hook up the wires, and check them twice, then three times, to make sure nothing went awry. "Well, do you want to be an angel and fly across the stage for the grand finale or not? Speak up! Speak up!"

Soraya almost fainted. "Yes," she squealed.

"Get her fixed up, Ernie!" Nathan roared. "We're counting down now, girls! Let's make this the best Christmas opening ever. Good luck."

Soraya followed Ernie in a daze and did just what he told her to do. Draped in the angel costume, with a gold halo attached to her back, Soraya danced around to see herself in all the mirrors. "Now what do I do?"

"You fly." Ernie laughed. "But first I have to put your wings on. Then I have to attach all the wires to the back of the wings. When the dance number ends, you'll fly across the stage. You smile and hold your hands in prayer. Oh, crap, you don't have any stage makeup on." He looked at her with a critical eye, then said, "You know what? You're pretty enough without it. By the way, does Trish know you're doing this?"

Soraya crunched up her lips. "No. I don't think so. She went off to get into her costume. Then that man made it all happen so fast. Won't she be surprised when I fly across the stage! Will you take my picture so I can send it to my brother when the show is over? Make sure you get a picture of Trish, too, in the same shot if you can."

"I'll have one of my assistants sit out front and do it. Trish will have my hide. What's your name?"

"Soraya. I know yours is Ernie. That's a nice name. What are those things on your face?"

"Freckles. I hate them."

"I like them. They give your face character. I never met anyone with red hair before. Is it real, or do you color it?"

"It's real. People with red hair usually have freckles. The kids used to call me carrot top in school. I got in a lot of fights."

"That's terrible," Soraya said, peering closely at Ernie's face. She reached up and touched a freckle on his cheek. Then she leaned over and kissed the same spot she'd just touched. Ernie almost blacked out.

"You are the most beautiful angel I've ever seen," he said hoarsely.

"Thank you for saying that."

"Three minutes!" came the announcement from the backstage speaker.

Soraya watched as the girls scampered to get in line.

"Two minutes!"

Soraya craned her neck to see Trish, but in all the commotion and chaos, she could see only the top of her head.

"One minute!"

"Thirty seconds!"

"Showtime!"

"We have to hustle now, Soraya. Follow me. I have to attach the wires. I will be the one controlling the pulleys. Just relax, and everything will be fine. Are you nervous?"

"Like a cat on a griddle," Soraya said truthfully. "Are you nervous, Ernie?"

"I wasn't until you kissed me. Now I'm jittery as hell."

Soraya laughed. "I can do it again if you like. On the lips this time."

Ernie almost blacked out a second time. "Yeah, like you'd really kiss me on the lips. Girls don't much like me, and my freckles and red hair."

"Well, *I do*. So there!" Soraya leaned over and planted a lip-lock on Ernie that made his spiked red hair move of its own accord. When she broke away, she giggled as she fluttered her wings. Ernie groaned. Soraya giggled again.

Somewhere in the back of his mind Ernie heard his cue to start the countdown. His voice hoarse, his eyes glazed, he managed to say, "On the count of one, you'll feel yourself being pulled upright. Just relax, and hang loose. Your body, your legs will be straight out. The mechanics do the rest. Just remember to keep a smile on your face and your hands steepled. Ready!"

"I am so ready, you dear sweet person."

And up she went.

Then across the stage she sailed. She saw Trish gaping in disbelief as she floated past her, then floated back again to the wild applause from the audience, all the while wondering if Ernie had captured her and Trish on film.

The moment the curtain came down,

Trish was at her side. "What the hell? How . . . Ernie!"

"It was Nathan's idea, Trish. Trixie was in a car accident on her way here this evening. There wasn't enough time to find a replacement. Nathan saw Soraya just standing there, so he hired her on the spot. So if you're going to yell at anyone, yell at Nathan. You're going to find out sooner or later, so you might as well know, she kissed me. On the lips!"

Trish didn't know if she should laugh or cry. "On the lips, huh?"

"Yeahhh. No one ever kissed me like that. My very own angel kissed me. She was great, wasn't she?"

"Soraya!" Trish thundered.

"How'd you like my debut, Trish? It was meant to be! I was just standing there, and all of a sudden I was this angel! I actually felt like one. It was my debut, and I loved it. Mr. Nathan said I can do the other two shows this evening. Trixie will be back tomorrow. In a million years I have never been this happy. Oh, I so hope the pictures came out good. I can't wait to send them to Malik."

"Didn't you leave something out?"

"Oh, you mean me kissing Ernie. Yes, yes, that was great, too. I'm going to do it again, too. He got all rubbery in the knees. I like his freckles. I never met anyone with red hair before. Why are you looking at me like that?"

"You will not kiss him again. Your brother is going to kill us both. This had better be one of those girl secrets. Understood?"

"No, I don't understand. I liked kissing him. I think he liked kissing me, too."

"I bet he did. No more."

"I will tell Malik, so do not worry. I will not promise, Trish. I am here to experience life. Malik said so."

Trish gave in gracefully. "Come on. Let's get changed and go get some supper before the next show."

Soraya whirled around when she heard her name called. Ernie handed her a camera and said one of his assistants was front-row center and managed to get all the pictures she wanted. "It's his camera, so you have to give it back. You can download them to your phone and send them from there. I have to go now. See you at the next show."

Trish couldn't believe her ears when she heard Soraya ask, "Do you want me to kiss you again or wait for the next show?"

Ernie took one look at Trish and ran. Both women laughed.

Half a world away, Malik bellowed for Rashid. "Come look at my sister. She is an angel. She just sent me a text explaining how that happened. And she tells me she kissed some fellow named Ernie. He's the young man I tried to entice to get me to Trish, if I recall. That means I know him, so I can't get upset that my sister kissed him. Do you agree, Rashid?"

"Well . . ."

"Cut the bullshit, Rashid. You have eyes for my sister no matter how much you complain about her being a pest. Do you think I'm blind to what I see? Maybe you need to kiss her. I see her looking at you when she thinks no one sees her. Aha! So I'm right. Blushing at your age, Rashid! Oh, golly, Miss Molly!" Malik cackled with glee.

Rashid stomped out of the room, his face fiery red.

Malik leaned back in his lounge chair and stared at the pictures of his sister and his betrothed. He smiled.

Life was perfect.

CHAPTER 9

It was just a few minutes shy of six o'clock when Trish walked down the steps to the kitchen to make the first pot of coffee of the day. She looked out at the new day, still dark. She clicked on the television, turned it low so as not to wake Soraya. Last night's weather report indicated snow today. In one way, for Soraya's sake, she hoped it would snow as she hadn't taken her to Tahoe as promised.

Six o'clock was always a good time to call Emma. At nine in the morning, East Coast time, Emma was just getting ready to head to work. Talking to her sister in the past had always been a good way to start her day.

Trish poured her first cup of coffee and swallowed a vitamin. She scribbled a note to buy extra vitamins to take with her to Dubai and stuck the note on the refrigerator. The list was getting longer. She'd probably need an extra bag just for things like that.

Trish removed her cell phone from the charger and hit her speed dial. She heard her sister's early-morning voice. "You guys freezing up there in Princeton?" were the first words out of Trish's mouth.

"It snowed during the night. Looks to be about four or five inches on the ground. I'm glad I have four-wheel drive. What's going on in Nevada?"

"Snow's predicted for today. Have you heard from Missy?"

"No. They leave today for Hawaii. Stop worrying, Trish. If she doesn't call, my world won't end. My heart will break a little more, but that's okay, too. I can't fight Jeff. He's the one with the money. I'm done with that."

"It's so unfair. We were never selfish like that, were we, Em?"

"No, Trish, we weren't like that. So, having said that, it's my fault, mine and Jeff's. We spoiled her. That's the bottom line. I don't want to talk about this anymore. How is your houseguest doing?"

The two sisters talked then of Soraya, the Christmas decorations in Princeton, and Las Vegas. They laughed a bit, but the laughter was strained, as Trish kept trying to figure out how to work the conversation around to Jeff and his business in the Middle East. She finally gave up when she realized that her sister was babbling about everything and nothing in an attempt to steer her away from anything involving her ex-husband.

Five minutes later, they said they loved one another and broke the connection.

Trish shivered. Then she realized she hadn't turned the heat up. She cranked it high and was rewarded almost immediately with the scent from the Christmas tree wafting through the house. Just for a minute, she felt like she was ten years old again, her eyes full of wonder at the sight of the tree and the gaily wrapped packages nestled beneath the fragrant boughs.

Trish made her way back to the kitchen and her second cup of coffee. She called Malik, but her call went to voice mail. She looked at the clock. She had time to do some more research on her laptop before Soraya made her way downstairs. If it was the last thing she did, she was going to find out what her former brother-in-law was doing in the Middle East. Jeff Davis was slick. Jeff Davis was manipulative. Jeff Davis was known to balance on the fine line between legal and illegal. Emma had told her that once, then sworn her to secrecy. At the time, she had agreed, hadn't given the words or the promise another thought.

Trish tapped furiously, going to Google, then on to other sites. She was reading with such intensity, she barely had time to click off when she saw a sleepy Soraya standing in the doorway. She hoped she didn't look guilty.

"Tonight is your Christmas party! I can hardly wait. And tomorrow is your Christmas Eve. I can't wait for that, either. And then it's Christmas Day! Are you excited, Trish?"

"I'm always excited when it comes to Christmas. I love it. But the best part is we are so ahead of schedule with my wrapping up all my business that we can now leave two days after Christmas. That's what *really* excites me, Soraya. It's going to snow today, and I'm really sorry I didn't get to take you to Tahoe."

"It's all right. Perhaps I will return someday and make the trip. I'm going to be sorry to leave, Trish. I've had the best time of my life, thanks to you. I truly feel as if you are my sister. But I'm not like Malik. I don't belong here. Given a choice, Malik would have stayed here until my father called him home. I'm actually homesick, believe it or not. I can't wait to get . . ."

"Back to Rashid?" Trish's eyes twinkled, and a big grin lit her face.

Soraya flushed a bright pink as she poured herself a cup of coffee. "Yes, that, too."

Trish closed her laptop, got up to refill her cup, and carried it to the back door. Dark, angry clouds that looked like shrouds were scudding across the sky. It was light enough now to see the snow flurries swirling about. She called Soraya to the door. "Snow!" she said triumphantly.

Soraya rushed to the window, then clapped her hands like a little girl.

"If the accumulation amounts to anything, we can go out and play in the snow. We'll build a snowman, and you can send a picture to your brother. Let's just hope we get enough, and we actually get to do it before we have to leave for the Christmas party. This is the one night of the year where all us girls get to go slinky and glittery, the more bling the better. New Year's Eve pales in comparison to the casino's Christmas party. This is also the night when they give out the Christmas bonuses. Management has always been very generous in the past with us, so let's hope this year they are just as generous."

Soraya clapped her hands again. She

raised her eyes upward. "Please, let it all be what I want it to be," she said under her breath.

"Well, then, let's get this show on the road," Trish said as she headed for the second floor to get ready for whatever the day held in store for her.

It was snowing when Trish and Soraya watched the driver load the bags and trunks into the minivan and the limo that would take them to the airport. Trish shivered inside her shearling jacket. She struggled against the wind, drawing the collar of the jacket against her cheeks. Soraya laughed as she tried to catch the snowflakes. Trish smiled when she saw the delicate white flakes coat Soraya's eyelashes.

"Before you know it, we'll both be swimming in warm water, wearing sundresses, and preparing for your wedding. I am so excited. Are you excited, Trish?"

Trish could barely hear her over the howling wind. She had turned so she could get one last look at her town house, at the place where she'd gone without, struggled to pay for her home all these years. Tears puddled in her eyes. She knew her home would be well taken care of by her friend. What she hadn't counted on and was still a bit peeved about, and a bit overwhelmed by at the same time, was Malik's Christmas gift, which had arrived on Christmas Eve morning courtesy of FedEx. Inside the padded envelope was the deed to her town house; Malik had paid off the mortgage, and she owned the building free and clear. Just for a little while, she'd felt intruded upon, that her life had been invaded. She knew Malik meant well, but it was a thorn in her side, and she knew that even though she'd tried to gush and thank him, her words didn't ring true. And Malik, very sensitive to her attitudes, had called her on it. In the end, she had confessed to how she felt, and he, in turn, had become subdued. They'd talked long into the night, and when she broke the connection, she felt okay with what he'd done.

Right now, though, she felt like she was saying good-bye to someone else's home. She shrugged inside her heavy jacket. She'd get over it in time.

Two hours later, they were airborne. The last call she'd made before boarding was to her sister, to tell her how much she loved her and would miss her. It was Soraya who had called Malik to say that they were boarding.

Once the private plane climbed to cruising altitude, Soraya unbuckled her seat belt and danced her way up and down the aisle before sitting back down. "Let's talk, Trish. The last few days have been so wild and hectic, I don't even know where to start."

Trish smiled. Her thoughts were, for some reason, on her sister and the tone in her voice when she'd called to say one last good-bye. According to Emma, she was just hanging. The Realtor for whom she worked had closed the office till after the New Year. The three new friends she'd met in group therapy had returned to work, and she was left to fend for herself. She'd jokingly said she was going to clean out her closets, take a walk or two in the snow, return a few Christmas gifts, sleep, and cook some food and freeze it for the nights when she worked late. For some reason, all of that had brought tears to Trish's eyes. She hadn't wanted to ask, but she did, anyway, wanting to know if Missy had called on Christmas. She was told no, and the subject was dropped. *Ungrateful little brat.*

Trish shook herself out of her reverie when Soraya poked her arm. "Earth to Trish!"

"I was just thinking about how sad my sister sounded. What do you want to talk about, Soraya?"

"Everything. Just absolutely everything. Malik laughed himself silly when he saw the picture of the snowman we made. He said he's going to frame it and put it in his cave, along with the pictures of you and me in costume. I just loved that whole experience. I loved the Christmas party and how glamorous everyone looked and how nice and friendly everyone was to me. Drinking champagne till three in the morning is something I won't soon forget."

"Neither will Ernie. How many times did you kiss him that night?"

"Seven!" Soraya said smartly. "I was honest with him and told him I was practicing on him, and he took it very well. I think on my return I will feel confident enough to kiss Rashid and . . . How do you say it? Blow his socks off. Ernie said he loved being kissed by a real-live princess."

"And did you also tell this to your brother?" Trish asked slyly.

"I did not! That's a girl secret. Christmas Eve and church was lovely. Christmas Day was just as lovely, with that wonderful dinner you cooked. I so enjoyed opening the presents and everyone laughing and smiling. You have delightful friends, Trish, who love you very much. They are going to miss you. Tell me, what did you think of Malik's

Christmas gift to you? He must have called me a dozen times to see if I would change what I described as your reaction."

"It was very thoughtful and kind of him to do that."

"But . . ."

"Girl secret?"

"Absolutely."

Trish explained her feelings about the gift.

"I understand. Now, if you had told me that back in Dubai, before I came here, I would not have understood. Malik should have known better. He spent more time here than I did and has a better understanding of the way you do things. Can you forgive him for what he's done?"

"Of course. It is no longer important. It is —"

"What it is. Your favorite saying," Soraya said, finishing Trish's statement.

In spite of herself, Trish laughed.

"Let's talk about your wedding dresses. How lucky you are that you get to choose two and you will have two ceremonies. Malik said in his last e-mail that the palace seamstresses are just waiting for you with their designs, their bolts of fabric, and their needles. I can't wait to find out what you choose. And you are to choose my dress also. I want something . . ."

"That will blow Rashid's socks off. Yes, I know."

The two women settled down to talk seriously about Islamic weddings, the protocol, and what was expected.

They talked for hours, until Trish's eyes started to droop. The last thing she heard was Soraya telling her that the groom in an Islamic wedding gave the bride a gift of money or jewelry. The bride did not give the groom a gift, but in a Christian wedding the bride could gift her new husband. "So that's when you give Malik the rattletrap, at your Christian wedding." Then Soraya's eyes, too, closed.

Neither woman woke until the plane was ready to make its descent into Dubai International Airport, the older of the emirate's two airports.

CHAPTER 10

Trish craned her neck to look out the window of the private plane. She smiled from ear to ear when she saw Malik in his white robe, Rashid next to him. "They're here!" she squealed in happiness. Soraya clapped her hands.

When the plane finally came to a dead stop, both women unbuckled their seat belts and were at the front of the plane in a nanosecond. The moment the door opened and the portable stairway was in place, Trish almost flew down the steps and into Malik's arms. He held her close and swung her around before he kissed her until she gasped for breath.

Out of the corner of her eye Trish saw Soraya advance toward Rashid. In the blink of an eye her lips were on Rashid's. Malik started to move in his sister's direction. Trish pulled him back. "She's practicing, Malik. She's in love with him. Let them be."

"But . . . but . . . ," he sputtered. In the end, he capitulated and only shot his sister a look of disapproval, which she totally ignored.

Rashid, his face flaming, was unable to look at Malik. Finally, Malik took pity on his second in command and laughed out loud. "She's all yours, Rashid. Now she is *your* responsibility. What? What? Did the cat swallow your tongue, brother?"

"You're enjoying this, aren't you, Malik?" Rashid hissed as he held the door open for Trish and Malik.

"Actually, Rashid, I am." Malik grinned like the cat who had caught the canary.

"I'll sit in the front with Rashid," Soraya said sweetly.

"No, you won't," Rashid grumbled. "It is not seemly. Malik . . . ?"

Malik was otherwise occupied with kissing Trish. He waved his hand to show that Rashid was on his own. Soraya giggled. Rashid pretended to glower, and Malik and Trish continued with what they were doing.

Day one of Trish's homecoming. As far as she was concerned, nothing could have been more perfect.

The minute Malik dropped Trish and Soraya off at the palace, they were surrounded by chattering women, who quickly spirited

160

them away to what Soraya said was the room where the wedding preparations would begin for both of them.

They spent hours picking and choosing materials, threads, and ornate trim. Needles and scissors flashed as the ladies stripped down both women to take measurements.

"It is so hard to choose. I have never seen such beautiful fabrics," Trish wailed. "How am I to choose?"

"Close your eyes, twirl around, and then just point." Soraya laughed. "I cannot choose my fabric until you make your choice. Remember, we have just two weeks until your wedding day. Tomorrow we will go into town so you can choose your Christian wedding gown. Two weeks is not much time, Trish."

Trish started to wail again as she contemplated the gorgeous materials laid out in front of her. She knew from all the reading she'd done that red was the color of choice for most Muslim weddings. She took a deep breath and pointed to an absolutely breathtaking red bolt of cloth that was shot through with gold threads. She looked at Soraya, and the ladies huddled together. She pointed her index finger at a luscious strawberry-red bolt of sheer material. A shout of approval went up, which told Trish she had made the right choice. Soraya chose gold fabric shot through with silver threads.

Hours later, they broke for a late lunch, during which the two women chattered and laughed like teenagers. They complimented one another endlessly until, as Trish put it, they got down to the good stuff. The *good stuff* meaning Soraya breaking Muslim protocol by kissing Rashid.

"Don't you get it, Trish? Now he has to make an honest woman of me. I am so glad Ernie let me practice kissing him. Now Rashid knows what to expect. I did good, didn't I?" she asked anxiously.

Trish choked on a date she was munching. "I think it's safe to say you blew his socks off. Your brother's as well."

Soraya just laughed and laughed.

The following day was more of the same when the two women were taken to an exclusive bridal shop in the heart of Dubai, where Trish had to close her eyes, twirl, and point to a gorgeous Vera Wang creation that looked like it was made especially for her. It fit so perfectly, there was no need for alterations. She chose a veil of dotted swiss that was softer than a baby's cheek.

"Malik is going to be over the moon when he sees you in this dress, Trish. Not that the red one isn't going to be gorgeous. It will be, but everyone wears the same thing. It's actually boring. This says it all," she said, pointing to the Vera Wang. Trish agreed with her 100 percent.

Trish looked at the price tag on the gown and almost fainted. "Oh, my God, Soraya, I can't afford this. It's twenty thousand dollars. We have to go somewhere else."

"Oh, you silly girl, this has all been taken care of. Don't fret, Trish. It is our way. Please, don't fight Malik on this. He's trying to please you."

Trish thought about the paid mortgage on her town house back in Vegas and winced. She felt as if a dark cloud had suddenly formed overhead. She looked down at the price tag on the Louboutin shoes — twelve hundred dollars. Soraya bought four pair. The cloud overhead got darker.

Trish stopped and looked down at her cell, where a text was coming in from Malik. It read, Hot dogs at seven in the cave?

Trish's response read, You got it.

Life was beyond wonderful. Well, almost.

On the ride back to the palace, Soraya was busy on her BlackBerry. "It seems that only Zack will be able to make the wedding. Possibly Tobias and Max. Things can change on a dime, he said. Malik does not know this. It is to be a surprise. Oh, one other

163

thing, the car should be in port in three days. I must talk with Rashid about where to have it taken and how to hide it. I don't know if he can keep a secret of this magnitude. I might have to kiss him some more."

"That sounds like a plan, Soraya. I must say, you are devious. Were you always like that, or are you going to say you learned that in the States?"

"Half and half. You must be relieved that the car is finally going to get here."

"I am. I didn't know you had invited Malik's friends to the wedding. I'm sure he will be pleased if they can make it. I look forward to meeting them. Zack was so helpful with the car part of things."

"Do you know the story of Zack and Malik's friendship?"

"I guess I don't. I just assumed they were roommates and grew close over the years."

"Yes, that is true. Zack always took Malik home with him for holidays. He has a big family, and they have a huge farm. Zack is the only one in the family who went to college. The other children chose to stay home and work their farm with their father. Malik and Zack worked the farm with the others during summer vacations. Malik loved riding the tractors and baling the hay and all that.

"Zack's father had a really bad accident, and Malik was with him. He knew what to do and had a medical team there within minutes, and they airlifted Zack's father to a special hospital, where surgery was performed, and they were able to save his legs. Malik saved his life. He paid all the medical bills, and, you know Malik, he paid off the farm but made the parents swear never to tell Zack. He set up scholarship funds for Zack's nephews and nieces, because Malik knows how important education is. Zack doesn't know that, either.

"Nor do any of his other friends know what he's done for them anonymously. My father told me all of this. Malik doesn't even know I know, and you must not let on that you know, either. My father was so proud of Malik. He has such a big heart. He lives to give to others. So, do you understand about him paying off your town house, and all the rest?

"Trish, you have no idea how much good Malik does for the migrant workers here in Dubai. He does it anonymously. He helps the expats, too. Again, anonymously. Before we left for the States, I asked him if he would help me get involved in women's rights issues, and he agreed. I took the liberty of telling him that you and I would be working on those issues on our return. After the wedding, of course. So, that's something else he's willing to do for you. But you must say nothing unless he mentions it to you first."

Trish digested the information Soraya divulged and tried to put her betrothed's generosity out of her mind. She loved Malik, so she had to learn to accept his ways in this new world she'd suddenly become a part of.

Either you loved unconditionally or you didn't love at all.

And she loved.

The day finally arrived.

The palace buzzed and hummed with activity.

It seemed to Trish that the entire populace of Dubai had turned out for the wedding of Sheik Malik bin Al Mohammed.

Seated front row and center were Malik's nine friends from the States. Soraya had confided two days before the wedding that Rashid had made all the arrangements for the guests as his personal wedding gift to Malik. Trish almost burst out laughing when she saw Malik's reaction when he spotted his friends. She thought for one wild moment he would break with tradition and rush at them. Instead, he grinned from ear to ear and gave a thumbs-up.

From there on in, it was all a blur to Trish. She knew that later she would be able to watch the video of her wedding. All she knew was that she was married to the most wonderful man in the world, whom she loved more than life itself, and she had the wedding ring to prove it. She was now officially Mrs. Malik bin Al Mohammed. She didn't know if she was a princess, a royal highness, a *shaykhah* — pronounced "cha cha" — or something else, and she didn't care.

When the wedding was over, and the bride and groom left the festivities, it was Rashid and Soraya's job to entertain the American friends, which they did till all hours of the night.

The Christian wedding was to take place the following day, with a candlelight ceremony at sundown.

It was a small private wedding in the church of Trish's choosing. She loved it when she got to walk down the aisle and saw Malik waiting for her. Even from the back of the church, she heard his gasp of approval.

Over and over, under her breath, she kept repeating, "Thank you, God. Thank you,

God. Please, always let me be as happy as I am at this moment."

All through the wedding dinner at the Burj Khalifa, or Khalifa Tower, a 2,716-foot-high hotel that had cost $650 million to build, Trish was so nervous and fidgety, Rashid finally took pity on her. He tapped his spoon against the glass in front of him for silence. When he had everyone's attention, he looked around the wedding table, his gaze finally settling on Malik. "And now, ladies and gentlemen, the bride wishes to present her new husband with a wedding gift. A gift from the heart, I might add."

What followed was a lot of hooting and hollering, with Malik's friends doing it along with Soraya, who had magically in the past few days learned to whistle between her teeth, thanks to Tobias, who, with the patience of a saint, had taught her.

Rashid made a low, sweeping bow as Trish got up and led the parade from the private dining room out to the hall, then to the special door with a huge EXIT sign in bright red letters.

Trish turned until she was just inches from her husband's face. She winked at him and whispered, "Don't you dare blow this one, Malik. A lot of work and effort went into this. I hope you can accept it in the

168

spirit in which I'm giving it to you. Now, close your eyes, take my hand, and do not open your eyes until I tell you. Promise!"

His heart beating trip-hammer fast, Malik did as he was told. Rashid opened the door. Warm evening air swirled inward. It seemed in that moment in time, everyone's hearts stopped beating.

"Open your eyes!"

Soraya, unable to contain herself, shouted at the top of her lungs. "It's the rattletrap!"

Malik swayed on his feet. Zack caught one arm; Rashid the other.

"Get in! Get in!" everyone shouted at once. "Turn on the engine!"

There wasn't a dry eye among the group as Malik walked around the front of the car. He gathered his pristine white robe about him and climbed into the driver's seat. It took him three tries before he could get his hands to stop shaking long enough to get the engine to turn over. It purred like a contented cat. His eyes were so wet, he couldn't see out of the windshield. As she watched him, tears rolled down Trish's cheeks.

Zack leaned closer. Trish liked the scent wafting off him. "We did good, Trish. Real good!" he whispered.

"All thanks to you," Trish blubbered as

she looked up into the bluest eyes she'd ever seen in her life. She'd been so busy since the Americans' arrival, she had barely had a chance to get to know them. What she knew in that instant was that she had a friend for life in the man standing next to her. She smiled, and he smiled in return and gave her shoulder a little squeeze. Trish felt like an electric current passed through her. Zack, as well, because he stepped backward, a strange look on his face.

And then Malik was scooping her into his arms and carrying her to the passenger side of the rattletrap. It took some doing, but with everyone's help, they managed to get the yards of material on her wedding dress secure inside the car.

"The game plan is you drive your car to the airport, we'll bring it back, and off you go to Switzerland for your honeymoon. We'll say good-bye now, bud. Your turn to visit the States," Zack said, a catch in his voice.

There were manly hugs, a lot of backslapping and handshaking before Malik climbed behind the wheel again.

As he peeled away, horn blaring, there were more hoots and hollers as the tin cans and trash lids that the American contingent had tied to the back bumper clanged and clanked. The sign on the back window said JUST MARRIED.

Malik laughed so hard, he had a hard time keeping the car on the road. "Do you believe those guys? Aren't they the greatest!"

"They are," Trish said, nestling close to her new husband.

"I don't know what to say other than thank you, Trish."

"That'll do it, husband. That'll do it!"

■ ■ ■ ■

PART TWO:
FOUR YEARS LATER

■ ■ ■ ■

CHAPTER 11

Trish woke in the huge bed, her arm stretching out, only to find an empty space. Malik was gone. He'd been gone for four days now. She lay quietly, her thoughts ricocheting every which way before they settled on one thought. Eleven months and fourteen days to give birth to a child or be banished from Malik's life.

It wasn't going to happen, and she knew it. Four years of trying and four years of doctors' visits and four years of tests and more tests were all the proof she needed to know she was not going to bear a child. No matter how many times she brought up the subject to Malik, all he would say was, "Time will tell." Well, time was certainly not on her side. Malik had done everything she asked; they had traveled far and wide to the best doctors in the world with no results.

Her eyes burned when she thought of Soraya's three lovely cherubs running around the palace, laughing and squealing. She was such a good mother, and Rashid was a doting father. Malik loved chasing the little ones, then swooping them up and swinging them high in the air. And they loved their uncle Malik and aunt Trish, as well. Often, Soraya allowed her to bathe the children, powder them, and tell them bedtime stories. And then she would cry when she had to return to her own quarters.

More often than not, these past months, she was alone. Malik seemed forever to be going somewhere and staying days, sometimes weeks at a time. He always called or would send text messages, but they, too, sounded *off* somehow to Trish. Not for the first time, she wondered if her husband was having an affair and looking for her replacement. That thought alone always brought a flood of tears.

Trish squeezed her eyes shut. She hated, absolutely hated, starting her day out by crying. She'd promised herself there would be no more tears, what would be would be. Still, she didn't understand how something so wonderful, so perfect could be destroyed by a stupid man-made rule. *Produce a child, an heir, or you're gone. With a time limit, no less.* None of the high-priced doctors would say definitively it was she who had a problem; nor would they say it was Malik's problem. Almost all of them had rendered the same opinion: "When it's time, nature will either grace you with a child or not." How did you fight something like that?

In the space of four years, Soraya had gotten married and given birth to three beautiful children, and she was once again pregnant, with her fourth child. It just boggled Trish's mind.

Trish swung her legs over the side of the bed as she thought about the day she was facing. Her days were all the same lately. She went to her language class for two hours. She was now as fluent in Arabic as Malik, and he constantly praised her. He would always hug her when she recited the Koran to him. She'd done her part. After her classes, she would go into town, meet with some of the expats with whom she had become friendly. She'd check in with some of the migrant families, with baskets of food and toys for the children. And when no one was looking, she'd slip money into the hands of the wives. Then, perhaps, she would have lunch, possibly shop a little, then return to the palace, swim by herself in the pool, and wait for Malik to return. She spent the waiting time either calling her sister or her friends back in Vegas to catch up on the stateside news, even though she read Dubai's English-language newspaper, the *Khaleej Times.* Her sister, Emma, was always doom and gloom, and it depressed her to talk at great length about her problems. Her friends were always upbeat, because, as Connie said, when you lived in the city that never slept, how could you not be upbeat?

Maybe what she should do was plan a trip back home. Malik constantly encouraged her to do so, but she'd never taken him up on the offer. This was her home; this was where she belonged. Although now she did have a reason to return. The friend she'd rented her town house to these past years was getting married and had moved to Seattle three days ago. She had assured Trish that she'd left the town house in impeccable condition. Connie had checked and had said that indeed, the town house was in excellent shape and asked if she wanted her to find a new renter. If she returned, she could stay in her old town house. She could see all her friends and make a trip to Princeton to see her sister.

Trish walked over to her little desk, where Malik always left notes for her. There was no note this morning. There hadn't been notes for many days now. For weeks and months, if she wanted to be accurate.

In the bathroom, Trish stripped down and made a point not to look at her naked body. She was thin, way too thin. There were dark shadows under her eyes that no amount of makeup could cover. Her hair was luster-less, where once it had really been her shin-ing glory. It had been so many months since Malik had run his fingers through her hair.

Something was wrong.

Eleven months and fourteen days was all she had left.

Suddenly, a bolt of anger ripped through her. *Enough of this bullshit.* If she was back in the States, she'd take the bull by the horns and swing it around and around until the bull was so dazed, it would wander back to its pen. When had she become this *wuss,* this person who didn't speak her mind?

Trish took the quickest shower of her life. She washed her hair only once, added conditioner, then dressed in one of her pret-tiest sundresses. She piled her wet hair on top of her head, lathered her face with some sweet-smelling moisturizer, and left her apartment. Her stride was long and pur-poseful as she waved off her maid, who was carrying her breakfast tray.

When she reached Soraya's apartment, she rapped once and burst through the door. Soraya, still in her nightclothes, her hair standing on end, just gaped at her sister-in-law. "What's wrong, Trish?"

"Everything! That's what's wrong, and do not stand there and tell me you don't know what it is. Rashid cannot keep a secret from you, and we both know it. I want to know what's going on. I have eleven months and fourteen days to become pregnant, which is one of the stupidest rules I have ever heard of. I can't believe I was stupid enough to agree to such a barbaric rule. My only defense is I was so in love with your brother, I would have agreed to anything.

"So, my question to you right now, this minute, is, are the advisers and the council preparing my walking papers? Where is Malik? Where does he go every day? His routine has changed. He's been gone this time now for four days, with only several texts. He's now gone days, weeks at a time. He doesn't call like he used to, doesn't text like he used to, and he no longer leaves me notes. We haven't been to the cave together in months and months. I need you to tell me what's going on."

"Trish, I don't know. I didn't know anything was wrong. Rashid tells me nothing about my brother. He's away as much as Malik. All he says is, it is palace business and not my concern," Soraya said, waving her hands about. "As you know, the little ones keep me busy, and I'm not feeling all that well with this pregnancy. I swear to you, I don't know what you're talking about. Let's get some coffee and go into the garden."

Her back ramrod stiff, Trish followed as Soraya waddled ahead of her, out of earshot of the servants.

After they were seated and a servant brought coffee for Trish and pear nectar for Soraya, it was Soraya who spoke first. "It breaks my heart to see you crying like this. Please, dry your tears, and let's talk. What can I do? I feel terrible that I wasn't able to be there for you. Why didn't you say something sooner?"

"Because . . . because it is so personal. I think Malik is looking for my successor, someone who will give him an heir so that when they shoo me off, this new person will step in. How cruel and unjust is that? I have had every medical test there is, as has Malik. I don't know why I haven't been able to conceive, because it isn't for lack of trying on both our parts. Look at you. Fertile Myrtle. Married four years and you have three children and another one on the way. You and Malik had the same parents, and you're the one with the children. The doctors said there is nothing wrong with me or Malik. If you were me, how would you feel?"

Soraya burst into tears. "I can go to the council, to the advisers, and plead your case, but it won't do any good. Still, I will do it. My father set that rule in stone. As I told you, he never married again after my mother died. If they do indeed banish you, Malik will never take another wife, so get that idea out of your head."

"God, what should I do, Soraya?"

Soraya rushed to Trish and took her in her arms and held her as close as her protruding stomach would allow. Trish sobbed into her shoulder.

"Where is he today? Do you know?" Trish asked through her tears.

"Malik didn't tell you that they were going to France? Rashid left at four this morning. He was very . . . grumpy. Very out of sorts, even though he is a morning person. Usually, I am the grumpy one. We need to put our heads together. Now, dry your eyes and let us see what we can come up with. But first, allow me to shower and kiss my babies good morning. And then I am yours for whatever good I can do."

Trish rang a little gold bell and asked Lily to fetch more coffee. "And would you mind going to my apartment and fetching my cigarettes?" Such a silly, stupid question. No servant would ever admit they minded. As silly and stupid as smoking cigarettes. She had never really smoked except under stress. The last time she'd had a cigarette was before her wedding. Sometimes, she thought, swiping at her eyes, a girl needed something to carry her through the trying times, and, for sure, this was a trying time.

Before she knew it, Trish was gulping at the freshly brewed coffee and puffing out smoke rings, one after the other, from cigarettes she didn't even want.

Soraya stood at the entrance to the private garden, her eyes wet as she stared at her sister. She had considered Trish her sister from the day she first set foot in the palace. In her opinion, they were closer than blood siblings. Right now, her heart was breaking for her sister because she knew there was nothing she could do to ease the hurt and pain Trish was feeling.

"That bad, huh?" Soraya said, motioning to the cigarette.

"Does the smoke bother you?"

Soraya smiled. "It is going the other way on the breeze, but no, it does not bother me. I called Rashid, but my call went to voice mail. I was not nice to my husband,

183

and my message was . . . How should I say this? . . . It was threatening. I know how to get under his skin and what nerves to pinch. So far, he has not responded, and so this may require one more phone call. I never, as in never, give Rashid two chances, so he knows I am serious. His first loyalty, I'm sad to say, is to Malik, not me. Do you have any idea how hard that is for me to swallow?"

Trish just nodded. "Where are the children?" she asked listlessly.

"At the little pool. They are like little fish," Soraya said proudly. "Ah, here is a text from my husband. I shall read it to you, Trish.

Dear wife, ha! It is never wise to threaten one's husband. I regret my inability to respond to you immediately. I ask your indulgence. You know I cannot discuss palace business with you. Suffice it to say I am here with Malik on personal business. I cannot discuss that with you, either. Our return is scheduled for three days from today. Tell me now if I should make other arrangements if I am not welcome. That is what your threat meant, is it not? My undying love, Rashid.

Soraya reread the text to herself again. She made a very unladylike sound in her throat, and to Trish, it sounded like she said, "Personal business, my ass."

She fired off a text in response. That's exactly what it meant, my husband. When it comes to us, there is nothing personal that I cannot know. I cannot bear my sister's unhappiness, and a pox on you and on Malik for thinking such a thing. I am not a forgiving creature, as you well know. I can have your belongings transferred to the bowels of the palace within minutes.

"That was rather harsh, wasn't it, Soraya?" Trish said, when Soraya handed her her cell phone so that Trish could read the text messages. She fired up another cigarette.

"We'll know the answer to that when we see how long it takes him to respond." Soraya eyed the peach nectar in the glass on the table. She alternated between pear and peach nectar all day long. "I'm sick of it!" she blurted.

The minutes ticked by. Both women tapped their manicured nails on the shiny glass-topped table. When Trish started to tap her foot on the colored flagstones, Soraya reared up and rang the bell on the table. Lily came on the run, breathless.

"Listen to me carefully, Lily. Pack up all my husband's belongings and transfer them to the . . . whatever it is that's under the palace floor. Set up a bed. Do not leave so much as a paper clip behind. Also, you may take all the silver-framed photos that have my husband in them. Leave none behind for me to glare at. Why are you still here? Go! Go and tend to this immediately."

Trish opened her mouth to say something, but Soraya held up a finger to shush her. "I learned this from you, my sister. Never make idle threats, and never give ultimatums unless you are prepared to carry them out. It's the only thing I can do for you, Trish. It will do Rashid good to spend some time reflecting."

Trish tried smiling to show her appreciation, but her heart wasn't in it. She toyed with the spoon in her cup as she stared off into the lush gardens.

"Ha!" Soraya said dramatically. "Wait till you hear this one!

So, my wife, you have ejected me from our quarters. That is so unkind of you. What will our children think? The whole palace is jabbering about it. How am I to face anyone on my return?

"You see, Trish, someone here in the palace has already notified my husband that he is to be relocated. He responded to that but not to my text. Men are such . . . What is that animal that stinks, Trish?"

"Skunks."

"Yes, skunks. Well . . . now I am angry. Angry for myself and angry for you. It is time for you to make a trip back to your home. I will arrange everything. All you need to do is get your things together. One way or another, we will find out what is going on. I want you to trust me on this. Can you do that?"

"Of course I trust you. With my life, if need be, Soraya. Just like that, you want me to go back to the States? For how long?"

"Yes, just like that! Until I tell you to come back. Those . . . *two* left for France on *personal* business and didn't tell either one of us, so yes, just like that."

Soraya fired off a response to her husband's text.

It is not everyone else you should worry about facing, my husband. You will be lucky if you are ever again allowed to gaze upon my beautiful face. No further communication from you will be accepted by me.

"Come. Let us prepare for your trip back to the States. Promise to give Ernie a kiss for me."

In a daze, Trish agreed she'd give Ernie a kiss, then followed her sister-in-law back to her apartments, where, in the blink of an eye, she called the airport and in rapid-fire Arabic set the wheels in motion for Trish's

187

return to the States.

Minutes after that, Soraya was tossing clothes on the bed and pulling things out of drawers. She snapped her fingers for the maids, who appeared instantly. "Pack these things and have them taken to the airport. Shaykhah will be leaving in ninety minutes."

Soraya turned to Trish. "Where are your winter things?"

Trish shrugged. "I don't know where the maids put them."

Soraya snapped her fingers again. "Find Shaykhah's winter clothing and put it all in a separate bag."

"Are you sure, Soraya, that this is the right thing to do?"

Soraya threw her hands in the air. "What's that saying you are so fond of? Six of one, half dozen of the other. If nothing else, your husband will wake up when he returns and sees you gone. You cannot allow him to take you for granted. That's what you taught me, Trish. That wasn't a lie, was it?"

"No, it wasn't a lie. Should I leave a note?"

"Absolutely not! I will inform my brother upon his return that you are gone. Let him . . . sweat! Be unavailable when he calls and sends you texts. Can you do that?"

"Yes, I can, but it will be hard."

"Then call me if you find yourself about

to respond, and I will talk you out of it."

Trish sat down on the bed and started to cry. Soraya stood by helplessly as she tried to figure out dozens of ways to strangle her brother upon his return.

CHAPTER 12

Basel, Switzerland

Rashid Zayed stumbled his way through the heavy snow across the street from the University Hospital of Basel. He pushed back the sleeve of his heavy jacket to look at his watch. Twenty more minutes, and he could go into the hospital and up to Malik's room. In twenty minutes, according to the rosy-cheeked doctor, Malik's tests would be complete, and he would return to his room.

Rashid jerked at the wool cap on his head. He hated the cold with a passion.

This was the third, and according to Malik, the last hospital and specialist to be seen in as many months. Then it would be a matter of choosing which hospital, which diagnosis, and which treatment to go forward with.

His heart heavy, shivering with cold, Rashid began the process of crossing the road and entering the hospital. He hated the heavy, bulky clothing he was wearing, as well as the storm boots, which felt like anchors on his feet. He was no stranger to Western clothing, having worn it for seven years in California, where he studied with Malik. He'd worn warm clothing there, but nothing like the cumbersome outfit he was now wearing. But more than anything, he hated the secrecy Malik had insisted on, secrecy that was now coming back to haunt them both. Rashid knew his wife would leave no stone unturned in order to find out what was going on. He shivered inside the bulky clothing. With fear. Only to himself would he ever admit that he was afraid of the spitfire he'd married.

Rashid was inside the warm lobby. He stepped aside to allow a solemn-faced family to go ahead of him. He removed his heavy coat and hat and walked into the coffee shop at the end of the corridor. He ordered a cup of hot chocolate. While he waited, he sent off another text to his wife, though he knew that it would be ignored. Still, he tried. He hated lying to her. Why had he told her they were in France when they were in Switzerland? Because he was a terrible liar, that was why. And because Malik had told him to say they were in France. "To throw anyone off his trail," as he put it.

They were incognito, which, in Rashid's opinion, was stupid; but again, Malik had insisted. "Too much is at stake right now," was how he put it. So, Malik had signed in using his best friend's name from the States, Zack Molton. Rashid himself was Duke Richards. American dollars had been deposited to cover all costs the moment they walked through the doors. The same thing had been done when they visited Sloan-Kettering in New York and the hospital in London two months ago.

Rashid sipped on his hot chocolate, which was so hot, it burned his tongue. He loved it, though, because the marshmallows had melted, and it was thick and creamy. He picked up one of the hospital brochures to be found behind the menus on every table and started to read it.

The University Hospital of Basel, it said, was one of Switzerland's leading medical centers. It had over fifty clinics, polyclinics, and institutes, all working together on an interdisciplinary basis and under one roof. It was known worldwide and had an excellent reputation for its state-of-the-art technology and systematic interdisciplinary approach to ensure the well-being of every patient.

Rashid continued to read. *The close co-*

operation between the oldest university in Switzerland on the one hand and the global life-science corporations based in Basel on the other guarantees the highest standard of treatment and innovation in all medical disciplines. The brochure went on to say that patients came from all over the world to be treated at this fine facility.

Basel, it read, *is situated in the heart of Europe, being the Swiss border town to Germany and France. The hospital is located in the center of the city, approximately fifteen minutes from the Basel-Mulhouse-Freiburg International Airport. Families are surrounded by numerous hotels and many shopping facilities. The hospital is known globally for its outstanding oncology, prostate, and renal specialists, as well as for its facilities for treating musculoskeletal disorders and its centers for the treatment of lung cancer.*

Rashid already knew all this. In fact, he had the entire brochure committed to memory. He had just read the brochure to kill time.

The coffee shop was full. Rashid looked around to see if anyone was waiting for his table. There was no line, so he sat a few more moments. He needed to meditate for a few minutes to try and get a good mindset before he walked into Malik's room. He

193

felt sick to his stomach, and he felt like crying. Crying! He couldn't remember when he had cried last or if he had ever cried. Surely he had. He just couldn't remember. He looked down at his watch again. *Time to go.* He got up, cleared off his table, and paid the bill.

Rashid walked slowly to the elevator. He felt like he had a giant boulder in the pit of his stomach. And his eyes kept burning. It was all so unfair. How was he going to walk into Malik's room with a smile on his face and adopt an upbeat manner? How? He also knew that the moment Malik was returned to his hospital room, he would be checking his cell for missed calls and texts. By now Malik would know about Soraya and would also know that Trish was winging her way back to the States. And that Rashid had been relegated to the bowels of the palace.

Rashid cursed, using all the American cusswords he'd learned while studying at Berkeley. He never cursed, because his religion forbade it. But at that moment, he just didn't care. He let loose, first in Arabic, then in English, and after that, in the four other languages in which he was fluent. Unfortunately, he did not feel one bit better; in point of fact, he felt worse because he'd used foul language.

Rashid rapped softly with his knuckles on the door. He drew in his breath and let it out with a soft *swoosh* of exhaled air. He walked into the room and wasn't at all surprised to see Malik texting on his phone.

Without looking up, Malik said, "Sounds like you stepped in the dung pile. I'll talk to my sister. You don't deserve her attitude. Pregnant women are very unpredictable, as you well know."

"You'll do no such thing. I can handle my own affairs, and need I remind you, Malik, I wouldn't be in this mess if you had been honest with your wife and your sister. This . . . this . . . secrecy is no good for you or for them. You can't keep something like this secret."

"Yes, I know. I have every intention . . . *had* every intention of talking to Trish and Soraya once I got back home. I wanted it all confirmed first."

"Well, Your Highness, you're a little late. Let me be the first to tell you that your sister does not have a forgiving bone in her body. Secondly, your wife is over the Atlantic by now on her way back to the States. She thinks you are — forgive me here — screwing around on her, looking to replace her because she cannot give you a child. I don't know if she has a forgiving bone in her body

195

or not. Only you know the answer to that. What is to become of her, Malik?"

Malik closed his eyes. "I need to think."

"*Think!* Is that what you said? You've had three months to think about all of this. I don't want to hear any more bullshit. Yes, I'm saying unseemly words. You should have heard me in the elevator. I will not apologize, either. You screwed up, Malik."

"Yes. I guess I did. No one likes being given a death sentence. I did talk to you. You refused to believe nothing could be done to help me. We both agreed, you and I, not to mention anything to either Trish or Soraya until we were certain of the diagnosis and the prognosis. By day's end, we will have that. Am I not right, my one true friend?"

"Yes. But . . . you gave off all the wrong signals to the women. You changed your patterns. Women are not fools, even though we sometimes think they are. Your wife missed your notes, you were away too much, and you didn't talk about your days and what you did or did not accomplish. You did not take her, or I should say invite her, back to your cave. Even a dolt such as I would have developed the same feelings the women got."

"So what you're saying is, neither Trish

nor my sister will forgive me when I tell them the truth? You're saying they won't care that I'm dying and are only concerned that I kept them in the dark?"

Rashid threw his hands in the air. "I know nothing about women. I don't know what to do. I've always known what to do before." His eyes started to burn unbearably. And then his eyes filled with tears. They rolled down his cheeks. Malik was off the bed and standing over his friend of forever, his hands on his shoulders. "I didn't know you knew how to cry, Rashid. Listen, I didn't mean that the way it sounded."

"I'm crying for you, you fool," Rashid blubbered.

"Yes, yes, I know that. The thing with the women, that was just a diversion to cover up your feelings."

"You're off the wall, Malik. I'm crying here like my baby son for the whole ball of wax, for you, for all of us, and, by the way, your ass is hanging out of that designer gown you're wearing."

Malik grinned, backed up to the bed, and scooted into it. "Now that we cleared all of *that* up, what should we talk about?"

"How about getting out of this godforsaken cold, which is eating at my bones? I don't think I'll ever be warm again," Rashid said, swiping his arm across his eyes.

"We must talk of this, Rashid, and then we can talk about the cold and leaving this place. I am in Allah's hands now, and we both know it. Treatment . . . will be carried out back home. Amir will discuss all of this with the doctors here. I decided that I like these doctors the best. It won't be easy, and it will be painful. Actually, we could leave now if you like, Rashid. I already know what the doctors are going to say later in the day. They pretty much already told me. I can leave instructions for all my records to be transferred to Amir. Of course, at that point, I will have to own up to the fact that I am not Zack Molton. But that is a minor detail.

"If you stop and think about all of this clearly, it could be a blessing in disguise. Trish will be able to remain in control at the palace, and she won't have to leave. I'll be gone before the five years are up, which is just eleven months and fourteen days from now. Yes, yes, I have been keeping track of the days, just as Trish has. There is nothing the council or the advisers can do then. Allah, as they say, works in mysterious ways. Now, do you want to leave or not?"

Rashid gasped. "Your time is that short?" He dropped his head into his hands and started to cry all over again.

"Keep this up, Rashid, and you'll turn into a crybaby. So, do we leave or not?"

"Yes. Yes, we should leave. I don't want you staying here one minute longer than you have to. Tell me what to do about Soraya and Trish."

"As soon as I figure it out, you will be the first to know. And if I catch you looking at my ass when I go into the bathroom to dress, I will make sure you never leave the bowels of the palace."

Rashid got up and left the room. He walked to the nurses' desk and informed them that Mr. Molton, whose real name was Sheik Malik bin Al Mohammed, would be leaving immediately, and all records were to be faxed to the sheik's doctor. He carefully wrote out all the information; then the nurse copied it into Malik's file.

"Thank you for taking such excellent care of His Royal Highness," Rashid said softly.

The little nurse nodded, her eyes full of sympathy.

Taking into account the time difference, both of the sleek silver jets landed in different parts of the world within minutes of each other. One landed at McCarran International Airport in Las Vegas; the other landed at Al Maktoum International Airport in Dubai. No smiles, only tears could be seen on the passengers' faces as they exited their respective aircraft.

Trish walked down the portable stairs, mindful of the last time she'd landed at this very same airport. Soraya had been with her then, her eyes full of wonder that she was actually in America and just moments away from what she considered the adventure of a lifetime. And for her it had been an adventure. She herself had been happy at that moment, too, yet sad at the same time because she had left Malik behind.

Trish climbed into the town car and buckled up. Thirty minutes from then, she would be walking into her old home. Knowing Connie, she knew there would be food in the refrigerator and wine chilling in a bucket. There would be a fresh supply of wood for her to build a fire her first day home. There might even be a Crock-Pot of chili simmering on the counter, along with fresh hard rolls, the kind she loved. The heat would be turned up to a temperature of her liking. Friends did these kinds of things for other friends. She had to admit, she missed Connie and the girls. Texting, even calling, just wasn't the same.

For the first time since getting into the car, Trish noticed that it was snowing lightly own house. It was then that she noticed two things: it was snowing harder, and there was a huge van that had pulled up right alongside the town car. Men hopped out of the van and started carrying bags and trunks up the steps. Trish blinked. And then her heart started to flutter in her chest. So many trunks and boxes. All her things? She'd thought she was bringing just her winter clothes. Had she been kicked out for good?

Trish ran up the steps and opened the door. "Just . . . just pile everything up in the foyer," was all she could manage to say. She looked around. Everything looked the same, the place smelled clean and fresh, and it was warm. She walked into her living room, and she'd been right. A neat stack of wood rested on the hearth. Before she could think twice, she went over to the fireplace and turned on the gas starter to ignite the logs, which were ready for burning. Connie had outdone herself.

Trish tipped outrageously, smiled, and thanked the men standing in the foyer. The moment she closed the door and shot the dead bolt, she started to cry. She counted the trunks and bags. Eleven in all. She had no idea she had so many belongings. She looked down at the small gold-lacquered

outside. She wondered what the weather report was. She leaned forward and asked the driver.

"They are predicting four inches. At least that's what the weatherman said early this morning. It's been bitter cold here for the past two weeks."

Trish thanked him, leaned back, and closed her eyes. She was torturing herself by not activating her phone. She'd promised herself when she boarded the plane for the long flight that she wouldn't check it till she was in her town house and settled in. It was one of the hardest promises she'd ever made to herself.

Trish's thoughts were all over the map as she wondered if she'd made a mistake in confiding in Soraya. She thought then of Rashid and his new quarters and how that was going to play out for him and Soraya. Would Malik intervene? She had no idea what he would or would not do these days.

She wanted to cry so bad, she had to squeeze her eyes shut. Crying, it was said, was cathartic. Well, she'd shed more than her share of tears these past months, and she didn't feel like cathartic was working.

Trish thought about her sister, Emma — anything to take her thoughts away from her own personal problems. She regretted that she and Emma weren't as close as they had been. Time and distance were the culprits. Each of the sisters had made a new life for herself. Calls these days were all on Trish's part because, as Emma put it, "I don't have the money for overseas calls, and I can't afford to put another plan on my cell phone, so you will have to call me." That was fine with Trish. She didn't mind, but every time she called, Emma was either with a prospective client or the call went to voice mail. And when they did talk, Emma never mentioned the estrangement from her daughter, who was now in college, or her ex-husband, who was, according to Emma, the devil incarnate.

She thought then about how gung ho she'd been back in the early days of her marriage, when she tried her best, with no luck, to figure out what Jeff Davis and his band of international lawyers were up to. In the end, she'd let it slide because her own life was more important. She wished now she had done more. Perhaps she could enlist the aid of some computer geeks while she was home and see what they could dredge up on Jeff Davis. With the twenty million dollars in annual payments that had been paid into her Swiss bank account, she would certainly have enough money to do whatever

she wanted to do. And that did not t
account the returns on the investm
had been made with that money
could spend whatever it would tak
out what the slimeball — that v
Emma had called her ex when she
to her last week — was up to. Er
know some computer people wi
ways things like that were done.
certainly be something for her to
the time until she decided if she
to return to Dubai or not. Just th
of not going back sent chills
spine.

If hackers could break into the
computers, surely there was so
there who could find out Jeff Dav
And she knew in her gut there w
She'd ferret them out, then pass
Emma. It was the least she coul
sister.

Emma was so damned stub
had lost track of the many tim
fered financial help. She'd even
cash, by overnight courier, only
sister return it. Finally, she'd g
their relationship was where
now, almost at the freezing poi

"We're here, miss," the drive
into the parking slot assign

chest with the impressive lock that Malik had given her for her birthday in the second year of their marriage. The chest was where she kept her jewelry, her banking records, the statements, and the endearing cards Malik had given her during their marriage. The key to the ornate chest was on her key ring.

It was almost dark outside when Trish meandered into the kitchen, the tears still trickling down her cheeks. She'd been so right. A bright red Crock-Pot, its ON light glowing brightly on the WARM setting, awaited her. She didn't have to lift the lid to know it was chili. On the counter, alongside the Crock-Pot, was a freshly made apple pie. She could smell the cinnamon. She knew there would be raisins and chopped nuts in the pie. Connie again. Connie loved to bake. The hard rolls were from the bakery, the seal still on the box. What more could a girl want, unless it was someone to share it with?

At that moment, Trish realized she was ravenously hungry. She quickly fixed a bowl of food, got out a tray, and carried it all into the living room, where she turned on the television for the early news. A fire, the news, food, and a flood of tears. What more could a girl ask for?

Sometimes, like then, life was definitely not a bowl of cherries, but a bowl of chili made for her by the loving hands of a dear friend.

CHAPTER 13

Trish slept away the better part of three days after her return to her town house. She woke, showered, ate, and went back to sleep. At sundown on the third day, she woke, finally feeling like her old self. She showered, washed her hair, and dressed in a comfortable old set of sweats that felt like an old friend. She made a fire, scrambled some eggs, and settled down in her living room, the television on low. Outside, it was snowing. She'd been stunned to see the accumulation since her arrival. She'd been equally stunned to see the three notes her friend Connie had left for her during the three days. They were bright and witty, so like Connie, she thought as she read one of them.

You really are a sleepyhead. I know, jet lag. I brought more food. I will continue to check on you until you're up and moving with a purpose. I hope your dreams are good ones.

Trish smiled. Tomorrow she would get back into the swing of things. She'd rent a car, go to the grocery store, and get down to business. She stared at her cell phone in the charger on the little table next to where she was sitting. She'd checked it once during her three-day sleeping binge. There were forty-two text messages from Malik and four voice-mail messages. Seven text messages from Soraya and nineteen voice-mail messages. All sounded urgent from brother and sister. On the second day, between bouts of sleep, she'd sent one simple text to each: I arrived safely. Will be in touch soon.

The word *soon,* she told herself, meant different things to different people. She allowed herself a small snort of laughter. Where had this shitty blasé attitude come from all of a sudden? From her sleep, from her dreams? She shrugged it off.

Trish finished the last of her eggs and carried her dishes out to the kitchen, where she made more coffee, then turned on the dishwasher. While she waited for the coffee to drip, she downed two glasses of orange juice. She sniffed and wondered if she had a cold coming on. *Damn, this is no time to get sick.*

Thinking preventively, she looked in the cabinet, and sure enough, there was a half bottle of cognac. She would lace her coffee with that, down some aspirin, and hope for the best. She moved over to her kitchen door, turned on the outside light, and saw the accumulation of snow on her little deck. She shrugged that off, too. Sooner or later, it would melt. By tomorrow morning, she knew, it would all look like a winter wonderland. Being warm, dry, and well fed was all that was important to her at the moment.

When Trish carried her coffee, which was more cognac than coffee, back to the living room, she stopped in her foyer to stare down at the trunks, suitcases, and the little chest. What was in all of them? Tomorrow was another day. She knew in her gut she needed to be clicking on all cylinders when she opened them. So much stuff for just a short visit. The words *short visit* were her words. The amount of baggage signaled a different phrase, *permanent stay.*

Coffee in hand, back in front of the fire, Trish curled her legs under her to settle down for another endless rerun of her favorite television show, *NCIS*. The phone in the charger rang. She craned her neck to see the caller ID. Zack Molton. Aha, Malik was calling in his big gun. Trish let the call go to voice mail. Five minutes later she heard the signal that a text message was coming through. Same caller ID, Zack Molton. She ignored it, too, and before she knew it, she was following the program playing out on the screen. She did love Leroy Jethro Gibbs and his fellow agents and the way they solved everything in sixty minutes. *Life should only be that perfect,* she thought.

The cell in the charger continued to ring throughout the evening. Trish sat engrossed in the continuing episodes she'd missed. At eleven o'clock, without another look at her cell, she got ready for bed. The two cups of coffee and all the cognac had made her sleepy all over again. She drank another glass of orange juice and popped some more aspirin.

Trish was asleep before her head hit the pillow. When she woke at seven the next morning, she lay there for a few minutes, trying to decide how she felt. She yawned elaborately and decided she felt full of spit and vinegar. Time to start the new day.

Trish brushed her teeth and headed for the kitchen, where she brewed coffee. As it dripped, she sent off a text message to Malik and one to Soraya. Both messages were the same. It's snowing. Looks beautiful. She typed in her name and returned the phone to the charger. She eyed her belongings in the foyer as she made her way back to the kitchen.

Mid-morning, Trish was dressed and ready to head out. Her new rental car was due any moment. She stood in the foyer, watching out the window for the people who had promised to deliver the car no later than ten thirty. She looked down at her watch. Five minutes to go. The building association had done a good job of plowing out the road and the parking spaces. She'd insisted on a vehicle with four-wheel drive, just to be on the safe side.

The car arrived at ten forty. Trish signed the papers, handed over her credit card so the courier could run it, and she was good to go.

At the last second, Trish ran back to the kitchen for another glass of orange juice and more aspirin. Finally, she was ready to face her old world again. She headed straight for the nearest mall, where she went to the Verizon store and bought a new phone. She signed a one-year contract for it, paid it in full, and was assured that if she returned in two hours, she would have full service. She killed time by walking around the stores.

There wasn't one thing she needed or wanted. Maybe she should get something for Emma, but what? It had been years since she'd set eyes on her sister. She had no idea what size she was these days. She scratched that idea. She stopped at Nordstrom, had a bite of lunch, then headed back to the Verizon store, where she pocketed her new cell phone and headed for home.

Back inside her cozy town house, Trish got down to work at the kitchen table. She opened up her laptop and put her plan into motion. An hour later, she called Connie and asked her if she'd stop by, because she needed to talk to her about something important. Connie agreed and said she'd be by no later than two o'clock. It would be so good to see her old friend in the flesh again.

When the doorbell rang at ten minutes of two, Trish almost killed herself running to the door. She opened it and squealed her pleasure at seeing her old friend. "Come in. Come in. It's so cold out there!"

They hugged each other, kissed each other, then hugged some more before Trish burst into tears.

"It can't be that bad, or are you crying with happiness at seeing me?" Connie teased lightly as she eyed the trunks and cases lining the foyer.

"Both, Connie. Come on out to the kitchen. I have coffee on. You look great. You haven't aged a day since I saw you last."

"I wish I could return the compliment, Trish. You look terrible. I have this great new makeup that will hide those dark circles under your eyes. And you lost weight. Well, I'm going to fatten you right up. Pour me coffee. Then let's talk."

And talk they did until well after five.

"Trish, playing devil's advocate here, what is it you're doing here? Are you trying to teach Malik a lesson? Did you try to talk to him, or did you hide in your shell and pretend everything was all right? Think back to when you say his indifference started. Can you pinpoint anything in particular that happened?"

"Just the business of me not getting pregnant. It weighed on my mind. It would on yours, too, if you were in my position. That's the only thing I can think of. As far as I know, palace business and the other emirates are okay. Malik really doesn't discuss any of that with me, except maybe in passing. He's not a worrier by nature. He . . . Something is . . . was on his mind, and he couldn't hide that fact from me. He tried, but it just didn't work. The big telling point was that we didn't go to the cave. We used to do that a lot.

"You know what else, Connie? I don't even know whose idea it was for me to come home, mine or Soraya's. All I know was that within hours, the plans had been made, and here I am. As well as all those trunks and bags and boxes. I can't bear to open them. I guess this is my swan song. But then, another part of me wants to know why all the voice mails and texts from both Malik and Soraya. Maybe it's one of those things, you know, where you don't know what you have until you lose it. That kind of thinking. Maybe they're both sorry about whatever it is they are sorry about. Does that make sense?

"I feel so . . . I don't know what the word is, Connie. Betrayed, maybe. Ignored? Did Malik fall out of love with me? Did he find a replacement for me, one who will give him an heir? I just don't know. What I do know is that I am not going to discuss my life, my future, over the telephone or by sending texts. Another thing is I have all this money. On day one I was told it would be mine forever, no matter what happened. And it's true. With all the successful investments the Swiss bankers have made for me, I have over one hundred million dollars in my name. And guess what? I have no will. I'm going to see to that while I'm here. Is this unbelievable or what? Paid for services rendered. That sucks, Connie."

"Oh, Trish, you don't know that for sure. For some reason, it's not computing for me. There's something here that isn't adding up for me. With everything you've told me over the years about Malik and your relationship, I just don't see him kicking you to the curb as you say. I grant you something isn't right, and I'm starting to think it's with your husband, not you, and he doesn't know how to handle it."

"Like what?" Trish snapped. "We've always shared everything from the day we got married."

Connie threw her hands in the air. "I don't know, Trish. My best advice, my only advice, is to go back to Dubai and talk it out with Malik. Hog-tie him if you have to and get to the bottom of it. Find out *exactly* where you stand regarding the childbirth issue. The man is the head of his country. He should be able to change a stupid ruling like that."

"You're right. I *am* going to go back, but I'll go back only when I'm ready and not one minute sooner. I'm going to stay a while, try to get my head on straight, and only then will I make my decisions. In the

215

meantime I plan to pretty much ignore both Malik and Soraya. I will send off a text from time to time. It's Malik's turn to sweat a little."

"Sounds like a plan to me. So you haven't looked into the trunks is what you're telling me. Plus, you didn't read or listen to any of the messages that have been left for you. You assume — I want to stress the word *assume* here — that you have been kicked to the curb because you can't bear a child for your husband. Is that correct?"

"Pretty much, yes."

"Well, let's just check it out, because I have to leave shortly. We have an eight o'clock show during January and February, as you know. Are they locked?"

"No."

Trish and Connie walked from the kitchen to the foyer where Connie dropped to her haunches and opened the first trunk and gasped. "Wow! Would you look at this! I have never in my life seen such gorgeous silk. There are bolts and bolts of it, every color of the rainbow." After opening two more trunks, Connie exclaimed, "This one has sets of gold-plated dinnerware. And this one is full of gold silverware. Are you planning on opening a store, and you didn't tell me? How did you get this stuff into this country without going through customs, or whatever it is you have to do?"

Trish threw her hands in the air. "I had no idea what was in the trunks. I thought it was my stuff. I guess it's gifts for my friends. This must be Soraya's doing. She oversaw the packing of my things. It was kind of a last-minute decision on my part to come home."

Connie opened several other trunks and described the contents to Trish. "This one has exquisite wall hangings and brocades. This one has gold figurines. I didn't know there was that much gold in the world. This has to represent a fortune, Trish. Okay, okay, this case has your winter clothes in it. And there's a lock on that beautiful little chest. Me thinks, Trish, you misinterpreted things. Perhaps you should spend the evening listening to those messages on your phone."

Trish chewed on her lower lip. She waved her arms about and said, "This doesn't mean I haven't been kicked to the curb. How do you explain Malik's strange behavior?"

Connie was already on her way back to the kitchen to gather up her notes. "Let's go through this one more time before I leave. You want me to find a computer hacker who can be trusted to ferret out your sister's ex-husband's financials. You know he's doing something dirty, and your sister got screwed by him.

"Ernie will be a big help on this. His day job is writing software for huge firms, and he knows just about everyone in the field. He is so good at that, but it's not what he wants to do. He wants to be a choreographer. I'll do my best. Are you going to wait for me to get back to you, or are you going to go to see your sister first?"

"I was thinking about leaving tomorrow and surprising her. You can reach me on my new cell phone." Trish ripped off a sticky note from a pad stuck to the fridge and handed it to Connie.

The two women hugged one another again as Trish walked Connie to the door. "Say hi to everyone for me and give Ernie a big hug. Soraya said to give him a kiss."

Connie laughed all the way out to her car.

Trish's heart felt lighter as she made her way back to the living room. She picked up the phone and started to scroll through the text messages. Several times she smiled and several times she frowned at her husband's messages. Soraya's just made her laugh out loud. The text and voice mail from Zack Molton was a puzzle, with Zack just saying that he wanted to check in to see how things were and that he had not been able to reach Malik in over a month. He went on to say he hoped everything was right as rain, and if she had a chance, to flip him off a text to reassure him that all was right in her corner of the world.

Trish puzzled over the text and voice mail. Malik hadn't been in touch with Zack, either. Normally, they were in touch several times a week. More puzzled than annoyed, Trish shelved her thoughts about Zack Molton and set about booking an airline ticket to Newark, New Jersey, where she would rent a car and drive on to Princeton. She crossed her fingers that her sister would welcome her with open arms.

Dinner was a ham sandwich and a glass of milk. Then she was back on her laptop, taking virtual tours of Princeton. She did a Google Earth search to see exactly where her sister was living. She winced as she hit one link after another to gain more information. Then she did the Google Earth search again to see Jeff Davis's new house, which he lived in with his trophy wife and her sister's daughter, her niece. She whistled to herself at what she was seeing. Compared to where Jeff lived, her sister was living in the ghetto.

"Well, we'll just see about that," Trish murmured under her breath.

She wished she was more computer savvy. She knew she was wasting time, but she kept at it, and finally she actually hit on a public record site that told her who held Jeff Davis's mortgage. She whistled again. A five-million-dollar house with yearly taxes that could feed a family of six, according to the Realtor he'd purchased the house from. He had a sky-high mortgage. He'd bought the house at the high-tide mark in real-estate prices, and the house's value was now depressed by 47 percent. The house was in a gated community called Bar Haven. It was precisely 8.6 miles from the ghetto where Emma lived.

Trish kept clicking and clicking, going from one site to the other until she found what she thought she wanted. Once again, she took a virtual tour of a gated community, Bar Haven's competitor, called the Enclave. The houses in the tour were Mc-Mansions, gorgeous, with four models that were fully furnished with top-of-the-line everything. The Enclave builders had been wise and had stopped building just as the economy took a nosedive. Not so Bar Haven's, who had finally had to stop their phase two section thanks to a lack of bank funding. The pictures she was viewing looked like a war zone.

Trish went to another site and clicked again as the virtual scene moved up one street and down another. Huge, bright red FOR SALE signs could be seen on just about every other house. On Jeff Davis's street alone, there were seven FOR SALE signs. Rich on paper only. All the more reason to get Jeff's financials.

Trish looked at the clock on the range and sighed. Twelve thirty! She shut down her laptop, warmed a glass of milk, shot the dead bolt on the front door, and went upstairs. Before she put on her nightclothes, she packed a small bag and carried it out to the foyer. All she had to do in the morning was roll out of bed, shower, grab a cup of coffee, and head for the airport.

No dreams invaded her peaceful night's sleep.

CHAPTER 14

Trish's flight from Las Vegas touched down in Newark, New Jersey, at a little past noon eastern standard time. She proceeded to rent a four-wheel-drive vehicle and was on Route 1 within thirty minutes for the drive to Princeton. The sky was overcast, the color of gunmetal. From time to time, she saw snow flurries and had to turn on her windshield wipers. At least for the moment, there was no accumulation of snow.

Caught up in her own thoughts, as well as the reasons for being where she was at the moment, Trish paid little attention to the changes in the area since she'd lived there as a teenager. She was hopeful she could do everything she planned in the three days she'd allotted herself in her old home state.

Trish registered at the Hyatt Regency, using her birth name, because she still had a credit card and her American driver's license in the name of Patricia Holiday. For some reason, she hadn't wanted to give up those things. Just then, she couldn't even remember if she'd told that to Malik or not. She opted for a suite of rooms when she checked in because of late she did a lot of pacing. She carried her own small bag to her suite, checked it out, washed her face and hands, brushed her teeth and her hair, and felt like she was good to go. Before heading out, though, she opened a can of juice from the minibar and gulped it down.

Her car was still parked at the hotel's entrance, so she was off within minutes. Her first destination was the gated community where Jeff Davis lived. She explained to the guard that she was meeting a Realtor at Jeff's address. He nodded lazily and let her drive through. She drove up and down the streets, stunned at the FOR SALE signs she was seeing. She found Jeff's house with no trouble at all. A devil perched itself on her shoulder as she pulled into her former brother-in-law's driveway. She marched up to the front door and rang the bell. She waited a minute and then rang it again. Finally, the door opened to reveal an incredibly tall, thin woman dressed from head to toe in designer wear. She was wearing so much makeup, Trish thought she'd need to go through a car wash to get it off.

"Hi. I'm Eileen Wilkerson. I'm a Realtor, and I heard through the grapevine that you and your husband are considering putting your house up for sale. I'd like to offer my services. I know how trying these times are for all of you living out here in all this luxury, and then, in a heartbeat, it's all taken away. Who knew this property, which you probably love, would be down forty-seven percent in only a few years? Everyone is underwater. Goodness, there are seven houses for sale on this street alone. And I heard another one is going on the market tomorrow. You have to have something outstanding to beat out the others. So, are you interested in listing with me?" Trisha said brightly. If this skin-and-bones person standing in front of her was twenty-six years old, she was old.

"I don't know what in the world you're talking about. My husband and I aren't selling our house. Who told you that?"

"One of your neighbors. I'm sorry, but I can't divulge his name, but my understanding is that he is a friend of your husband's. He said — and I probably shouldn't even tell you this, but you seem like a nice person, and sometimes husbands don't tell their wives everything — but he confided that money was in very short supply because of this perilous economy." Trish almost danced a jig at the look of panic on Jeff's trophy wife's face.

"Well, that just stinks," the woman said. "Neighbors gossiping like that. Jeff will be terribly upset. It's not true. I will admit that it's very sad seeing all those empty houses on the street. There's never anyone around. Look, it's cold, and we're not selling our house, so there's nothing more to say."

"Okay," Trish said happily. "I understand you don't want to talk about it. I'll come back in a week or so, and maybe you'll be more amenable to talking then. You know, after you speak with your husband. Now, here's a little tip, and I don't usually tell people things like this unless they're clients, but you look so . . . worried, I'm going to tell you. This place is sinking. No one wants to live here anymore. The place to go is the Enclave. They're *solvent.* Right now, you can buy a five-million-dollar house for practically nothing. You have a nice day now, Mrs. Davis. I'm sure we'll be talking soon."

If Trish hadn't already been half turned around, the heavy mahogany door would have slammed her in the face. She laughed all the way back to her car. She was still laughing when she drove up to the gate of the Enclave, thanks to her GPS. She told the guard she was interested in one of the houses and was meeting a Realtor at the office. He waved her through without a problem.

Trish consulted the map she'd printed off the Web site, and drove around till she found the street named Nightstar Lane, where there were four model homes on display. She liked the fact that the four homes were on a cul-de-sac, the lots were heavily treed, and the landscaping, even in the winter, was lush and full. She knew it would be beautiful in the spring. The builder, she could tell, had tried to save as many of the trees as he could.

Trish continued her drive around the Enclave. She saw only one FOR SALE sign. The clubhouse was absolutely gorgeous, from what she could see of it, and there were tons of cars in the parking lot, which meant the residents of the Enclave had it going on. She saw the two Olympic-size pools, the three tennis courts, and, off in the distance, a nine-hole golf course. She also saw a shuttle bus parked in the lot. She did one more drive around, then headed for the sales office.

A bored little man was sitting behind his desk, watching something on his computer, when Trish walked in and introduced herself. The man, who said his name was Dudley Enwright, shook her hand and motioned for her to take a seat. Directly in Trish's line of vision was a giant map of the Enclave. Red Xs marked the available properties, and there weren't that many.

"I'm here to make your day, Mr. Enwright. I want to buy all four models, along with the furnishings. I'm prepared to pay cash within the hour. I can wire the money into your escrow account immediately if we can agree on a price. Are you interested? I don't want you wasting your time. I can drive over to Bar Haven and pick up four houses for pennies on the dollar. I mean that literally. So, let's start to negotiate." This was where all she'd learned from Soraya, who had taught her how to haggle at the souks, came into play.

Enwright's eyes popped wide. "Well . . . this is . . . extraordinary. I might have to call my boss. He's the one who will have the final say. All four, eh?"

"Yes, all four. Call him now so we don't waste time. I am in a hurry, and as I said, Bar Haven is not all that far from here. I can cut the same deal within minutes over there."

Enwright made the call and said his boss was on the way. Negotiations that weren't

227

really negotiations got under way. Trish held firm at her price and didn't budge. Twice, she got up and headed for the door. The second time her hand was on the handle when the door opened and the boss was standing in the doorway.

"Ten minutes, gentlemen, and I'm out of here." The men left to go into a back room. Trish remained standing by the door, her eyes on her watch. "Always," Soraya had said, "be prepared to walk away, and make sure your eyes reflect the decision."

The two men were back in eight minutes. "We have a deal, Miss Holiday," said Enwright.

Trish whipped out her laptop and tapped furiously the moment Enwright gave her the bank's routing numbers. Everyone signed in fifty different places, and the deal was consummated.

"I know a lot more goes into this, but I really do not have the time to do it all. Emma Davis is the Realtor, and as such she will get the realty commission. The new tenants will be moving in tomorrow, so I will need the keys. All those pesky details can be cleared up with her. So, we're good, gentlemen?"

The boss, whose name was Stanley Peabody, managed to croak, "We're good, Miss

Holiday."

Enwright handed the keys to Trish, who dumped them in her purse. She was fifteen million dollars poorer, but she felt wonderful.

"I can see myself out, gentlemen. A pleasure doing business with you."

In a daze, the two men watched Trish leave with only limp-wristed waves.

Back in her car, Trish headed to Route 1 and the Mercedes car dealership. She breezed in and within an hour purchased four Maybach top-of-the-line Mercedes-Benz automobiles. A promise in writing of delivery by eight the following morning to each of her four driveways at the Enclave was all Trish needed to know another deal had been cut in stone. Once again she whipped out her laptop and typed furiously, transferring $2.5 million to the dealership coffers.

Trish was back on the road and headed for her sister's apartment by four thirty. *Now,* she thought, *comes the hard part.* Convincing Emma and her three loyal friends that what she was doing for them was right and just. And a way to get even with the dirty scoundrels who had kicked them to the curb for trophy wives.

It was five thirty when Trish pulled into

the parking area of the complex where her sister lived. It was so depressing, she wanted to turn around and run. And she didn't know if Emma was even home. Not too long ago, Emma had said her hours were eight to five during the week, half a day Saturday, and half a day Sunday. And she'd said she didn't live far from the office she worked out of. Trish found the unit building and crossed her fingers as she made her way through the parking lot to the apartment. It was fully dark by then, but she could see a light in the window. She let loose with a sigh and rang the bell at the side of the door. Within seconds, it was opened by her sister.

The two women stared at one another, and it was Trish who broke into tears. "I need you, Emma," she said, at which point Emma also burst into tears.

The small apartment was stiflingly hot. It was as depressing as the outside. Trish knew she couldn't stay here one minute longer. "This is what we're going to do, Emma. Call your friends. Tell them to meet us at . . . whatever restaurant you want. I have such good news for you and your friends. Don't give me any bullshit, either. Later, you can ream my ass out as much as you want, but right now this is about *you*. Are we clear on that?"

Emma nodded and made the calls. And then she directed Trish out to the parking lot and an Outback restaurant several miles down the road.

By six thirty, introductions had been made. Trish decided she liked her sister's friends, and knew she hadn't made a mistake by doing what she'd done. They all looked weary and beaten. Probably, they thought the same thing about her. They ordered drinks, and Trish made the toast.

"To your new lives!"

"I think you need to explain that, Trish," Emma said quietly.

Trish explained. In excruciating detail. The women just gaped at her. Emma started to cry. Trish dug around in her purse and pulled out four sets of keys. She read the labels and handed them out. The girls' hands shook so badly, they could barely pick up the keys. Clare Hart, a breast-cancer survivor, actually kissed the key, then started to cry. When Trish fished again in her purse for the extra sets of keys the dealer had given her for the Maybachs, Alice Gamble turned white and said she was driving a 1986 Ford with 250,000 miles on it. Robin Olsen sat in a trance, trying to take it all in. Emma just kept crying.

"Time for another drink, ladies!" Trish said. Toast after toast was made until their food arrived, huge steaks, thrice-baked potatoes, and coconut shrimp. Considering the shape the ladies were in, Trish was surprised that they cleaned their plates. She was even more surprised that she cleaned hers.

It was ten o'clock when Trish called a halt to the evening. "We are drunk, ladies, and that means we cannot drive, so this is what we're going to do. We are going to call a cab, and we're all going to the Hyatt Regency, where you will sleep for the night. Emma, you will bunk with me. You are going to go back to those shitty apartments only to get your personal belongings after breakfast. Then I will take you to your new homes, where you will settle in.

"I'm going to give you two hours, and then one of you will drive the others into New York, where you have appointments at the Red Door for *the works.* I am giving you each a check to do some shopping for new things. I want you to buy whatever you want. And then I'm giving you each another check to jump-start your new bank accounts. Ladies, you are going into business for yourselves. We can talk about that tomorrow night, when you get back from New York."

Everyone started to cry, even Trish. Who knew that being very rich could be so much fun?

It was one o'clock in the morning and Emma was sound asleep when Trish pulled out her cell phone and sent a text to Malik. It read: I just spent eighteen million dollars. Maybe nineteen before I'm finished.

The return text was almost immediate. It is being replenished as I type this. Are you all right? I miss you. I love you.

Trish burst out laughing.

I love you and miss you, too. Good night.

CHAPTER 15

Trish woke to see her sister staring at her from the bed across from her. For a moment she was a child again, sharing a room with her big sister. She smiled at her, and Emma smiled back.

"What am I going to do with you, Trish? This is all so . . . I don't even know what the word is. Beyond generous. You don't even know my friends, and yet you took us all under your wing and turned our lives upside down in minutes. When I opened the door and saw you standing there, I almost blacked out. And then you said you needed me. Did you just say that so I wouldn't turn you away? Why would you suddenly need me, of all people? I guess I am stupid, like Jeff says, because I don't understand."

"I do need you, Emma," Trish said, turning and propping herself up on one elbow. "But I wanted to . . . to help you first. We can get to me later. Remember when you said you never saw it coming? You said it was the same with your friends. Was that true, or were you trying to convince yourself you didn't see the signs? It's important for me to know the truth, Emma. I never understood how you could have missed those signs everyone talks about.

"I came here, Emma, because I am experiencing those signs, and I need my big sister to help me out here." Trish's eyes pooled with tears. "I thought I had the love of all time, you know, the kind they write books about and make movies out of. Our love was so special, and it never wavered or faltered. I was Malik's life, and he was mine. Forget the money, the wealth, the power. None of that mattered to me. I would have lived in a tent in the desert with him if that was all I could get. He said he felt the same way. I suppose it's easy to say words like that when you know it will never happen.

"Malik is torn between two cultures, his and ours. His time here in the States won over, I think, but duty is something else. And we somehow weathered that together. Three months ago, possibly four, things changed. Malik was away more and more. For years he would call and would send charming, witty texts to me no matter where he was. Then that stopped, almost on a dime. When he returned, he was withdrawn, *spacey,* kind of, if you know what I mean. Like he had things on his mind and was on overload.

"He used to leave me little love notes on my desk, under my pillow, on my vanity. He would bring me silly presents that made us both laugh. We'd go for rides in the rattle-trap. Then it all stopped, but it was a gradual process, almost unnoticeable if you weren't paying attention. Fortunately, I was paying attention. I tried talking to him, and all he would say was that it was palace business or emirate business, and he would try to do better.

"And, of course, the fact that I haven't been able to get pregnant wore on both of us. I expected him as the ruler to change that man-made law, but he didn't. In eleven months, I will be banished from Dubai, as antiquated as that may sound. I'll have to leave because I can't give Malik an heir. I knew that going in, but I was so in love, I never thought I wouldn't have a child. It was ridiculous to think such a thing. Both of us were tested by the best doctors in the world. None of them could find a reason why I couldn't get pregnant. I was told to relax, that I was too tense, and Malik was told to slow down and go on holidays where we could unwind and relax. We did that a dozen times, and I still didn't get pregnant.

"I came here on a whim. But the more I think about it now, the more I'm convinced Soraya goaded me into it. Trust me, it didn't take much to convince me. I didn't leave a note or anything. I just left. Tit for tat, that kind of thing. Very sophomoric on my part, but at the time, I didn't think so. I didn't call Malik or text him, either, that I was leaving. He burned up the wires once he found out.

"Soraya took matters into her own hands and kicked Rashid out of their apartment, and as far as I know, he's still living in the bowels of the palace as we speak. She did that because he is not supposed to keep secrets from her, and yet he did not tell her anything about what's going on, and we both know he's Malik's right hand and knows everything. There are not supposed to be secrets between married couples.

"That's why I'm here, Emma. I see the signs. I'm doing something about it. Did you or didn't you see the signs when things went awry with Jeff? I need to know, Emma."

Emma swung her legs over the side of the bed. "Let's order some room service. I need coffee before I can deal with this. You order, and I'll hit the shower. Order some yogurt and fruit, too. By the way, I don't want to go to New York today, and neither do the girls. Can we cancel and do it next week? This is all just way too overwhelming for us. We need time to catch our breath."

"Sure, no problem. Go ahead. I'll order and use the other bathroom. Let's have our breakfast in our robes, like we used to."

Emma leaned over and hugged Trish. "You are such a romantic. That's why I love you so much."

Both women were seated in the sitting room, in the hotel's fluffy white robes, when room service rang the bell thirty minutes later.

"Coffee smells good," Emma said when the door closed behind the waiter. She poured for both of them. Trish took it black, and Emma added real cream and sugar. "Oh, this is so good. Best cup of coffee I've had in years. Okay, yes, Trish, I've had years to think about what you asked me. Yes, there were little signs that at the time, I ignored because they didn't seem *all* that important.

"Jeff started leaving the house at five in the morning. Climbing that corporate ladder bullshit was how he explained it. He never got home till around midnight. I couldn't stay up that late. He never saw Missy, never went to any of her school functions. Told me that was a mother's job. After that, my household allowance was cut almost in half. Said his firm had cut back, and we had to economize. Then he cut off the charge cards for the same reason. I rarely if ever charged anything, anyway, mostly just stuff for Missy or the house. You know me. Mom taught us to be frugal.

"By the time he dumped me, I had no money, no credit, no cash, and while he gave me the house in the settlement, I couldn't make the payments, so he took it back. What he gave me in alimony was a joke. So, yes, the signs were there. I just didn't want to believe them and hoped he was telling the truth and it was just a rough spot he hit and things would go back on track. It didn't work out that way. I'm still paying off my share of the divorce. I have no credit. I live day to day, paycheck to paycheck, and before you can ask, yes, I cashed in the monies from our parents' insurance and that little CD I had. It's all gone now."

"Did . . . did you fall out of love with Jeff?"

"I did. I just didn't know it at the time. I was operating on wounded pride for way too long. I thought it was love, but the truth is, there was no love for either one of us. One time, I smelled perfume on his clothes. He gave me some silly story about a woman in the elevator who was mashed up against him and was drenched in perfume."

"I still love Malik. I will always love him. I think I might be one of those people they write songs about. You know, one true love and all that."

"Then you need to go back, Trish. Talk it out. I don't want you to have regrets down the road. If it's not meant to be, you need to be able to walk away on your own. Anything else is too painful and debilitating. I don't want to see you go through what the girls and I and many, many other women have gone through. I don't know what to tell you about the pregnancy issue. To me, that rule is barbaric, and it's a manmade rule, so it should be one that can be changed. Maybe that's what your husband is trying to do, and his people are fighting him over it. If he's the supreme ruler, I don't see what the problem is."

"I got a text from him last night, and he said he misses me and that he loves me. It made me smile. I know I have to go back. And I will when I'm ready. First, we have to get you guys squared away. I think you all should go into business for yourselves.

Emma, think about all that stuff I told you about in my foyer. You could sell one-of-a-kind things, like those fabulous silks. You're a Realtor, right? Even though you are still working as a real-estate salesperson, look into finding a building, and I'll buy it, and you and the girls can set up shop. You'll be your own bosses. Just check your listings, and I bet before the day is over, you'll find a suitable building.

"You all need a job, you need good health insurance, and there are four of you, so you can get a group policy. I've set up bank accounts for all of you. You have good credit cards now. I've paid the taxes and the home owners' insurance for three years for each of you, so that's a good buffer for all of you until you can get a business up and running. If the economy doesn't rebound, you at least have a buffer.

"Make everything outrageously expensive. I've seen and found over these past few years that the more it costs, the more people want it. Try and figure that out. You have to see to all the paperwork, and, by the way, you get the commission on those properties I bought. Win-win, Emma! Jeez, I almost forgot. I have to go back to your apartment complex and pay off your leases. Once you get your things out of there, I don't want you to go back. If you don't want to go to New York today, what are you going to do?"

"Go to Walmart or Target and outfit my new house. What are you going to do, Trish?"

Trish thought about the urgent text messages that had come through from Connie and Ernie yesterday that she hadn't responded to. "I have some things I need to take care of. I'm going back to Vegas tomorrow. I booked an early morning flight before I went to sleep. I want to know I'm leaving all of you settled and happy."

"Trish, I can never thank you enough, nor can the girls. You have literally saved our lives."

"Tell me something, Emma. What do you think you would feel or think, the girls, too, if you found out your ex-husbands were going to go to jail?"

Emma's hands started to tremble. She set the coffee cup down on the table and stared at her sister. Trish wasn't the least surprised at her response. "Missy will be devastated."

"That's not what I asked you, Emma. I asked *you* what *you* would feel and think."

Her eyes wide, Emma stared at Trish. "What aren't you telling me here?" Emma's voice verged on the hysterical. "Why are you asking me this?"

"Emma, I want you to trust me, okay? I have suspicions, a very serious distrust of Jeff. I might as well admit it to you now. I always did distrust him. Things just don't add up for me where he's concerned. Get back to my question, okay?"

"I'd like to see him languishing in some prison in the general population. I know I can speak for the girls, too, if that is going to be your next question. I don't like to think I'm the kind of person who feels and thinks like that, but these last years have been a horror for us all. If Jeff had just been a little bit kind, if he'd helped me just a little, but he didn't. He stripped me bare, then stole my daughter from me. There, you asked me, and I told you."

"Okay, then, let's get dressed, pick up the girls, then recover my rental car from the Outback parking lot and get this show on the road. I'll take you all out to the Enclave, and you can do what you have to do, and I'll do what I have to do. Let's meet up at, say, four o'clock. We'll have a happy hour somewhere, a good dinner, and call it a night, if you're all agreeable. I'm anxious to get back and . . . to see what my future holds for me."

The two sisters hugged tightly.

"It's nice to know you can always count

on family, isn't it?" Trish whispered.

Emma released her hold on Trish. She squared her shoulders, looked her sister in the eye, and said, "Damn straight, little sister."

It was eleven o'clock when Trish entered the hotel and headed up to her room. She'd done all she could for her sister and her sister's friends. Emma would follow up with all the pounds of paperwork the Enclave was holding for her. She'd paid off the leases, the girls had collected their personal belongings, and they were all at their new digs. Credit cards with high limits in hand, they were embarking on a shopping spree to fill their cupboards and closets. Trish didn't think she'd ever seen four happier women in her whole life. Well, perhaps one happy woman, Soraya.

The first thing Trish did when she kicked off her shoes was to call Connie. She listened intently for a good twenty minutes and finally said, "I'll call Ernie first thing tomorrow morning. I'll be back sometime tomorrow. Thanks, friend."

When she woke the next morning, after eight o'clock, she called room service for a pot of coffee. She was too nervous to eat anything just yet. She waited for it to arrive before she called Ernie. It was still early in Vegas. Ernie could be a bear, she'd heard, early in the morning. Nonetheless, nine o'clock Vegas time wasn't *that* early.

Trish poured her coffee. As she was bringing the cup to her lips, she had a wild thought. Could drinking a lot of coffee prevent her from getting pregnant? The thought was so ludicrous, she gulped at the coffee in her cup and finished it in two long swallows. She poured a second cup, leaned back in the chair, propped her feet on the coffee table, and called Ernie.

The two old friends talked for a good thirty minutes, playing catch up. They talked about the cold weather, the snow, the skiing in Tahoe, the latest casino gossip, and a new dance routine he was trying to perfect. They switched over to Soraya and how things were in Dubai. Then he talked about his new wife and how happy he was.

When there was a lull in the conversation, Ernie said, "Talk to me, Trish. I need precise details, your objectives, what exactly you want and expect. I know. I know. Connie explained it all, but I want to hear it from you, too. Your reasons don't matter to me or to the person who will be working with you on this. We just all have to be on the same page.

"I have to tell you straight up that this guy is one expensive dude. His fee is whatever slice of beachfront property he has his eye on. I think I can safely say he's never taken a job for less than seven figures. Tell me now if that is going to be a problem. It could be quadruple that amount, so you need to know that before I put you in touch with him."

"What kind of guarantee does he give that he can get the information I want?" Trish asked.

"There are no guarantees in this life, Trish. You know better than that. I will tell you this. He, to my knowledge — and I would have heard otherwise — has never failed to deliver. There's no one better. Now, having said that, you might not like his results, but boo hoo to you. You will get what you ask and pay for. The results are something he cannot control. So, should I call him to pave the way or not?"

"Beachfront property, huh?"

"Oh, yeah," Ernie drawled.

CHAPTER 16

Trish sat and twiddled her thumbs and sipped coffee, her gaze on the huge window in her hotel suite. Snow flurries were swirling about. That had to mean it was going to be cold outside. She thought about turning on the television to check the weather. *Why bother?* Snow flurries meant it was around thirty-two degrees. As she sipped at her still-hot coffee, she wished she had asked Ernie if the nameless person would call her soon or later. No sooner had the thought entered and exited her head than the phone rang. With the words *beachfront property* swirling around inside her head, she answered her cell phone, but not before she took a huge deep breath.

Trish wasn't quite sure what she expected to hear, but the soft, cultured voice that said, "I'm a friend of Ernie," wasn't it. "He asked me to call you. Tell me how I can help you."

"Ah, yes. Did Ernie share our conversation?" Trish asked. She took a moment to wonder why she was feeling so jittery and nervous. Maybe because she knew she was breaking the law, and the voice that was speaking to her was going to help her do it.

"Only that you needed help and could afford my fee."

Trish cleared her throat, her eyes on the snow swirling outside the hotel window. She wondered where the man talking to her lived. Probably on some luxurious secluded island that he owned, basking in warm sunshine. "It's complicated. It's just not one person. It's four people, maybe five. I want . . . It's a package deal. Does that mean four or five beachfront properties or just one?"

The voice on the other end of the phone laughed. It was a nice sound. Trish found herself relaxing. "One fee. Now, tell me what you *need.* Then tell me what you *want.* After that, tell me what you will *settle* for."

"I can't settle, and what I want isn't relevant. I need what I am about to tell you."

"Well, that's settled, then. Do we have a time frame?"

Did she have a time frame? She hadn't thought of it in those terms. "Well, my plans right now are rather vague. I'm planning on leaving the country possibly by the end of the week. I'd like this put to bed before I leave. I guess I should say I'm flexible."

"That's good to know. Tell me now what it is you need. I don't want to know the why of it, so be concise."

Trish licked at her dry lips. She could feel her heart fluttering in her chest. She could change her mind, back out, decide not to break any laws right now. All she had to do was break the connection.

"I can't tell you what I need without telling you some of the why. So here goes. Five years ago this man, Jefferson Davis, divorced my sister and took her to the cleaners. Since then, she has lived below the poverty level. He hid his money, while my sister had to scrimp and scrape just to get through each day. He gave her the house, but she couldn't afford to keep it. This is all because when they got married, he insisted she give up her job to be a wife and mother. After the divorce, he got himself a trophy wife, and then, because he had the money, he took my sister's daughter, my niece, too.

"The story is essentially the same with the other three men and my sister's friends, who were left in the same position. These four men are all lawyers, so the deck was stacked against the women from the get-go. They all

249

made sure that the women didn't have the funds to hire decent lawyers. In the end, they just gave up. The four men were friends prior to their divorces, though they worked for different law firms. They all resigned and formed their own firm, and now they're international lawyers.

"I think they are laundering money in the Middle East, but I don't have any way to prove it. I just have suspicions, but my gut instinct has always been good. I don't think I'm wrong. I want you to find out where the money is, how much there is, and how we can make it disappear. By disappear, I mean just some of it. Actually, I'm not sure what I mean in regard to the money. If there's a way to do it with no blowback, we can give it to children's charities, women's shelters, that kind of thing. I want what those women were cheated out of to be given back to them. I hope I said that right.

"Then I want the IRS and the authorities to invade their lives. Long prison terms would make everyone but the four men, and anyone else involved who has to serve them, happy. I would not be devastated if you could find a way for their identities, as well as their money, to disappear. In other words, I want their lives reduced to rubble. I'd also like to see them lose those fancy houses they live in with their trophy wives. And if you can find a way to cancel their country-club memberships, do that, too. And while you're at it, I'd like some misery to befall the *skanky* lawyer who represented all four men in their divorces. Just make it five in total. I'm sure your fee will reflect all five men. I don't want any of the fallout to touch my sister or her friends. They have to be kept out of it entirely."

The silence on the other end of the phone bothered Trish. Finally, she heard the cultured voice say, "It's all doable. My best estimate would be three days, possibly four. If it goes longer, I will apprise you of the fact. I'm going to need to know where you want the proceeds — let's call it the ladies' severance — to go."

"I thought about that. I'm going to open a bank account in Las Vegas when I return tomorrow. I assume you want me to have Ernie be our go-between. When I have it all set up, I'll be in touch. Unless you can come up with something better."

"I think I can come up with something better. I'll be in touch. But I will need the amount of money you want allocated for each woman. I assume you want interest, and money for the misery they endured, to be added to the total amount." Trish loved

251

the amused tone in the man's voice.

"You assume right. I have to figure out the amount. It will be fair. Maybe on top of the interest and misery, we could add a bonus, not outrageous, but a bonus nonetheless."

"Doable. Tell me why and how you think these men are in the money-laundering business."

"You said you didn't want to know the why or to get into personalities."

"I did say that, but I need something more to go on."

"I just know bits and pieces I've picked up on. The emirates are known for money laundering. I live in Dubai. I understand that before I moved there, His Royal Highness, along with the leaders of the other six emirates, signed a deal with these four lawyers to bring new business to them because the oil will be running out soon. A contract was signed. When my husband's father died, he took over the reins. He was educated here in the States and knows business. Actually, he has a doctorate, as does his second in command. I heard them talking and, as I said, picked up things here and there. I think the contract is up for renewal soon. I know that sounds vague, but it's all I have."

"Does Mr. Davis know you are married to the current emir of Dubai?"

"I don't know. My sister assured me that she never told anyone, not even her three friends. Even my niece didn't know. I asked my sister yesterday if that was still true, and she said yes. Jeff isn't stupid, though. He's slick, and he's manipulative. If their contract is up for renewal, I can almost guarantee that my husband will not go along with it. As emir of Dubai, he is also the prime minister of the emirates, with veto power over really important national policies, as enacted by the legislature. So, if he balks, the other leaders will go along. It's the best I can offer up."

"It's enough for a start. I'll do my own research. Now let's discuss my fee. Here is what I propose. For something as complicated as this, my fee would usually be five million dollars. But considering the details of what you want done with the monies liberated and the potential size of those funds, I suggest that after whatever the total amount to be distributed to the four ex-wives is deducted, I retain five million dollars plus five percent of whatever is left. So, if, say, one hundred five million is left after distributing money to the ex-wives, I would keep ten million — five million plus five percent of a hundred million. As long as the amount I receive that way is at least five million dollars, I will return your fee. In other words, your fee will be treated as a deposit. Does that sound fair to you?"

Trish listened, swallowed hard, and managed to squeak out a verbal okay.

"Do you have a pen handy?" When Trish said she did, the voice rattled off wiring instructions. "When your fee slash deposit is confirmed, I'll send you a confirmation, and I'll start working on your case. Is that acceptable?"

"It is."

"Then we should hang up. I'll be in touch."

Trish's hands were shaking when she placed the cell phone on the table. She opened the coffee carafe. The coffee was cold. She called room service and ordered a fresh pot. Then she paced around the suite until the coffee arrived. She gulped at the first cup she poured. Then she opened up her laptop and flexed her fingers. She squeezed her eyes shut. So much money, and she was breaking the law in the bargain. She knew she could still back out if she wanted to. All it would take was a phone call to Ernie.

Before she could change her mind, Trish

tapped out the letters and numbers that would allow her to transfer five million dollars to a man she didn't even know, so he would do something that could put her in jail for the rest of her life.

Done!

Still dressed in the hotel robe, Trish reached for one of the hotel's notepads and pens. She scribbled numbers, then added them, subtracted some, added more, until she was satisfied that she had something worthy enough to run by her sister. If the numbers worked for Emma, they would work for Clare, Robin, and Alice.

Trish was momentarily distracted when her cell pinged, the signal that a text was coming through. Malik. Two words.

Good morning.

Trish supposed it was a good morning. Did he text her because he'd just been informed that she had wired out a very large sum of money? Probably. The thought annoyed her. She grew more annoyed, the more she thought about her husband being apprised of everything she did the moment she did it. He probably wouldn't even mention it unless she did. She decided to ignore the text for the moment.

Trish concentrated on her pad and the numbers she was scribbling. The marital home Emma had lived in with Jeff and Missy had been sold for three million dollars when Jeff took it back. Emma's half should have been half of that. Five years' salary of roughly sixty thousand dollars had been lost. If she had worked at her modeling career, it would have been more. Perhaps a small bonus on top of the salary. A new car. Medical insurance. Wardrobe. Miscellaneous costs.

Trish totaled her numbers. She stared at the bottom line — $2.5 million. She pursed her lips, then chewed on the end of the pen. The number sounded good, but it wasn't enough. She decided to round it out to an even three million. The girls would need good tax attorneys. If they invested their money wisely, they would be able to get by in the years to come without worrying about going on a breadline. Especially Clare, with her perilous health condition.

Satisfied that she'd done all she could for her sister and her sister's friends, Trish closed her laptop, ripped up the papers with the columns of numbers, and flushed them. She decided she had had enough coffee for one morning and wheeled the cart out to the hallway, then headed for the shower. She heard her cell ping just as she was stepping into the shower. She knew the incoming text would be from Soraya. Just enough time had gone by since Malik's for him to have gotten in touch with his sister.

Under the needle-sharp spray of the shower, Trish's thoughts were all over the map. For sure, she wasn't happy. But she wasn't sure if returning to Dubai would make her happy, either. She felt like she was in a no-man's-land. The bottom line was that she would have to return and talk things out with her husband before she had a chance at the happiness she'd once had.

It wasn't that the love she had for her husband had wavered. She still loved him heart and soul. But she had to be sure Malik still felt the same way. If she had to leave the emirate, then she would leave. It was that simple.

Trish took her time toweling off and getting dressed because she didn't want to have to look at Soraya's text. Or reread Malik's.

Dressed now for the day in wool slacks, boots, and a turtleneck sweater, Trish felt brave enough to face the world, her sister, and her sister's friends, to update them on the latest. At first she had thought she'd keep her activities secret, but she had nixed that idea pretty quickly. The women had a right to know that the wrath of one Trish Holiday Mohammed was bearing fruit. Not

257

for the first time, Trish realized the power of money and what it could do. And yet, she'd give it all up, every single penny, if she could just go back to the life she'd had with Malik before. . . . *Before . . . what?*

Her head hurt from thinking about her husband. Still, she had to read Soraya's text. It was so like her sister-in-law. The message was simple. Are you all right? Can I do anything? Is it snowing?

Trish knew she couldn't answer Soraya unless she also answered Malik's text. They were both being so political by not asking her when or even if she was coming back.

Trish looked out the window. The flurries were gone. Now it was actually snowing. She hoped there would be no accumulation to prevent her from flying out tomorrow morning.

Trish drew in a deep breath and prepared to send a text to her husband.

Good morning to you, too, Malik.

The second message was a tad longer.

I'm fine. No, there is nothing for you to do for me. Thank you for asking. It is snowing as I type this.

Trish's last text was to Ernie. It read, Tell your friend the amount is three million each. For now, offshore. I'm going to be unavailable for the rest of the day. I'll see you tomorrow, upon my return.

A soft knock sounded on the door. She heard the maid say, "Housekeeping."

Trish gathered up her jacket and purse. She looked down at the two cell phones and decided to leave them on the desk. At the last second, she picked up the Dubai phone and put it in her purse. She might need it if an emergency cropped up out on the road. She wanted to spend her last day with her sister without interruptions. Who knew when she'd see her again?

It was dusk when Malik walked out to his own personal garden and sat down. He was tired, and there was no point in hiding it. The relief he felt showed on his face when he sat down and put his feet up. Rashid was there in an instant. He had two bottles of beer in his hands.

"I have corrupted you, have I not?" Malik said.

"You have, but I allowed it. Have you taken your meds this evening? Dare I ask if you are permitted to drink this beer?"

"You dare, and the answer is yes. I have taken the medicine. It makes me very tired. But there is no pain. Yet. We must make plans, Rashid."

"Have you heard from your wife?" Rashid

asked bluntly.

"A few moments ago. But it was in response to a text I sent her. I wished her a good morning, and she wished me one back. I still don't know when she's coming back or *if* she's coming back. I had no idea I hurt her so badly, if what my sister tells me is true. She has spent so much money these past few days, it boggles my mind. Just an hour or so ago she transferred four million dollars to some offshore account. That's on top of the nineteen million she spent yesterday. I, of course, replenished it. What do you think she's spending it on?" Malik asked fretfully.

"From what I know of your wife, she isn't spending it on herself. Off the top of my head, if I had to guess, I would say it's her family. She has a sister and a niece, does she not?"

"That's what I thought. But why?"

"Ask her." Rashid smiled.

"I can't do that. I promised her I would never ask what she did with her money. She's so frugal. I think you're right. I am also wondering if something is wrong, and if that's why she returned to the States."

Rashid snorted. "There might be something wrong, but she just worked that into her return because of what you did. I now know things about women I didn't know before. You are at fault here, and it doesn't matter the reason, so just accept it and go from there."

"I can't do that if she doesn't return, now, can I? I'd make the trip to the States, but I'm just not up to it. This . . . this thing is sapping all my energy. I hate the pills. They just make me sleepy. I do not want to sleep away what's left of my life. Tell me, how goes it with you and my sister?"

"You know damn well how it is going. All you have to do is say the word, and I am back in her good graces. What kind of friend are you, anyway?" Rashid grumbled.

"I did that an hour ago. You are free to go to your apartments, where your wife is waiting with open arms. Do not look at me like that. Go now and tell her the truth, the whole truth, and nothing but the truth. That is an order, Rashid.

"But before you do that, would you mind fetching me another beer? No, wait. I think I'll go to the cave, and I can open my own beer. You're still standing here. Go!"

"Wouldn't it be better coming from you, Malik?"

"No, my friend, it wouldn't. She will need to weep and feel your arms about her. Tomorrow she can squeal at me. Be brave, in case she hits you. She might, you know. Pregnant women do strange things. Speaking of pregnant women, the council has agreed with me that the law my father initiated is archaic, and it has been rescinded. Trish and I are in the clear on that. I should have done that years ago, and I take responsibility for my wife's angst these past years. I hope she can forgive me."

"Forgiveness is an act of love, Malik."

"And you learned this . . . where?"

"From you, that's where. Come along. I'll walk you back to the cave. I want to see you settled before I go before the dragon lady."

Rashid hated leaving Malik alone, but he desperately wanted to see his wife and children. When he left Malik, his feet had wings on them as he raced to his apartments. The children were already in bed, and his wife was standing in the doorway, her arms folded over her protruding stomach. She glowered at him.

Rashid shuffled his feet and bit down on his lower lip as he struggled to find the words he needed to say. Finally, he just blurted it out, then reached to take his wife in his arms. "I am so terribly sorry. Malik swore me to secrecy. I had no choice, my love. I begged him to tell you himself, but he said you needed to vent to me first.

Tomorrow morning will be time enough. We now need to sit and talk. We have to call Trish and tell her to come home. I think you are the one to do that. Can you? Will you?"

"Of course. Of course I will, but that is not something you speak of on the phone. I will send her a very carefully worded text. But, Rashid, I'm not sure where she is. She could be with her sister in Princeton, New Jersey, or she could be in Las Vegas. I know. I will call Ernie," she blubbered into her husband's chest.

"I'm not sure I like that idea," Rashid said glumly.

"Do you have a better idea? You need to get over your jealousy of Ernie. I just used him for practice. You got the benefit of all my practice. Come, come. Let's go to the sitting room. While I do this, will you get me some peach juice? That way, you won't have to hear me sweet-talking Ernie. By the way, Rashid, Ernie is married now to a lovely young lady."

Rashid grumbled some more just to keep in practice as he sought out one of the maids to fetch the peach juice. He stopped in his children's bedrooms and smiled as he brushed their hair back from their foreheads. He bent over to kiss each of them on the cheek. "I am so blessed," he whispered to each of them.

When Rashid returned to the sitting room, Soraya was smiling through her tears. "Trish is in New Jersey with her sister. I sort of explained things to him, but I made him promise not to tell Trish. He did promise. Now, what you have to do is make arrangements for a private plane to bring Trish home. Do it now, and I will text her. I need to be alone to do this. This is girl stuff. Do you understand?"

Rashid didn't understand, but he said he did. He trotted off a second time so that his wife could compose the message to Malik's wife.

Tears streaming down her cheeks, Soraya knew that what she was about to write was probably the most serious message she would ever write during her whole life.

Dearest Trish, I wish I wasn't writing this to you, but Rashid has said I must. Arrangements are being made as I type this for you to return to Dubai. Just go to Newark Airport. Do not delay. You must return immediately. Please, do not think for one instant, one moment, that this is a ploy or a trick to get you to return. It is urgent that you return *immediately.* I have the answers to all your questions and mine, as well, but I have been forbidden to discuss them at this time. Rashid has informed me that the silly pregnancy law has been done away with. He said he saw the council's declaration himself. It has been stamped and so ordered. I know you are full of questions that I cannot answer right now. I know how mysterious this must sound to you, but Rashid has said you are not, I repeat, you are *not,* to get in touch with Malik before your return. Please text me when you are on the plane. As you Americans say, my one true friend, fly with the angels. Much love from me, Rashid, and all the little ones, who miss you.

Soraya's fingers were shaking so badly that she had to hit the SEND button twice before her text made its way across the world. She felt drained as she tried to imagine Trish's reaction to the message once she got it.

Rashid returned, a glass of peach juice in his hand. Soraya waved it away.

"I just sent you for that to get you out of my hair. I sent it, Rashid. Now we wait. Sit here by me. Put your arm around me. Oh, the baby just hopped from one side to the other." Then she burst into tears. Rashid's eyes were wet as they snuggled close, waiting for a return text.

Trish cut the engine, gathered her purse and gloves, and was about to get out of the car when she heard her cell phone ping. Thinking it was either Ernie or the nameless, faceless man she'd spoken to earlier, she clicked it to read the message. She blinked, then shook her head to clear it. She read the text a second, then a third time. She looked out through the windshield, which was suddenly full of snow. She thought she could see her sister standing in the open doorway of her new house. The cell in her hand, she got out of the car and ran to the door.

"Look at this! I don't know what to do. God, Emma, what do you think it means?"

Emma closed the door, turned on the foyer light, and read the text. "I think it means just what it says, Trish. You need to go right now. Wait, wait! First you have to respond. Tell her you're on your way to the airport. Another few hours, and everything will be delayed. Do you hear me, Trish?"

"Yes, of course I can hear you. Something terrible has happened. I just know it."

"Maybe not terrible, just serious enough for you to return. You need to go now."

"Okay, okay. I have to stop back at the hotel to get my things. I'll call you from the airport. I have to turn the car in."

Emma was crying as she hugged her sister. "Call me as soon as you know something. Promise me, okay?"

"I will. I promise. I had other stuff to tell you. It will have to wait, Emma."

"Whatever it is, it can wait. This is more important," Emma said, tapping the cell phone. "Go now. Thanks again. God, how inadequate that sounds."

"Say good-bye to your friends for me. Okay, okay, I'm going. I love you, Emma."

"And I love you, Trish. Like Soraya and Mom always said, fly with the angels."

Trish opened the door and ran down the steps and out to the car. Emma stood in the doorway, the snow spiraling inward to wet the wooden floor. Emma didn't care. She watched her sister until the rental car's back lights were just faint pinpricks of pink light. Only then did she close the door and clean up the floor. Her shoulders drooped as she made her way to the kitchen, where she put on a pot of coffee and called her friends. "Please come now. Unexpected emergency." Then she mumbled a sincere prayer from her childhood that things would go well for her sister.

CHAPTER 17

Rashid looked at Malik and smiled because
he looked fresh, bright-eyed, and alert. He
knew for a fact that Malik hadn't taken any
of his medicine, because he wanted to be
seen as strong, even though he knew that
rumors about his health, which he and
Rashid had tried to squelch, had already
circulated.

"I'm glad you had the good sense to call
this meeting in Dubai, instead of in one of
the other emirates. Even I am feeling the
stress, and don't tell me it's because Soraya
is about to give birth. Are you absolutely
sure, Malik, that the other emirs are going
to vote with you?"

Malik threw his hands in the air. "They
assured me they would. When I explained
the whole world would be coming down on
us over here if we didn't put an end to
what's going on, I think they saw the light.
Look, we're never going to stop the money

laundering, but we can certainly scale it back. I, for one, have always taken umbrage at the fact that Dubai is known as the Little Switzerland. And as much as I hate to have to admit it, we're in the position my father put us in. I owned up to that little fact with the others. If our facts and figures are correct . . . and, Rashid, we went over them time and again, until we were blind . . . The bottom line is, numbers don't lie."

"The others are *old*, Malik. They like the status quo. They don't like upheaval. They could switch up at the eleventh hour. Then what do we do?"

"We talked about this, Rashid. We simply refuse to sign and renew the contract with those thieves. That's what we do. International Alliance Capital has ripped off the emirates, taking over a billion dollars. That's a billion, with a *b.* Remember that American phrase we learned when we first went to the States? We didn't understand until Zack explained it to us."

Rashid laughed. "Money talks and bullshit walks. Those four are snakes."

"Right, and what do you do when you find a snake in your midst? You cut off his head."

"Hold on, Malik. A text is coming in." Rashid scanned the brief text and frowned. It was from the pilot of Trish's plane.

We're grounded in London due to severe weather. Twelve hours more on the ground before we can take off, and even that's not certain.

Rashid typed a terse reply. Keep me apprised.

Malik frowned. "Is something wrong?"

Rashid hated lying, but he lied, anyway. "It was Soraya saying she thought she was going into labor, but it's a false alarm."

"What will you call this one, Rashid?"

Rashid laughed. "Malik if it's a boy, and Patricia if it's a girl. Now if it's twins, we have it going on. Soraya thought you would be pleased."

"I am pleased. Has she heard from Trish?"

Another lie rose to Rashid's lips. He was sure Allah would forgive him. "If she has, she has not told me. She is not in touch with you?"

"I'm afraid not. Perhaps today," Malik said wearily. "Tell me, wise one who professes one minute to know everything about women, then in the next minute, he says he knows nothing about women, how could something so wonderful go so bad in such a short time?"

Rashid straightened his shoulders. He was glad not to have to lie again. "Because you were stupid and didn't tell her the truth at the beginning. That's how."

"I should cut your damn tongue out, but, alas, it's true. Tell me the truth now. Do you think I can make this right? Providing Trish returns."

"Of course you can make it right. Trish loves you the way Soraya loves me and the way I love her. End of story." Rashid looked down at his watch. "Ten minutes, Malik, till we beard the lions. And before you can ask, yes, you look forceful and on top of your game. One last question, Malik. When and how are you going to tell the emirs that you are turning the reins over to your wife, your sister, and me?"

Malik smiled. "At the end of the meeting, after everything is signed, and the emirs ask if there are any other housekeeping details to be discussed. They have no say. I rule Dubai. Sometimes the things that are *not* said aloud are the most important. They all know you will be the driving force, and you will run our country as I would. New blood will begin to take over the other emirates. Educated young blood like yourself. That's where the real power is, Rashid, in education. Even my father saw that when he sent the two of us to the States. He saw the day coming when night would have to give way to light, as he put it. I have not one single worry that the three of you will do all that is right for our country and our people."

Rashid's vision blurred for a moment as he tried to imagine his life without Malik in it. The lump in his throat was so big, he could barely swallow. He nodded and made a sweeping motion with his hand to indicate they needed to head to the meeting room at the other end of the palace.

Trish entered the VIP lounge at Heathrow and settled herself. A twelve-hour delay! She was beside herself with worry. What was going on? She had sent three texts to Soraya since she'd stepped off the plane and had received only one in return, which was almost laughable.

I'm kind of busy right now. I think I'm going into labor.

Trish wasn't sure how she should respond or *if* she should respond. She decided to wait a bit to see if Soraya, or possibly Rashid, would send another text. She walked over to the bar and ordered a ham and cheese sandwich and a scotch and soda. She carried both back to a comfortable area that was virtually empty. As she chewed, she checked her other texts. Ah, one that said the sender was unknown. Hoping it was from Ernie's nameless, faceless friend, she felt her heart take on an extra beat. It was. It was simple and to the point.

Making headway. Check with Ernie twenty-four hours from the time of this text.

Trish didn't know if she should respond or not. She thought about it for a few minutes, and by the time she finished her sandwich, she had sent off a text.

Am on a twelve-hour layover in London on my way home. Will do as you say.

Trish finished her drink, disposed of her trash, and decided to take a walk around the airport just to have something to do. She wanted to pick up some reading material in one of the shops to occupy her during the remainder of the flight back to Dubai. And to pick up something for Soraya's children and Soraya herself. If nothing else, it would give her something to do. Twelve hours seemed like an eternity at the moment.

Trish strolled along aimlessly, gazing into shop windows, stepping aside more than once to get out of the way of passengers racing toward their flights. She wondered why they were in such a hurry, since most of the planes appeared to be grounded. Finally, she stopped in a bookstore, bought a book by Stella Cameron, her favorite author, a copy of the *London Times,* and three packages of Life Savers. She was pocketing her change and reaching for the bag the clerk was handing her when she felt a hand on her shoulder. She whirled around, her eyes almost bugging out of her head.

"Zack!"

"Trish! I thought it was you, but I wasn't sure. What are you doing here?"

Trish's first thought was, *How big he is, how handsome.* She'd never seen such blue eyes in her life. "I'm on my way back to Dubai, but the plane got grounded because of the bad weather. What are you doing here?"

Zack took hold of Trish's arm and led her away from the long line of people waiting to pay for their purchases. Out in the middle of the terminal, he smiled down at her. "Right now the same thing you're doing. My flight was grounded two hours ago. No clue when I'll get out. I've just been rambling around to kill time. Let's go somewhere we can talk. Can I buy you a drink?"

Trish's somber mood lightened. This would be a good way to pass the time. "Let's go into the VIP lounge, although I'm sure it's crowded by now, but not as bad as out here. I imagine every bar seat has been taken."

"I think you have that right," Zack said,

looking around. "Lead the way. I'm right behind you."

"What are you doing here?" Trish asked.

"There was an international conference, and I had to give a speech. Boring as hell, but it was something to do to break up the winter blues. You know how that goes. So, you were stateside, eh? You should have called to say hello. How are things in Dubai? That husband of yours isn't big on staying in touch of late." He said this half jokingly, but Trish saw the concern in his eyes. "Plus, you didn't answer my last text."

Trish was relieved when she opened the door to the lounge and saw that the seating area she'd been in still had two vacant seats. She rushed forward and claimed them. Zack laughed out loud at the speed with which she moved. She thought he had a wonderful laugh, and her mood lightened even more.

"When it's crowded like this, a steward will come around and take your drink order. They serve food, too, if you're hungry. I had a very good sandwich a little while ago."

A steward appeared out of nowhere, a fussy little man wearing a bow tie, his gaze swiveling about as he tried to calculate his tips. Trish ordered another scotch, and Zack ordered a bourbon on the rocks with a turkey club sandwich.

Zack leaned forward, his blue-eyed gaze sharp and intent. "Things aren't quite right, are they?" he said bluntly.

Trish squirmed in her chair. "What makes you say that?"

"Well, for one thing, you have dark circles under your eyes, you're a lot thinner than in the last picture Malik sent to me, and you're traveling alone. In addition, you look like you have the weight of the world on your shoulders."

"Wow. All that in five minutes," Trish said lightly. "It was more or less a rush trip home. I went to see my sister, who lives in Princeton, New Jersey. Jet lag, burning the candle at both ends, not eating right, and now this. As for the weight, a lady can never be too thin. At least that's what all the fashion magazines say."

"Yes, you can be too thin, and who cares what fashion magazines say! You are too thin," Zack said bluntly.

"Why don't you tell me what you *really* think?" Trish teased.

"What I *really* think is, something is wrong, and you don't want to talk about it. How's zat? My mother takes great pride in the fact that she didn't raise any dummies."

In spite of herself, Trish laughed out loud. "Okay, my sister had some problems. I stepped in and am trying to help. It got complicated. Things back in Dubai could be better. I left to go stateside to help clear my head a little."

"Did it work?" Zack asked as the steward removed the drinks and food from a silver tray.

Trish winced. "I really didn't get a chance to find out. I was summoned home, and that's why I'm sitting here. My sister-in-law said it was urgent that I return immediately, and she stressed the word *immediately.* They hired a private jet for me, so I guess it is important. Other than that, I know nothing. It goes without saying, I'm worried."

"What do Malik or Rashid say?"

Trish winced again. "Soraya said I wasn't to get in touch with either of them, and made me promise. Now you know everything I know." To show her disgust, she downed her drink in two long gulps. Her eyes started to water with the effects of the alcohol.

"I'm sorry, Trish. I just want to help. I can't believe I bumped into you like this. Malik has been on my mind a lot lately. I've tried calling him, but he doesn't respond. The other guys tell me the same thing. I'm sure you know we were always a tight group, and that didn't change once we all went our separate ways. We were all in touch almost daily up until a few months ago. Then things sort of got shot to hell. I can't explain it any better than that."

Trish nodded. "Yes, that's when things started to change. At first, it was barely noticeable, then just a tad subtle, then nothing. I thought it had something to do with that archaic law about me not having a child in five years, but that wasn't it. By the way, that's been done away with. Malik saw to that, but only just recently. I wish he had done it sooner. It would have saved me a lot of angst. Guess they won't be kicking me to the curb, after all. Then again, you never know."

Zack digested her rapid-fire dialogue and smiled. "Malik always was able to figure out a solution faster than any of us when we were in school. Listen, would you like me to return with you, talk to Malik? I'm more than willing. I have time coming to me, and I can do it if you want me to."

"That's so kind of you, but no. I will promise you, though, that I will let you know what is going on as soon as I find out. Lord, can you imagine Malik's expression if the two of us walked off the plane together?"

Zack grinned. "I think that's a visual I can do without."

Trish laughed. "Yeah, me too. So, Zack, tell me about how it was when you all were in school. I've heard Malik's version a thousand times, but I'd really like to hear yours. In case you don't know it, he considers you the best thing since sliced bread. Don't ever tell this to anyone, but I think if it was a toss-up between you and Rashid, he'd pick you."

"Really!"

"Yes, really. In his heart of hearts, Malik is American. Unfortunately, he takes his birthright very seriously. He's happy, but he's not happy. Does that make sense?"

"Absolutely. Malik and I have had long discussions on that very subject. I totally understand."

"So, tell me all you guys' secrets."

"Well, there was this one time when . . ."

The four men who made up International Alliance Capital were pacing in the luxurious room they'd been assigned until they were called into the meeting with the seven emirs in Dubai. Not only were they dressed almost alike in five-thousand-dollar Hugo Boss suits, John Lobb shoes, and top-of-the-line Rolexes, but they all also carried the same pricey hand-tooled briefcases crafted from antelope skin. Four of anything garnered a steep discount, as Jeff Davis was fond of saying. And these four men knew a thing or two about discounts.

All four men were tall, muscular, looked fit and trim, and were heavily tanned. Although all of them were approaching the fifty mark, they could have passed easily for forty. The golf courses in the Middle East were better than a tanning bed in the United States. And anyone with half a brain knew more deals were cut on the golf course than in the boardroom.

Jason Hart, Clare's ex-husband, hissed to the others, "I don't like this. Something is going on. And I think it's this guy here in Dubai who is stirring the pot. He's been the most vocal since he took over after his father passed. And on top of that, I got an e-mail from the American embassy telling me to stop by because there was something wrong with my passport. Did any of you guys get that e-mail?"

"No, but I got an e-mail from my wife this morning, saying our mortgage company is foreclosing on the house in thirty days because we didn't pay our mortgage. We are up to date on everything. She's having a fit. Seems the sheriff stuck some kind of paper on our door, and you go to jail if you take it down. Ashley said all the neighbors saw it.

What the hell is that all about?" Josh Olsen asked in a jittery voice.

"Hell, I can top that," Jeff Davis said. "Simone sent me a text from the club and said she was denied entry. She went there for lunch with some friends. She said they had canceled our membership. Look, that's all just bullshit. Someone is screwing with us at home. Jealousy is a terrible thing, as we all know. We'll figure it all out when we get home. Let's just concentrate on the here and now and what line of bullshit we're going to give these guys. We need to renew this contract. Do you all understand the word *need*?"

"Oh, Jesus," John Gamble said, looking down at a text that had just appeared. "Gabriella said the bank refused to cash a check for lack of funds. She ran right to the bank and they showed her a zero balance. There was eighty-six thousand dollars in that account when I left to come here."

Always the doomsayer of the group, Jason Hart looked at his three partners. "It's karma. It's coming to bite our asses. I knew all this was too good to be true. I knew it the minute I dumped Clare after her breast-cancer surgery. What kind of person does a shitty thing like that?"

"Someone shitty like you, Jason. No one

told you to do that. In fact, I told you to stick it out till Clare recovered, but you were so head over heels for Krystal, you just couldn't wait. So suck up your karma and stay focused," Jeff said.

"Easy for you to say, Jeff. It isn't your passport under scrutiny. Getting bounced out of the country club isn't quite the same," Jason replied.

The leader of the Four *J*s, as Jeff liked to call his little group, grimaced. "I repeat, let's just stay focused. I do agree that something here is not quite right. They've never let us cool our heels like this before. Focus and stay confident. The first one who wimps out in there will feel my wrath. Understood?"

"Oh, Christ," Olsen murmured. "I just got an e-mail saying that I also need to go to the American embassy to straighten out something with my passport. Oh, man, I can just see the four of us being detained here for *months.*"

Davis and Gamble looked down at their respective BlackBerries and acknowledged that there were also issues with their passports.

Jeff Davis's eyes narrowed. Maybe it was true, the rumor he'd heard that his ex-wife's sister was married to the emir of Dubai. When he'd first heard the rumor, he'd laughed out loud. It was so ludicrous that he hadn't even bothered to check it out. Now, right that minute, he wished he had checked it out. His sister-in-law had always hated his guts. His mouth pursed into a tight line, he fired off a text to his daughter, Missy, which was simply one line.

Do you know where your aunt Trish is these days?

The return text came immediately. No. Las Vegas, I assume. Do you want me to find out?

Jeff's return text was simple. Yes.

Jeff's step quickened as he continued to pace. For the first time in his life, he felt jittery, out of control. The return text came in.

Mom says it's none of my business where Aunt Trish lives. Mom moved. She lives in the Enclave now.

Jeff swore under his breath. How the hell could his ex-wife afford a house in the Enclave? Unless . . .

Jeff was saved from further thoughts when the massive doors opened and a man in a white robe said, "The emirs are ready to see you now, gentlemen."

CHAPTER 18

Zack Molton got up, rolled his shoulders to ease the stiffness, and walked around the VIP lounge, which had become so crowded that it was almost wall-to-wall people. Food, he'd heard a few minutes ago, was in short supply, but the liquor was holding up, and soft drinks were going quickly. He looked at his watch. He was nine hours into his wait since meeting up with Trish, with no word coming over the loudspeaker as to when his flight would be able to leave the ground. He completed his full circle and sat down again before someone snatched his seat. Trish was asleep, curled up in her chair. He knew she was going to have a doozy of a stiff neck when she woke up.

Zack wished he could sleep, but the only place he could sleep was in his own bed. Even when he traveled, he tossed and turned in strange beds for hours on end, falling asleep only when it was time to get up. He struggled to make his big frame comfortable in the club chair. His cell vibrated in his pocket. Thank God for cell phones and friends to text. The text coming in now was from his friend Duke. He looked at the bars on the phone and knew he was going to need a charge very soon. He'd put his name on the list at the desk to charge his battery, but so far, they hadn't called his name. He took a moment to wonder how low Trish's battery was. Without stopping to think about it, he got up again and walked to the desk, where a clipboard rested, and wrote in Trish's name. She was number thirty-six on the list. He was number thirty-three, which meant two more people had added their names to the list after him. He refused to calculate the hours he had to go, with each charge lasting only fifteen minutes. He sighed. He could be here for days if the weather didn't let up.

He was back in his club chair within seconds. And then, to his own surprise, he felt himself nodding off.

Two hours later, Trish felt a nudge to her shoulder. She struggled to open her eyes and focus.

One of the stewards bent low and whispered, "You're to go to the gate. Your plane is ready to leave."

That was all Trish needed to hear. She got up, gathered her gear, then looked down at Zack, who appeared to be in a deep sleep. She hated to leave without saying good-bye, but still, she didn't want to wake him. She took a minute to fish around in her purse for a pen, then scribbled a short message on a napkin, which she tucked under his chin. Hopefully, he would find it. If not, she'd send him a text when she got on the plane, before takeoff.

Trish ran down the gangway and almost tripped as she skidded to a stop at the open door, where a hostess grinned at her. "In a bit of a hurry, are we?"

"It's been nineteen hours," Trish grumbled.

"That it has. That it has," the hostess said, commiserating. "Let's get you seated and buckled up. We're number two for takeoff. They're deicing the wings as we speak. Then we can taxi out to the runway. How about some nice fresh, hot coffee and some delicious made-from-scratch cinnamon buns loaded with butter and frosting?"

"Sounds good. Yes, I'd like that very much." Trish realized then that she was ravenous. They'd run out of food in the VIP lounge hours and hours ago. It seemed a shame that she was the only passenger on board the flight when so many of her fellow passengers back in the terminal were still waiting to fly to their destinations. She wondered when Zack would make it out.

At that moment, though, all she wanted to do was wash her face and hands and brush her teeth. Combing her hair might help a little, and perhaps a little makeup. She looked out the window to see all the busy maintenance workers and the heavy-duty snow-removal machines, all working at full capacity. She crossed her fingers and said a prayer that the plane would lift off without a problem and climb until they were out of the storm.

She was going home.

The meeting with the lawyers from International Alliance Capital had been over for hours already. The angry, disgruntled men with their fancy briefcases were gone, and Malik and Rashid were playing host to the emirs at a lavish late afternoon dinner.

The eighty-year-old emir of Abu Dhabi fixed his watery gaze on Malik and asked in a frail, reedy voice, "How did you know, my son, that those men were thieves and that they were robbing our emirates blind while placing us in the precarious position we now find ourselves in?"

"Study, watchful eyes, and common sense, Your Highness. We can make it right. I have already alerted the authorities, and matters will be taken care of. Having said that, we must take responsibility for turning a blind eye to what was right under our noses. As it is, the world is watching us very carefully. We do not need any more bad press. We all need the tourist dollars, but there are better, more honest people to help us with that."

The second-oldest emir spoke up, his voice as reedy and frail as his predecessor's. "What did those men mean when they said we were" — he looked around fretfully as he tried to remember the phrase Jeff Davis had used — "sabotaging them by way of their passports and their bank accounts? What do we have to do with their country clubs and eviction notices? I didn't understand any of that."

"Nor did we understand, Your Highness," Malik said. "I think they were referring to things that were happening back in America. It's all a mystery to me. What I still need to know is where they got the idea that we are hiding sixty-three billion barrels of oil and keeping it in reserve. Perhaps the Saudis are hiding it. It is not us."

A third emir, younger by only a few years,

spoke next. "They are foolish men who think that is a possible bargaining chip. For us to keep them on our payroll. I, for one, am glad to see the last of them. I want a guarantee that we are rid of them and that we won't be getting any bad press or people poking into our business over here."

Rashid stepped forward and spoke hesitantly after a nudge from Malik. "When a snake invades your personal space, the only recourse is to cut off the snake's head. I think all of you did just that by not renewing International Alliance Capital's contract. When you are dealing with billions of dollars of laundered money, there is not all that much we can do but take our share of responsibility. Accounts here in the emirates have been frozen as of early this morning. For now and in the days to come, it will have to be business as usual, until we can sort through everything to see just how much havoc these men have caused us monetarily."

"Life was peaceful until your father agreed to work with those men," the oldest emir grumbled. His tone was just as fretful sounding as it was the first time he spoke. He popped a grape into his mouth and chewed as he looked around the table to see if the others agreed with him or not.

They did, their heads bobbing up and down, even Malik's.

Malik's voice was strong and a little impatient because they had gone over this many times in the past six months. "What you say is true, Your Highness, but you must remember that my father partnered with International Alliance Capital when things were bad here. We needed new business, and we needed the tourism. It all went bad when the money started to flow faster than we could handle it. I hesitate to remind you that I was not here, and I also understand that my father's sins fall to me. What we've done now by chopping off the head of the snake is given ourselves breathing room to make wise, educated decisions from here on in. There is no rush."

The last emir sitting at the round table, a particularly close friend of Malik's father, looked at Malik and said, "I sense much trouble for these men. My heart is telling me there are other forces at work here, not just us sitting at this table."

The other emirs nodded sagely, although truth be told, none of them had a clue. They were just ready to get rid of what they called a blight on the United Arab Emirates.

The emirs grumbled among themselves for a few more moments. Then, as one, they nodded.

The meeting was over, the lavish and bountiful meal on the table barely touched.

The emirs' departure was grand and a bit pompous, their pristine white robes swishing importantly as they strode through the palace, Malik and Rashid behind them.

When the emirs were sent off with seemly bows and touches to the forehead, Malik dusted his hands dramatically. "I thought that went rather well. What do you think, Rashid?"

"What I think is, the Four *J*s pissed someone else off besides the emirs, and whoever it is, is about to collect some blood. Not our worry, Malik. You up for a beer in the cave?"

Malik's voice sounded tired, but he put on his game face. "Nothing I would like better. Then I will take my medicine. Stop watching me like an expectant father."

"Who else is going to watch over you?" Rashid snapped, his patience at an end. He had to deal not only with a temperamental pregnant wife, Trish and her plane, which was finally airborne again, but also with His Royal Highness.

The moment they entered Malik's cave, Malik ripped at his headgear and pulled off his robe. He was wearing cargo shorts and a white T-shirt that said MÖTLEY CRÜE on the back. Rashid was dressed the same, except his shirt said NEW YORK METS.

It was Malik who uncapped the beer and handed one to Rashid. "We're both going to go straight to hell, with no stops on the way, for this. You know it, right?"

"I do, and right now I don't give a good rat's ass!" Rashid said as he clinked his bottle against Malik's. Malik laughed so hard, Rashid had to pound him on the back to get him to stop coughing.

"Okay, one more, and that's it. Sit, Rashid, and talk to me. Why do you keep checking your phone? I thought you said Soraya said it was a false alarm."

"I have calls in to the American embassy, to the members of the council, to everyone I could think of. I want to make sure those men get out of here and that they go empty-handed."

"Ah, I see. What or who do you think the outside sources are that are causing problems for the Four *J*s?"

"I wish I knew so I could shake their hands."

"The money laundering is never going to stop, Rashid. But for now, we put a lid on it. If we stay vigilant, we might be able to contain it. That's going to be your job. You do understand that?"

"I do, and I will do my very best. And now it's time for your medicine. I'll fetch it."

Rashid handed over an assortment of pills, together with a glass of water. Malik ignored the water he was offered and swallowed the pills with the last of his Bud Light. Rashid didn't even argue, because he knew Malik's response would be, "At this stage of the game, do you *really* think it matters if I swallow those damn pills with water or beer?"

"Go to your wife and hold her hand and tell her how much you love her. I'm going to take a nap and dream about *my* wife."

Malik was asleep even before Rashid exited the cave. Carrying his formal clothing, he tromped down the palace corridors, daring anyone to say a word or even look at him. Inside his apartments, he saw his wife pacing around in circles. Rashid started to quake in his sandals as he perceived his wife giving him the evil eye.

"What did I do now?"

"You made me pregnant is what you did. I am miserable with heartburn, and my stomach is cramping. How could you do this to me?"

"If I remember correctly, you were a willing participant at the time."

"That was then. This is *now!*" Soraya shrilled, knowing full well the cramping was the first stage of labor. "This is it. I am not going through this again. Do you hear me, Rashid? I told the doctors to tie my tubes."

Rashid turned white. "You can't do that!"

"You just watch me! Owww!" she screeched, the sound ricocheting off the apartment walls. "Don't you dare walk away from me, you coward! You stand right there and watch me suffer. Do you hear me, Rashid?" Soraya bellowed at the top of her lungs.

"The whole place can hear you. They already know you are the worst patient in the whole world. Did you call the doctor? Are they waiting for you?" At his wits' end, Rashid flapped his arms as he, too, started to pace in circles. "If I tell you a secret, will you shut up and allow me to wheel you in the chair to the clinic?"

Soraya stopped bellowing long enough to say, "What kind of secret?"

"All secrets are good," Rashid said as he pushed his wife down into the wheelchair a maid had fetched as soon as her mistress started screaming. "I will tell you the moment I get you to the clinic, so you will have something to think about instead of terrorizing those poor doctors and nurses. No cursing this time, Soraya."

"This better be a really good secret, Rashid, or you will find yourself below level again."

Rashid was breathless as he sprinted down the corridors, pushing his wife so fast, she didn't have time to scream. The moment he reached the clinic and the doors opened, he gasped, "She's all yours!"

"The secret, my dear husband!"

Rashid leaned over and whispered, "I am leaving now to pick up Trish at the airport. I think we'll make it back in time for me to welcome our new addition. If not, carry on without me."

Soraya forgot about how miserable she was. "Truly, she's almost here? Did you tell Malik?"

"No. I want it to be a surprise."

Soraya started screaming and bellowing again as she let loose with every cussword she knew, which was a lot. She stopped long enough to scream, "Go!"

Outside the clinic doors, Rashid, his face dripping with sweat, leaned against the wall and slowly sank down to his haunches. "Why me, Allah? Why me?" When there was no answer to his question, Rashid pulled himself to his feet and walked back to his apartments, where he donned the white robe and his headgear. He called for a car and a driver and left the palace. He imagined he could hear his wife's screams ricocheting off the palace walls. It wasn't until he was inside the car that he let loose with a heartfelt sigh of relief.

CHAPTER 19

It was almost midnight by the time the chauffeur-driven car dropped Trish and Rashid off at the entrance to the palace. The deeper they moved into the palace, the quieter it became, until they turned the corner to head toward the clinic. They both stopped, looked at one another, and listened.

"She's not screaming," Trish said.

"I don't know if that's good or bad," Rashid said, his voice jittery. He knocked softly on the door. A nurse opened it, her eyes wild.

"What?" Rashid asked.

"False labor. The princess is sleeping now. The doctor feels the baby will arrive by sunup. Please, please, do us all a favor and do not wake your wife."

"I wouldn't think of it," Rashid said, drawing Trish away from the door.

The two looked at one another.

"He was in the cave when I left for the airport."

Trish nodded. "I'm going to take a shower and get cleaned up."

"Come. I will walk you to your apartment. I did not tell Malik you were arriving this evening. Soraya said not to tell him. You know it is worth my life not to listen to my wife."

"I do know that. Are you sure there is nothing you want to tell me?"

Rashid sucked in a deep breath. Instead of speaking, he simply shook his head.

At the door to her apartment, Rashid did something he had never done before. He hugged her. Puzzled, she looked up to see only sadness and tears in his eyes. "Good night, Trish. I am going to leave you now. I have this . . . this . . . I need to see my children." He whirled, his white robe rustling with the breeze he created.

Trish frowned. Was he that worried about his wife? Not knowing the answer, she shrugged and entered the altogether familiar apartment, where she'd been so happy. She looked around; nothing had changed.

She smiled when she saw that the huge bed was turned down, a fresh nightgown on her pillow. She knew even before she entered the bathroom that the tub would be filled with her favorite bath salts. Not that she wanted a soak just then. What she wanted was to wash her hair and take a nice long hot shower to wash away the smell of the airport and the stale air of the plane she'd been in for so many hours.

Forty minutes later, Trish was perfumed and powdered and dressed in what she called her favorite muumuu, a long sky-blue gown. Her wet hair was piled on top of her head. She wore soft, comfortable slippers. The little clock on the night table told her the time was ten minutes past one in the morning.

Her heart pounding in her chest, Trish left the apartment and walked down several corridors, knowing full well that there were many sets of eyes watching her. Like she cared.

The cave was dimly lit. Malik was sprawled on the oversize chaise. She smiled at the cargo shorts and the MÖTLEY CRÜE T-shirt, his favorite cave wear. He'd kicked off his sandals. She saw the four empty bottles of Bud Light. She tiptoed over to the chaise and sat down on the floor, her legs folded under her. She stared at her husband, her heart so full of love, she thought she would explode with the feeling. Silent tears rolled down her cheeks. She made no effort to stop them. Nor did she make an effort to wipe the tears with the sleeve of her gown.

Malik looked thinner. But, then, so did she, according to her sister, Emma. She leaned closer to stare at her husband's face. In sleep, it looked drawn and gaunt. She chewed on her lower lip as she tried to understand why Malik would have lost weight. She understood her own weight loss but not her husband's. She thought about Rashid's sad, moist eyes, and her heart started to pound in her chest. Still, she didn't move.

Something in the cave changed. Malik shifted in his sleep, his legs straightened out, and then his eyelids fluttered. "Trish," he whispered.

"Yes?"

"Why are you sitting on the floor? Why are you crying?"

"I was watching you sleep. I don't know why I'm crying."

"I missed you. You didn't say good-bye."

"I'm sorry about that. I was upset with you."

"Yes. It is I who should apologize. I'm sorry, Trish. We need to talk."

"I know we do. I wish we had done that earlier. I needed to leave and to think about things, you know, to get my head on straight. What went wrong, Malik?"

Malik struggled to sit up on the chaise. "Something no one is prepared for. At least I wasn't. I didn't know how to handle it."

"I would have helped you, whatever it was . . . is."

"I didn't want you to know," Malik said softly.

"But why? I thought we agreed that there would be no secrets between us. You shut me out, Malik. What could be so terrible that you couldn't share it with me? I love you. Together, we could have dealt with it. Secrets are for people who don't trust each other."

"Not this secret. There's no other way to say this other than to just tell you. I'm dying, Trish. When I left the palace, I was going from doctor to doctor, searching for a cure, but there is no cure. I don't have much time left on this earth. Can you forgive me? And if you can't forgive me for shutting you out, can you at least tell me you understand?"

Trish didn't trust herself to speak. Her world was spinning out of control, and there was nothing she could do about it. She nodded. Neither moved. It was as though they were both rooted to some unseen object that prevented either of them from moving.

Somewhere deep inside her, way down in the depths of her soul, she had thought perhaps it was something like this, but she had never allowed herself to give voice to the horrible thought. Something so perfect, so wonderful couldn't end like this. It just couldn't.

"Specialists in the States," she whispered.

"Been there, done that," Malik said gently.

"Switzerland. They have cutting-edge . . ."

"Been there, done that. I went to the best. I didn't overlook anything. It is what it is, Trish." Malik reached for Trish's hand. She scrambled to her feet and literally threw herself at her husband. He clutched at her, his whole body trembling as he held her. Their tears mingled as they crooned to each other, the words indistinct, but neither cared.

A long time later, Trish managed to whisper, "What do we do now?"

"I don't know, Trish. I've all but turned everything over to Rashid. I'll just be a consulting figurehead. When I'm gone, you will assume my role, and Rashid, along with Soraya, will be your adviser. Unless you don't want to do that."

"That wasn't what I meant, Malik. What I meant was, what do you and I do? What are your limitations?"

Malik shrugged. "I think it's one of those things that you work at as you go along. I'm hopeful that there will be good days along the way. It goes without saying, the bad days will outnumber the good. Can you do it, Trish? I don't know how strong I will be mentally. You might have to carry my burden, as well."

Her heart breaking, Trish did her best to smile. "I will never leave your side. That's a promise."

And then they slept, their bodies pressed tight in the oversize chair, their tears mingling, their hearts beating as one.

Jeff Davis looked across the linen-covered breakfast table at his three partners. "This is how I see it, guys. We just simply leave the hotel and head for the airport. We leave our luggage behind, all of our winter clothing. This way, the staff will think we're coming back. I'm in no mood for a fight with the credit cards. That goddamn American Express said if we took out their famous Black Card, the Centurion, we could buy a yacht on it. Since it's been shut down, we can't pay for the hotel rooms. After that bullshit with our passports at the American embassy, we're lucky we're going to be able to get out of here in one piece. You guys have any thoughts on this?"

"What the hell happened? In just two days, our lives have been shot to hell. Do these Arabs have that kind of power?" John Gamble hissed.

Jeff's eyes narrowed as he picked at the bacon on his breakfast plate. His head was spinning as he tried to figure out how many bills they'd racked up here in Dubai since their arrival, bills that they weren't going to be able to pay. Five-thousand-dollar-a-night suites for four, each for four nights. The elaborate dinners, with pricey wine, at Dubai's fanciest restaurant, Al Muntaha, which sat two hundred meters above the Persian Gulf. Those dinners ran into the thousands. And the rental cars. They'd racked up close to a hundred grand, and they were skipping out on the bill.

Josh Olsen stopped texting long enough to share his thoughts. "I don't think it's the Arabs at all. Yeah, they kicked our ass to the curb and told us to get out of their country. Truth be told, we deserve to get kicked out. I'm just surprised we lasted as long as we did in this gig. I thought for sure our money was safe offshore, but now it's gone. These guys aren't into that. No, our problems are coming from stateside. I don't know about you three, but it looks like I'm destitute. Ashley told me she spoke to your wives, and all of us now have foreclosure notices plastered on our front doors. I have sixty-four dollars in cash in my wallet, and that's it. But who is smart enough to pull something like this off?"

"My ex-wife, that's who," Jeff said. "With the aid of her sister, His Royal Highness's wife, my dear former sister-in-law. That rumor about her — it's true. I checked it out last night. There is no other explanation that makes sense. Think about it."

Jason Hart thought about his ex-wife, Clare, then. He'd been thinking about her way too much of late. "Clare, Alice, and Robin are best friends with your ex-wife, Emma. Let's be honest here. After what we did to them, I can see their wanting their pound of flesh. The tables have turned. Looks to me like the only things they missed are our licenses to practice law."

"By the time we get home, *if* we get home, we'll have correspondence from the bar association in our mailbox. I think that's a given," John Gamble said.

Jason Hart stood up the moment he drained his coffee cup. "I hate this place. It's so goddamned ostentatious and gaudy at the same time. You can take the Khalifa

Tower and shove it. My gut is telling me we won't ever, as in ever, be staying in a place like this again. More like never. Motel 6 is more like it from here on in, or even a tent in some field."

Jeff eyed his partners. "A defeatist attitude will get you nowhere. Be aware, gentlemen, that there are many eyes watching us. Let's go to our respective rooms, gather our briefcases and laptops, and split this place. Walk confidently, smile, and make small talk. Once we're out of here, we do what the attaché told us to do, go to the embassy, and they will escort us to the airport, make nice with the customs officials, get our passports stamped, and we board the flight. Thank God we have first-class tickets. Once we get home, we can deal with the passports. Are we all clear on this?"

The partners nodded.

An hour later, the four partners who made up International Alliance Capital were escorted through security at Dubai International Airport, where their passports were stamped. Then another stamp, which said FINAL in red ink, was slammed down. Jeff asked their escort from the embassy what it meant.

"When you get to the United States and

306

clear customs, your passports will be confiscated. My advice is not to kick up a fuss, or you'll be detained. Settle in, and then fight it out. What the hell did you guys do, anyway?"

"Not a goddamn thing. Her Royal Highness just happens to be my ex-wife's sister. You figure it out," Jeff Davis snarled.

"Ooh, that's not good." The young guy smirked.

"Yeah, well, you asked. Now you know. Is this flight on time?"

"It is, and you four will be the first to board. They're opening the Jetway right now. My orders are to stay here till your plane lifts off." He motioned for the four partners to move forward.

The young attaché, whose name was Lester Baker, sat quietly, vigilant, until the Jetway door slammed shut, at which point he walked over to the window and watched the huge silver plane back out of its assigned slot. Only then did he heave a sigh and turn to make his way out to the parking lot, his mission accomplished.

CHAPTER 20

The Four *J*s, having been renamed the Four Jerks by John Gamble, were the first four passengers off the plane. They headed straight for customs, went through the rigmarole, and didn't utter a sound when their passports were confiscated. All four men were cold and shivering in their light-weight Dubai clothing.

They huddled out of sight and hearing of the other passengers as they tried to figure out if they had enough money to get their cars out of the lot.

Jeff eyed the bills, calculated the amount in his head, then shook it. "Okay, this is what we do. We take my car, head straight for Solomon's office, and borrow some money. We let him deal with this mess. We've paid him an outrageous yearly re-tainer, so let the bastard earn it. Then, and only then, do we head home. Do you all agree?"

The Four Jerks nodded their heads as they danced around, stomping their feet, in an attempt to get warm.

"Damn, it's snowing," Jason Hart said. "I don't think I'll ever be warm again. I used to love snow."

"Shut the hell up, Jason. I'm in no mood for your commentary right now," Jeff snarled. Hart clamped his lips shut as he hugged his arms to his chest.

"People are staring at us," Josh Olsen said through chattering teeth. "It's like they *know.*"

"Sometimes, you are so stupid, I can't believe I even know you. They're staring at us because we're wearing Palm Beach attire and it's snowing outside," Jeff said.

"Who died and appointed you God?" John Gamble barked. "Just remember, Jeff, we're all in the same boat here. Civility goes a long way, so knock it off."

And then they were in the car, the motor running. "We'll sit here a few minutes, until the engine warms and the heater kicks in," Jeff said. "Look, we're all on edge right now. I'm sorry. I'm as upset as you all are. I don't know what our next move is. Let's hope Solomon can figure it out and get everything reinstated. I have to tell you, whoever did this to us, and I'm betting it was Mrs. Emir of Dubai, must know some pretty interesting people, never mind having the money to pay said interesting people to pull off what they have pulled off."

"How could anyone get to our offshore accounts? Those accounts were so well hidden, I couldn't even get to them without the instructions, and even then, I had to jump through hoops. All I wanted to do was check the account, not add to it or take anything out. I'm not getting any of this," Josh Olsen said.

"You want to beat a dead horse, be my guest," Jeff said. "I told you, the only explanation I can think of is that my ex-wife's sister hired someone to do this. I'm thinking she has access to what amounts to all the money in the world. Money talks. Money is power, so it is not out of the question that she found people capable of ruining our lives. I bet her friends in Las Vegas could have put her in touch. Bitch!" he seethed.

A strong gust of wind whipped through the garage, snow swirling in every direction from the strong wind. The heater finally kicked in with a loud blast of sound and warm air.

"I love this heated steering wheel," Jeff said. "Buckle up, guys. We're outta here."

Forty minutes later, Jeff roared into the parking lot of the high-rise office building where Ben Solomon had his law offices. The men ran, their pricey John Lobb shoes skidding on the slushy snow in the parking lot. The snow was coming down harder by then, the wind was howling, and the skeletal trees dotting the perimeter of the parking lot were bent almost all the way over from the force of the wind.

The Four *J*s raced to the elevator, savoring the warmth rushing through the vents. And then they were on the sixteenth floor. The elevator doors slid open. Two minutes later, they were in the exquisite marble-and-mahogany reception area, where a stunning blond receptionist usually greeted clients. Today, though, her desk was unmanned. The phone console was silent. No red or green lights flickered. The partners stood silent, listening for a sound from anywhere.

The Solomon office wasn't huge, but it was elegant. There were only Ben Solomon, the lead attorney, three associates, four paralegals, plus an office manager and a receptionist. From somewhere down the hall, they could hear a voice, but the words were indistinct.

Jeff ventured to the doorway and called out, "Ben, are you here?" The hallway went silent, and then they heard footsteps.

The usually dapper, expensively dressed attorney glared at the Four *J*s. "What are you doing here? Did we have an appointment? Jesus, you guys look like crap. Why are you decked out like that?"

The Four *J*s sighed as one.

John Gamble said, "It's a long story, but we need your help. And the reason we're dressed like this is we just got in from Dubai. We had to skip out on our hotel bill because some asshole stole our identities and cut off our money supply. We couldn't even go back to the hotel to get our winter clothing."

Ben Solomon gaped at the men standing in front of him. At one point in time, several years ago, he had referred to the men standing in front of him as the Fabulous Four, because the money was rolling in faster than they could count it. At present, they didn't look anywhere near fabulous, but then, neither did he.

Solomon raked his fingers through his spiky gray hair, which was already standing on end. He needed a shave. He'd lost his tie hours ago, and his shirt looked like he'd been wearing it for a few days, which was true. "Must be something in the air, then, because the same thing happened to me a few days ago. I am at my wits' end. I have spent twenty-three out of every twenty-four hours trying to figure out what is going on. On top of that, the bar association just sent a notice that they have canceled my license to practice law. Want some coffee? I just made it. Don't know how good it is, since making coffee is not a specialty of mine. I sent everyone home the minute this shit started going down. It's just us here."

In Solomon's office, which was as elegant and over the top as that of the CEO of any multibillion-dollar corporation, Solomon motioned for the Four Js to take a seat while he poured coffee at a lavish bar nestled in the corner. "Talk to me," he growled.

The Four Js started talking at once, but Solomon was able to get the gist of it all. "Well, you saved me the trouble of telling you my story, because it's exactly the same as yours. Who the fuck is doing this to us?"

"I'll tell you who," Jeff Davis snarled. "My ex-wife's sister, that's who. She's married to the sheik, His Royal Highness, or whatever the hell he's called, in Dubai. She's got money blowing out every orifice of her body. This is her payback for the divorce settlements *you* negotiated on *our* behalf."

"You need to get over yourself. I don't

care how the hell much money she has. She still couldn't pull something like this off. Don't you guys get it? We've been *erased* from society. It's like we suddenly don't exist. Whoever did this had to have a network of people who knew what they were doing and how to cover their tracks. As it stands, everything has been erased. That means it was never there. You can't argue with that, now, can you?"

"Where did the money go from all the accounts? Where was it wired to? There has to be a trail. You can always follow the money, Ben," Jeff said.

"Not this time, boys. Not this time. It's gone. When something was never there to begin with, how do you trace it? Now do you get it? I, like you, have twenty-eight days before my house is foreclosed on. Every check I wrote bounced. My credit cards are invalid. The bank called in the Feds. They think I'm part of some kind of conspiracy to launder money or some such shit. Then they threw in the credit cards, and they're planning to charge me with everything in the book. I can't even figure out how to fight this. It's some invisible force. And, oh, yeah, my wife is packing to leave me, along with her nest egg of jewelry and her paid-off car. Everything else is mortgaged to the hilt. Just like you guys. Well, will one of you say something?"

Jeff's expression turned ugly. "If it's not Trish, then who? You said a network. What network? I don't have those kinds of enemies. Hell, I've had clients who didn't like me, but none of them are capable of something like this. I'm telling you, it's got to be Trish. It's the five of us she went after. And by the way, my ex is now living in the Enclave. My daughter told me that in a text. I had a text from her this morning saying her tuition check bounced, and unless she pays up, she's out."

Josh Olsen walked over to the bar and poured himself another cup of coffee. He looked at the empty pot and set about making a fresh one. "I agree with Jeff," he called over his shoulder. "She just went after the five of us. By the way, none of us have been home. We came straight here."

"Well, by the time you get there, don't be surprised to find out that your wives have split," Solomon told them. "You'll be lucky they didn't sell off your antiques, the paintings, and whatever else you have of value."

John Gamble gasped. "In two days!"

"Hell yes! Do you live under a rock or something? When women smell defeat, they close ranks, and it's every man for himself.

Women are vicious. They don't just grab you by the balls. They squeeze them until you cry uncle. What? Have you guys been living in a cave?"

"So what do we do?" Jason Hart asked, his voice so choked up, he could barely get the words out. "Should we go to the police? File a report? What?"

Ben Solomon laughed so loud, he lost his breath. "That's exactly what you *don't* do," he said when he was finally able to talk. "If you are all certain in your own minds that it was your former sister-in-law who did this, then I suggest you go talk to your ex-wives. See if you can cut a deal. Then again, they probably didn't do a thing. If the sister did it, that's who you go after, but you can't even do that now since your passports were confiscated. Talk about a rock and a hard place. I gotta tell you. For the first time in my life, I honest to God do not know what to do, say, or even think."

Four sets of eyes zeroed in on Jeff Davis. Gamble voiced their thoughts. "Since you're convinced this is all your former sister-in-law's doing, and since she's the sister of your ex-wife, I guess you need to speak with your ex and try to get to the bottom of this."

"And do it quickly, before the Feds pay *us* a visit. We can't represent ourselves, we need to get lawyers, and you know what that's going to cost," Solomon said as he swiped at the moisture pooling on his brow. "I can't believe this shit. I read about it every day, but until it happens to you, there's no way to even begin to understand it all."

"I feel like squatting in a corner, sucking my thumb, and crying, all at the same time," Jason Hart said. "They say payback is a bitch. Well, boys, this payback doesn't get any better than that for our exes. I'm going home. I want to take a shower and get on some warm clothes. Let's agree to a conference call around six."

The others agreed.

Ben Solomon watched the Fabulous Four, who were far from fabulous, leave his office. He dropped his head in his hands and wept.

Jeff Davis dropped his partners off one by one, then drove home on the slippery roads. He was thankful when he arrived safe and sound. He pressed the garage door opener that was on his visor and drove into the garage. He sighed with relief when he saw Simone's car parked in her own bay. At least she hadn't left yet. But she would; he knew that as surely as he knew he needed to take another breath to keep on living. What he had to do immediately was to get hold of all the costly jewelry he'd given her and sell it.

Simone was waiting for him in the sterile kitchen, which was never used. He was stunned to see a box of cornflakes sitting on the counter. He wondered if it was her breakfast or her lunch. Not that he cared. He looked at his wife, waiting to see what she would do, which was nothing. There was no "How are you?" No "Glad you're home." No "Gee whiz, I missed you." Not even "What the hell is going on?" Not a peep. But her heavily made-up eyes were narrowed, and he knew she was ready to do battle.

Simone was beautiful. There was no question about it. She spent her days getting facials, massages, hair treatments, manicures, and pedicures. With the hours that were left over, she shopped or lunched with her friends. That day, she was dressed all in white cashmere, with at least ten strands of *real* pearls around her neck. He knew the pearls were real because he'd paid for them. And the cashmere — seven grand easy. One day, she'd joked to him that she would never go out of the house unless her turnout was in the seven-thousand-dollar range. *Excluding* jewelry. He'd laughed, because back then he was pissing money away. He wasn't laughing anymore as he pondered how much he could get for the pearls.

When it became obvious that Simone wasn't going to say anything, Jeff said, "Nice to see you, too." Then he stomped his way through the house and up to the master bedroom and shower.

Under the steaming spray, Jeff soaped up not once, not twice, but three times, until the water started to run cold. He hopped out, toweled off, shaved, and dressed in warm clothing. Then he closed and locked the bedroom door. He rummaged everywhere until he found his wife's jewelry box. He closed his eyes as he tried to picture the various items he'd purchased for her since their marriage and the months before, when he was wooing her. Some of it was in the safe, and he was the only one who had the combination. In the safe was twenty thousand dollars in cash for emergencies. Well, this was an emergency of the first order. He debated about taking it out and securing it somewhere else in the house until he remembered Ben Solomon's words about vicious women. Better to leave it where it was for the moment. He stuffed the jewelry from the box into the corduroy cargo pants that had six different pockets. She'd have to wrestle him for the jewelry, and he doubted that would happen, because she might break a nail in the process.

In the kitchen, he looked inside the refrigerator. A package of cheese slices, two oranges, and a pint of skim milk. The cabinet overhead was just as bare, but he did find a can of organic tomato soup and some oyster crackers. At least he wouldn't starve. The next day, however, was another story.

He risked a glance at his wife, who was pretending to read the writing on the cornflakes box. She looked up. "What's going on, Jeff? I think I have a right to know. Your daughter has been calling and texting every few minutes. You need to get in touch with her."

Jeff removed the soup from the stove and poured it into a bowl. He added crackers, salt, and pepper, and sat down to eat. "I don't know what to tell you other than someone stole my identity and wiped me out. All I have is the money in my pocket. Text Missy and tell her she has to sell the Porsche to pay her tuition. The car is paid for, so she should get a good price for it. She's a selfish little shit, so let's see if she does it or not."

"You made her that way, Jeff. She was a sweet kid when she came to us. You gave her the moon and the stars. You talked bad about her mother. You reap what you sow," Simone said softly. "I don't think this is as simple as someone stealing your identity. I know this because I've spoken to Ashley, Krystal, and Gabriella, and they said the same thing is happening to them. That leads us all to believe that four of you at International Alliance Capital have done something wrong or illegal, and this is a payback of some sort. We aren't stupid, Jeff. Tell me what's going on before I lose what little respect I still have for you."

Jeff turned around and reached inside the kitchen drawer for a pack of cigarettes. He fired one up, blew a perfect smoke ring, and said, "The long version is we're broke. The short version is we're broke." He pawed through the mail on the counter until he saw the letter from the bar association. He closed his eyes and sighed, but he didn't open it. Why bother? He knew what it said.

"Are they going to turn off the utilities?"

Jeff shrugged. "Do we have any firewood?"

"I have no idea. If we do, it is probably covered up by the snow. Have you looked outside? They're saying there's going to be a blizzard by morning."

"Then if I were you, I'd get cracking and go dig some out, unless you want to freeze to death. They might not turn off the utilities for a few days, but the power is sure to go out. If you recall, the generator fritzed out last year, and I never got it fixed."

Simone started to sputter. "Well, what are we going to do, Jeff? How are we going to live? Our credit cards aren't valid, and our checks are no good. We have no cash. Are they going to take our cars?"

"I don't know. I have never been in a situation like this one before. As to the cars, yeah, they'll probably take them sometime this coming week. I guess this is where you'll get to use all those muscles from the stationary bike you ride for hours, but this time you'll be pedaling your ass off on a real bike. That's assuming we even have a bike."

Simone burst into tears, her mascara running down her cheeks. Jeff got up and left the kitchen to go to his office. He needed to call his partners and come up with a plan.

But even he knew that there was no plan in the universe that could help him out of the mess he was in, but he at least had to try.

Plan B.

Plan B had to be Emma, to have her get in touch with Trish to call off the dogs of poverty.

Ha!

CHAPTER 21

The former Emma Holiday Davis, once again just plain Emma Holiday, sampled the stew she was cooking on the stove. Always, from the time when she and Trish were little girls, stew with dumplings, along with a freshly baked apple pie, had been for snowy days. She'd even carried the tradition into her married life. She'd made the pie earlier, with fresh apples, lots of cinnamon, butter, raisins, and nuts.

Satisfied that the stew was bubbling along nicely, Emma walked over to the kitchen door to look out at the falling snow. Memories going back to childhood and following through to this very moment attacked her. She wished Trish were there. She wished that more than anything. She hadn't heard a word from her sister since she'd returned to Dubai other than a brief text saying she had arrived safe and sound.

The snowflakes, which had started out

earlier as big, flat ones, were already minuscule pinpricks of frozen ice. No longer really snowflakes at all, but sleet, to be more precise. She turned away from the window to look at the stove. What *was* she going to do with that huge pot of stew? In the blink of an eye, she had her cell phone in her hand. She called the girls one by one and invited them to dinner. "Put on your snow boots and trudge on over here so we can admire each other while we stuff ourselves."

They all agreed immediately. She was, of course, referring to the morning they'd spent at the Red Door, getting "the works." They all had newly styled hairdos; they had all been made up, given manicures, pedicures, and massages. She had loved the facial and had actually fallen asleep while the cosmetician worked on her. She couldn't remember when she'd felt as good as she did at that moment. Years and years ago, maybe, when she had been in the middle of her career as a model. In other words, a lifetime ago.

A new outfit hadn't hurt her ego, either. She knew that she looked just as good as she felt; the girls had said the same thing. That night they would drink a thank-you toast to Trish. Thank God she'd had the good sense to pick up several really good bottles of wine when she'd done her grocery shopping.

Emma walked into the family room and turned on the stereo. She adjusted the surround sound and listened for a moment. Soft, soothing, mellow sound wafted throughout the house. Perfect. Absolutely perfect.

Emma turned on the outside lights so the girls would be able to make it across the yards in the swirling, darkened night. Maybe they'd have a sleepover if they overindulged in the wine. She looked around at the house that was now hers. It was so big. So beautiful. So *hers.* So lonely. It wasn't that she minded living alone; she really didn't. She had learned over the past few years to enjoy her own company. But there were times, like the present, when she felt the need to have friends around her. Perhaps *need* was the wrong word. The word *share* came to mind. That was it. She wanted to share her good fortune, her good feelings, with the friends who had seen her through her dark days, the same friends who understood what she was going through, because they had been and were going through the same thing. Her support group through thick and thin, through the good and the bad, through the dark into the light. And she, along with the others, owed their present improved circumstances to her baby sister.

Emma was back in the kitchen, wondering where she should serve her first dinner in her new home. In the formal dining room, with her good china as a way of celebration, or in the kitchen, with her brand-new colorful Fiesta dinnerware? She'd always been a kitchen kind of person, and the kitchen in this McMansion was the stuff of which dreams were made.

Not only did she have a fireplace in the kitchen, but she also had a one-of-a-kind back staircase. The builder had created a rustic kitchen with brick and slate, strong beams overhead that were perfect for hanging green plants, and a breakfast nook that was ideal for sitting with morning coffee and the *Daily Princetonian.* No reading the newspapers online for her. She liked holding the paper and getting newsprint on her hands. She felt the same way about reading books. She wanted to *hold* the book, smell the scent of the paper. Maybe she was a Neanderthal, as her daughter called her. She didn't care. She was what she was, and if Melissa did not like it, that was just too bad.

When the doorbell rang, she ran to answer it. The girls trooped in, took off their outer gear, and pulled off their snow boots. Each of them was carrying her high heels.

"A party is a party!" Clare said happily. "And guess what else. Right before you called me, Emma, guess who called me. C'mon, c'mon, girls, guess! Okay, okay, I'll tell you. Ethan Wylie, that's who. He asked me to dinner this Saturday, and I said yes. He knows about . . . you know," Clare said, touching her chest.

The women gushed and laughed and hugged Clare. They all liked Ethan Wylie, who was a widower and a deacon at the church they all attended.

"Well, that will be two toasts to make this evening. So, do we dine in my new dining room, or do we chow down in my new kitchen, ladies?"

"Wherever the wine is, my friend," Robin said as she beelined for the kitchen.

"The kitchen! Do you have a fire going?" Alice asked.

"As a matter of fact, I do have a fire going. It is downright toasty in the kitchen, and yes, that's where the wine is. So let's have at it, ladies. May I say one more time how beautiful you all look. That makeover at the Red Door was just what we all needed. We do look fashionable, if I say so myself."

"I think I must have spent an hour looking at myself in the mirror when I got home. After I made a fire, that is. I guess that we really let ourselves go," Clare said.

Emma whirled around. Her tone was fierce when she said, "Don't you dare say that ever again, Clare. We did not *let* ourselves go. Our ex-husbands, may they rot in hell forever, pushed us into situations where we had no choices. We no longer had any money for fancy this and fancy that. What little money we had went toward survival. We were always clean and neat. So what if we weren't fashionable? So what?"

"Whoa there, Emma. I just chose the wrong words. That was exactly what I meant," Clare said gently.

Emma calmed down immediately, assuming the role of camp counselor. "Someone set the table. Someone open the wine. Someone put some more logs on the fire, and I'll put the bread in the oven and spend the rest of my time watching all of you, but first I am going to turn on the floodlights outside so we can watch the snow and sleet come down while we eat. I love watching it snow. Makes everything look so clean and so perfect, like God's doing it just for me, if you know what I mean. I cooked, so you guys clean. Deal!"

"You bet," the other three girls agreed

cheerfully.

They laughed, they ate, and they finished off the first bottle of wine. Dinner was wonderful, they told Emma.

It had already been decided that they would indeed have a good old-fashioned sleepover, so they didn't have to walk home in the snow. The girls were trying to decide if they should eat the pie immediately or wait till later when Emma's cell phone rang.

They looked at one another, surprise — no, shock — written all over their faces. No one ever called them in the evening. Ever. Besides, they were all there, sitting at the table.

"Answer the damn phone already!" Alice prodded.

Emma reached over to the counter, looked at the caller ID, and gasped. "It's my ex!"

Clare said, "Don't answer it!"

Robin said, "Answer it!"

Alice, her eyes wide, shrugged.

Emma answered the phone. "This is Emma Holiday," Emma said briskly.

The voice on the other end said, "Don't you mean Emma Davis?"

"Not on your life, buster. I took back my maiden name. Yours was nothing but a reminder of how bad tainted meat smelled. What do you want, Jeff? You must want something. Otherwise, you wouldn't be call-ing me. A pint of my blood, some more skin, my soul? Get to the point right now, or I'm hanging up. And if I do and you call back, I'll have you slapped with an order of protection before you can say 'sheik of Araby.' " Emma looked around the table at her friends, who were grinning from ear to ear.

Emma heard her husband suck in his breath. "I need to talk to you, Emma. I can be there in thirty minutes."

"And I would agree to talk to you . . . why? Have you looked outside? We're hav-ing a storm. There must be five inches on the ground already."

"I have four-wheel drive. This is . . . urgent, Emma. I really need to talk to you. Missy told me you moved, so it might take me only twenty minutes."

"Oh, I bet it is urgent. For you. Certainly not for me. I don't much care if you want to talk to me or not. I have some free time next week. Call me then."

"Emma, for Christ's sake, listen to me. Don't hang up. I hate sounding melodra-matic, but this is life or death."

Emma laughed then, a bone-chillingly evil sound that made the girls rear backward in their chairs. "I hope it's your life or your death we are talking about. Tell me on the phone. I really do not want to see you. Your very presence offends me. My God! Are you crying, Jeff?" Emma's clenched fist shot high in the air. The girls grinned.

"No, I'm not crying, for God's sake. I'm catching a damn cold. I just got home a few hours ago and went from hundred-degree weather to subfreezing temperatures. Please, Emma. I'll be there in twenty minutes. I have the address." The phone went silent.

Emma looked down at the phone in her hand. "He's coming here. He said he'll be here in twenty minutes, and it's life and death. His, I assume. Wonder what else Trish did," she said, bursting into laughter. "Okay, girls, let's get this cleaned up. Then you all hide out in the laundry room so you can hear everything."

The women hustled and bustled, then ran to the foyer to grab their outerwear and snow boots. Emma wiped up the floor with one of her new towels, then threw it in the washer. She craned her neck to look out the side window. The girls' tracks had already filled in.

"Ooh, I dreamed about a day like this," Emma said as she swooped around the kitchen like a happy bat looking for a place to roost.

"Ya know, there are four of us. We could wrestle him to the floor, strip him naked, and toss him out in the snow," Robin said, glee ringing in her voice. "Maybe then it would really become a matter of life and death."

"We should tape the conversation," Alice said. "I can do that on this super-duper phone I bought yesterday. I say we do it so later on he can't say he didn't say whatever he's going to say." The girls high-fived one another.

"And here we thought this was just going to be another dinner and sleepover. Entertainment such as this is what women like us live for. Just make sure you scorch his balls," Alice said.

"Don't you worry, honey. I've got five years coming to me, plus your guys' five years to get off my chest. I like that part about wrestling him to the floor, stripping him naked, and throwing him out in the snow."

Emma whirled around to check the kitchen. Satisfied, she looked at the girls and burst out laughing. "He *was* crying. Trust me on that one. A cold, my ass. This is how we have to look at it, girls. The mountain has come to Mohammed. I may be the first, but I can guarantee you will all be getting calls from your exes sooner rather than later."

Their eyes on the kitchen clock, the girls uncorked the second bottle of wine. Alice poured generously.

Robin held her glass aloft. "To some serious ass kicking this evening!"

"Hear! Hear!" the girls hooted, Emma's voice the loudest.

"He's late!" Alice said, pointing to the kitchen clock. "If we're lucky, he ran off the road and is in a ditch somewhere."

Ever practical, Emma said, "There are, unfortunately, no ditches between where he lives and here. Oh, I forgot to call the guardhouse to put his name on the list of people to allow through."

Within seconds, that small feat was accomplished. Fifteen minutes later, the front doorbell rang. As one, the girls jumped, then immediately headed for the laundry room.

"Baby, this is your shining moment," Robin said. "Make the most of it. We're just a few feet away if you run into trouble."

Emma grinned, her eyes sparkling with what was to come as she hugged her friends. She smoothed down her cashmere sweater, which showed off her slim, toned body, and took her own sweet time walking to the front door. Opening it as if expecting to see an encyclopedia salesman on the other side, she saw her ex-husband huddled in a sheepskin jacket, a wool cap with earflaps covering his head.

"Take off your boots. Leave them there by the door."

There were no hellos, no "How are you doing?" and no comments along the lines of, "It's been forever since we've seen one another." Just, "Take off your boots," followed by Jeff's comment that something smelled good.

"That's right. You always made stew and an apple pie when it snowed."

"I'm surprised you would remember something so . . . *trivial*," Emma said, leading the way to her beautiful lived-in kitchen. Lived in only a few days, but it looked, nonetheless, like she'd been there forever. It practically screamed, "Emma Holiday lives here now." Emma motioned for Jeff to take the chair closest to the laundry-room door. It was good that his back was to it, so the girls could crack the door if necessary.

"A cup of coffee would be nice," Jeff said.

"It would be if you were a friend whom I had invited here, but you invited yourself. This is not a social call. You are taking up my valuable time right now, so get to the point so you can leave. I *did* not want you here. I *do* not want you here. This is *my* house. Not yours, not ours, *mine.*"

"You've come up in the world, haven't you?" Jeff said, looking around. He sniffed then like a hound dog. Emma knew he was hungry, and his eyes begged for some of her homemade stew. He'd always loved her cooking. She totally ignored what she was seeing.

"If you mean from the ghetto where I was living, then yes, I have. Of course, we both know who was responsible for putting me there, don't we? And we both know there was no earthly reason why it had to be done the way it was, the way you and that shyster you employed chose to do it. That's something I will never forget. Nor will I ever forgive you for that, Jeff. These last five years were not good for me. So, whatever you're about to ask me, just remember that."

"I'm sorry, Emma. I really am. I wish I could turn the clock back and undo a lot of the things I did back then. Unfortunately, I can't do that."

"Oh, I just bet you're sorry. *Now.* And if you think for one minute I believe you're really sorry about what you did to me, then you must have me mixed up with someone else. Now, why are you here and what do you want? Don't make me ask you again."

"I want you to call off the dogs. You've made your point. You've brought me to my knees. I understand you want your pound of flesh for the way I treated you, and you got it, plus a few pounds extra."

"What are you talking about? What point? What dogs? You don't look like you're on your knees to me. You're sitting in my house, in my chair, on your ass and talking in riddles."

"Like you don't know what's going on. It's your sister. She's ruined me and International Alliance Capital. This is a personal vendetta on her part. Money talks, and she's got more money than God. I know who she's married to. Why did you try to keep that a secret, anyway, Emma?"

"Because my family is none of your business, that's why. You may have stolen my daughter, you bastard, but she is the one and only member of my family you will have any contact with."

"Well, your sister damn well ruined us, all four of us. The whole damn company. Somehow, she managed to erase our identities. She confiscated our bank accounts. The money is gone. IAC is being charged with money laundering, the Feds are on our backs, they confiscated our passports, our credit cards are no good, the country club canceled our memberships, our houses are in foreclosure, and the mortgages are now owned by some Belarusian yahoos, and they want their money. Belarusians no less!"

There was such outrage in Jeff's voice that Emma smiled.

"Ah, you're smiling. I knew it. You were in on it, too. I want to know how she got to the bar association for them to lift our licenses."

Emma shrugged. "Boo hoo!" She got up to pour herself a cup of coffee but didn't bother to offer one to her ex-husband.

"I'm going to go to prison. I don't have the money to hire a lawyer, and that's another thing. She got to Solomon, too."

"That skank lawyer who took us to the cleaners? Well, I can't say that I'm sorry to hear that. Oh, boo hoo again. Can you prove any of this fairy tale?"

"You really are a coldhearted bitch, aren't you?" Jeff snarled.

"Appearances can be deceiving sometimes. My friends don't think I'm a coldhearted bitch. In case you happen to have missed it, Mr. Jefferson Davis, so-called great-great-grandson of a traitor, I hate your guts. If that makes me a coldhearted bitch, so be it. Do you understand that?"

"Yeah, I do, and that's why you put your

sister up to all of this. You just wanted to get even. Well, you got even, okay? So now call off the dogs so we can both get on with our lives. This is some fancy house. How'd you afford something like this?" Jeff snarled, not liking it that his ex-wife had the upper hand.

"Maybe I won the lottery. It's really none of your business how or why I got this house. It is mine, and it is paid for. That means there is no mortgage that Belarusians, or anyone else, can claim. By the way, that's hysterically funny. Belarusians? Who would have thunk it?

"And just for the record, my little sister wouldn't have a clue as to how to do all the stuff you just mentioned. I think you might have pissed off a few people during the past five years, the way you pissed me off, and now they're retaliating against you. I can just see you languishing in a federal penitentiary. In the general population no less."

"Where's my fucking money, Emma? I want it back," Jeff shouted as he came up and out of his chair, his face dark with hatred.

"I don't know where your fucking money is, Jefferson, nor do I care."

"Stop lying to me. I'm ruined. For God's sake, Emma, appeal to your sister. I know you two are behind this. Please, help me out here, or we're all going to go to prison. Me, Jason, Josh, and John. You don't want that on your conscience, do you?"

"I think this is where I tell you to hit the road, Jack. Enlist the aid of your trophy wives to help you out. Or maybe you can send Missy out to get a job to help pay the rent. We're done here."

Emma stood up and was starting toward the front door when Jeff grabbed her by the arm and swung her around.

The door to the laundry room swung open as if a tornado had invaded the room, and three women, brandishing brooms and mops, started swinging them. It wasn't a pretty sight. When Jeff Davis was firmly on the floor, spread-eagled, with stilettos pressing on his neck, Robin asked sweetly, "Now can we strip him naked and toss his ass out in the snow?"

"Well, yeahhh," Emma drawled. While the girls were proceeding, she looked out the front window. "I think it might take him a good ten minutes to clear off his windshield."

"Is that a fact?" Alice grunted as she and Robin hauled Jeff to his feet.

"I am so tempted to shove this mop up his ass," Clare singsonged, pushing the mop handle into Jeff's back to push him forward. Emma opened the front door wide, and together, they all gave a mighty shove; Jeff was propelled forward like he was shot from a cannon. Emma threw his outerwear and boots after him, then locked the door and shot the dead bolt.

"I think that went rather well, don't you, girls?" Emma said.

"We drank all the wine. You got any more?" Alice asked.

"I do, but it's not as good as the other two bottles."

"Oh, who cares? It's wine, isn't it? Right now, I'd drink that stuff that comes out of a box to celebrate," Clare said.

"Would you really have shoved that mop up his ass, Clare?" Robin asked.

"I would have given it my best shot," Clare responded smartly.

And the party was on, with toast after toast, all of them to Trish in one way or another.

CHAPTER 22

It was three o'clock in the morning when Emma donned her robe and tiptoed downstairs, but not before she looked in on her guests to make sure everyone was sleeping soundly. They were. In the kitchen, the fire that had blazed all evening was just hot embers, the flames long gone. She threw in two logs, made herself a cup of hot tea, then sat down in the rocking chair next to the fire. She stared into the flames as she tried to calm down. The meeting with her exhusband had stirred up all the old hatred, the five long years of not knowing if she would make it or not. So many times she had thought she might have to apply for public assistance or food stamps. Even now, five years later, the thought made her cringe in shame.

She didn't think she'd ever be able to let go of the hatred for her ex-husband, but somewhere, somehow, at some point in time, she realized that she had, in fact, let it go. Then, when she was sitting in front of him earlier in the evening, she'd been stunned to realize she felt sorry for him. *What goes around comes around.* She smiled to herself in the near-dark kitchen. She looked to the window and realized the floodlights were still on. She got up and walked over to the garden window to see mountains of snow. It looked beautiful, clean, quiet, and peaceful, and it was still snowing. She took a moment to wonder how Jeff had made it home and if he had hypothermia. Did Simone wrap her arms around him to give him her own body warmth? She laughed out loud at the thought. Simone was stick thin, without an ounce of fat on her lean frame. Poor Jeff.

Emma looked into the teapot; satisfied that the tea leaves had steeped long enough, she poured a cup and added some honey. She carried it back to the rocking chair. In the early days of her marriage, after Missy had come along, some of the best, the most pleasurable moments of her life were rocking in the chair, her child cuddled to her chest. So long ago, so many memories. All gone now. She hoped that new memories would surface, that her life would settle down and she could be happy again.

Happy? Exactly what was happy? She had to admit to herself that she didn't know the meaning of that word. At that moment. Emma closed her eyes and thought about Trish. She calculated the time difference in Dubai, reached for her phone, and pressed the number one on the speed dial. She listened to the phone ring on the other side of the world. She was about to hang up when she heard her sister's voice.

"It's Emma, Trish. I'm calling to give you an update. Are you okay? I haven't heard from you. By the way, it's snowing to beat the band here. I think we probably have around eight or nine inches by now, and it is still snowing," she babbled nonstop.

Her sister's voice was crystal clear, but it sounded strained to Emma's ears. She repeated her question. "Are you okay? Did you and Malik talk? Did you resolve things?"

"We did. Listen, Emma, can I call you back in, say, an hour? This isn't a good time, and yes, I do need to talk to you, but not right now. I promise I will call you back, okay? By the way, why are you still up at this hour? Maybe I should be asking you if you're okay, instead of the other way around."

"That's what I wanted to tell you. Jeff came here in the middle of the storm. But all of that can wait for you to call me back. Are you sure you're okay, Trish? I'm not liking what I'm hearing in your voice."

"I'm fine, Emma. You know me too well. I will call you back. Good-bye."

Emma looked down at the phone in her hand. She blinked. "Well, little sis, I don't believe a word you just said." Emma's thoughts turned wild and crazy. Then, as she tried to imagine what was going on, on the other side of the world, that would make her sister sound so . . . Her mind searched for the right word, and *sad* was the best she could come up with. Whatever it was, she'd know in an hour.

With nothing else to do, Emma decided to cut the pie, which, in the excitement following dinner, no one had touched. She cut a generous slice, replenished her tea, and took her seat again by the fire, but not before she added another log. She loved the niche carved into both sides of the fireplace, which was stacked high with good-burning hard oak wood. She made a mental note to call someone to deliver more wood later in the week. So many things to do. So much to tell Trish.

Her teacup empty, her slice of pie finished, Emma leaned back and let her thoughts take her back to her past. Eventually, she dozed off, only to wake when her phone, which was still in her hand, chirped to life. She blinked and clicked it on. She heard her sister ask if she was still awake.

"I am. I dozed a little while I waited for your call. Something is wrong. Am I right, Trish? I could hear it in your voice."

"Tell me your news first, and then I'll tell you mine."

Emma let loose and told her everything that had transpired during Jeff's visit. She expected her sister to hoot with laughter, but she didn't. Instead, all she said was, "It serves him right."

"How did you do all that, Trish? I'd really like to know. And, someday, I'd like to shake your hand for doing it. I had no idea marrying a sheik would make you so powerful. The girls are over the moon with what's going on. They keep saying karma is a bitch. I guess it is. Now, tell me how you did it?"

"Emma, I didn't do it, but I did pay someone to do it. I guess he deserves the reputation he has, because he pulled it off and made it work. All it took was a lot of money. Now, listen to me. Check your e-mails daily, and if you see some strange ones, check them out. Do not assume they're spam. Open them, and you'll get instructions as to where your . . . *severance* money is. Three million each. Make sure you all get a good tax man to represent you. Did you find a building for your new venture?"

Emma's brain was reeling. "Did you say three million *each*?"

"I did say that, and did you hear the part about getting a good tax man?"

"I heard that. I will. We will. Oh, my God! I don't know what to say."

"About the building . . ."

"Yes, I did find one right on Main Street, but the rent is ridiculous. We would be better off buying the building. There's an apartment on the second floor. We could rent that out, and it would help with the cash flow. The first floor is seven thousand square feet. The building is in good condition. Now, mind you, I haven't had time to look at it in person — I just took the virtual tour online — but I think it's perfect."

"Then by all means, let's buy it. Set it all up and let me know. One other thing. Connie is sending you all the things that I brought back with me. It's coming by UPS, so you should have it all by the middle of next week. I've already talked to Soraya, and she's excited to help. She needs a few weeks of downtime. She just had her new baby, a girl, and she's calling her Patricia

Ami. She named her after me. Isn't that sweet?"

"Very sweet. Now it's your turn. Tell me what's wrong. Is it what you thought, what you worried about?"

"Not even close, Emma. Malik is dying. He doesn't have . . . long. When he went away, he . . . he was going from doctor to doctor all over the world. His mind was someplace else, and he didn't want me to know. That's the bottom line. And before you can ask, I'm handling it. Maybe I should say that I'm trying to handle it. I swear, Emma, Malik is handling it better than I am. Rashid is . . . a basket case. Soraya and I are the strong ones, if you can believe that."

"Oh, dear God! Do you want me to come over there? I will. I can make plans to leave as soon as the snow lets up and the airports reopen. What can I do? I need to do something for you. The girls will agree."

"I appreciate it, Emma, but there's nothing for you to do. There's nothing I can do but be here. Malik is holding on well right now. He takes a lot of medicine, and he sleeps or naps a lot. He is doing his best to eat. We sit in the garden, we talk, we laugh, and we drink beer, which he is not supposed to do, but he said he doesn't care. He lets me drive the rattletrap, and we go for drives. We watch a lot of old movies. Soraya brings the kids over a few times each day, and Malik holds them and sings to them. It's beautiful to watch.

"Oh, Malik changed that crazy-ass rule that was in place about me not having a baby in five years. That's now off the books. And listen to this, when Malik . . . when Malik is . . . gone, I'm going to be the ruler of this emirate. Imagine that!" Trish said as she burst into tears.

Yeah, imagine that, Emma thought. Tears rolled down her cheeks as she listened to her sister sob her heart out. There was nothing to say or do, so she wisely remained silent until Trish was done crying.

"Sorry, Em. I can't let Malik or the others see me cry. There's no place here that is secret, where I can go and howl my guts out."

"Yes, I'm sure, Emma."

"No, Emma. I think Malik would think the end is nearer than it is if you showed up. I appreciate the offer, though. The time will come, I'm sure, when I will need your shoulders to cry on. But until then, let's just leave things as they are, okay?"

Emma sniffled into a paper towel she'd ripped off the roll and managed to say,

"Okay, if that's the way you want it."

"That's the way it has to be, not that I want it that way."

"Did you tell Malik's friends? You mentioned how close they are. Do they know?"

"Not to my knowledge. I agree with you, though. I don't think Malik wants them to know. I'm thinking that he's thinking the whole bunch of them would drop everything and hightail it over here. Guys are . . . Guys are guys. You know what I mean, Emma. They can't handle things like this. At some point, I will get in touch with Zack. I just don't know when that will be."

"Do you know —"

"No one will tell me. But then, I haven't actually asked, because I don't want to start counting days and hours, that kind of thing. Listen, Emma, I have to go now. If I don't call you, don't worry."

"What?" Emma all but screeched. "You drop something like that on me, and then you tell me not to worry! Let's get real here. I was born to worry. Okay, okay, I'll try not to worry."

The sisters, both crying, told each other how much they loved each other, and then the call ended. Emma swiped at her eyes, then looked up to see her friends standing in the doorway. She wailed louder now that they were all awake, her shoulders shaking. They swooped down on her like avenging angels, wrapping her in three sets of arms.

She told her friends the news between her broken sobs. And then they, too, cried and wailed for the unfairness of it all.

That was what friends did. They rallied around in support, Emma thought. And that was the mark of a tried-and-true real friend. And then she had a second thought. She thought about Malik's friend Zack and how upset he was going to be when he found out his best friend was dying and no one had told him so he could tell the others. What was that old adage? *Sometimes the best-laid plans of mice and men . . .* Emma never finished that thought, because she didn't want to cry again.

"What would you like to do now, Malik? How does a banana split sound? We can go to town and sit at one of those little outdoor cafés and watch the world go by. Are you up to it?"

"I am, but I'm not really in the mood for a banana split. I'd much prefer a nice cold bottle of beer and some really salty chips, and I'd like to do it out in the garden. That's if you don't mind. And I think it's time for you to tell me something that I can see is bothering you. You should know by now that anything you do or say is not something I will be uncomfortable with. So, what do you say?"

Trish laughed. "And what palace snitch told you something is bothering me?"

Malik laughed. "The snitches, as you call them, would be terribly upset if I didn't listen to them when they feel they have news to report. Most times, I don't even listen. I just pretend, to keep them all happy. It's a way of life, Trish. Tell me what is troubling you. It isn't the money you spent, is it?"

Husband and wife walked along, arm in arm, down the palace halls and out to one of the many gardens. Trish bit down on her lip. How much should she confide, or should she just blow it all off? If she did that, Malik, she knew, would drop it, but she felt the need to unload her worries. At least some of her worries. She struggled as to how to respond to his question.

"In part. In the whole of my life, Malik, I never spent more than fifty dollars at a time without hours and days of anguish. Should I? Shouldn't I? That kind of thing. Then in a few hours I blew nineteen million dollars and didn't bat an eye. I did that, I spent nineteen million dollars of *your* money, and you never once asked me what I did with it.

That just blows my mind, plus the fact that you replenished the money. So, to answer your question, partly, yes, it bothers me, but I did not spend it on myself.

"Sit down and drink your beer. See? That's what I mean. We were whispering, and here is the beer on the table even before we got here. Someday, I want to know how that *really* works. Someone around here must be clairvoyant."

Trish waited until Malik was halfway through his beer and salty chips, which he wasn't supposed to be drinking or eating, before she continued, "Do you want the long or the short version?" she quipped.

"We have all night, my dear, so let's go with the long version."

Trish started to talk then. She was like a runaway train as she recounted her and Emma's life up until her last visit home to Princeton. Malik listened intently but said nothing as Trish purged herself. When she finally stopped to catch her breath, Malik asked a question.

"First of all, it is your money, not mine, and you can spend it any way you want. Why didn't you step in sooner?"

"I tried. Emma is so proud. She thinks because she is the big sister, she has to do it all. And she was humiliated, ashamed, embarrassed. I understood all that. As for Jeff, that's a whole other story. Until this last visit home, I had no clue that there was anything I could do other than give her money, which she simply would not accept. Networking, Malik, is where it's at."

"Explain that, Trish. I know what networking is, but how did you make it apply to your sister and her ex-husband?"

Trish rattled on again about the nameless, faceless person whom she'd paid five million dollars so he could buy beachfront property. She stopped in her monologue when Malik started to laugh and couldn't stop. Thinking Malik thought she was gullible, she responded defensively.

"Aha, you think I bought a pig in a poke, eh? Well, you might need another beer for the rest of the story. But I will tell you this much up front. You will be surprised to learn that the five million I paid is already back in my account. What do you think about that, wise guy? And the whole thing went down as you were serving your walking papers on International Alliance Capital. You and your sheiks were, innocently, of course, providing the interference needed to bring it off without anyone being the wiser. So listen up now."

Malik listened, his eyes getting wider by

the second. He was so stunned, he was speechless. Finally, he found his tongue. "You didn't make this up? That all really happened?"

"As God is my judge. They're destitute. All four of them. All it would have cost was the money to buy a fortune's worth of beachfront property, and even that was refunded." This time, Trish laughed herself, but she was laughing more at the expression on her husband's face than at the actual deed itself and its aftermath.

Gasping for breath, his beer forgotten, Malik managed to gasp out, "And you did this all yourself? I wouldn't have known where to even begin to put something like it in motion."

"Well, let's be honest here. I had a lot of help. I just used your money to make it happen."

"Again, my dear, it is *your* money, not mine. Let's be clear on that. Why do I have the feeling that there's more?"

Trish burst out laughing. "Because there is more. That's why. Now listen up. This happened last night. Emma just called me a little while ago to tell me. Seems she was too wired to sleep, and she wanted me to know."

Malik's eyes twinkled. This was the most

animated she'd seen her husband since her return. She told him then about Jeff's visit, the way the women attacked him, then stripped him down and pushed him out into the snow. "Emma said it took Jeff over ten minutes to clear the snow off his windshield, in his birthday suit. When he was finished, mostly because she wanted no reminder of his visit, she threw his clothes out the door. He scooped them up, got into the car, and drove off."

This time Malik rolled off his chair onto the grass and kept on rolling, shrieking with laughter. Inside the palace, hundreds of eyes watched these strange goings-on. Then more eyes appeared when Shaykhah joined the emir and started rolling in the grass, their laughter bouncing all over the place.

"What the hell are they doing out there?" Rashid hissed to his wife.

Soraya tried not to laugh. "Maybe we should try it and see what happens." Rashid looked at his wife as though she had sprouted a second head. "I think in America this might be called a mating dance, even though they aren't dancing, but rolling around. I think it's the same thing. I'm game, Rashid, now that I'm *fixed*."

The panic on Rashid's face was palpable. "Well, that . . . that's not going to happen anytime soon."

Soraya pressed on and started to shed her clothing. "Just remember how lonely and cold you were down in the bowels of the palace." A shoe went flying. "And how angry I was." The second shoe joined the first. "And how you gasped in delight when I allowed you to take me in your arms." Her top sailed up, then down, to land on top of a fluted lampshade.

"I can't. . . . You can't. . . . This is . . . I am the acting emir now. *Stop that right this instant!*"

Soraya stepped out of her skirt, picked it up, and started to twirl it as she undulated her hips. Then the skirt sailed across the room. She stood in all her glory in the push-up bra from Victoria's Secret that she'd purchased in Las Vegas. The leopard-skin thong was so skimpy, Rashid covered his eyes as Soraya danced around.

Out in the garden, Malik stopped long enough to glance down at a text that was coming through. He blinked, tried not to laugh, then blinked again. "C'mon. This is something we both need to see. It's happening right now, outside my sister's apartments."

Trish had to run to keep up with Malik's long-legged stride.

"Shhh, not a sound now. This is the perfect spot. It's called spying, Trish."

"Oh, my Goddd," Trish hissed as Malik clapped a hand over her mouth. He covered his own mouth with his other hand.

"You need to stop this right now, Soraya."

Soraya ignored her husband and his words. "Ooh, I wish I had some music. I could really do a number with music." Soraya giggled as she moved one way, then the other. Rashid tried to catch her, but she nimbly danced out of his way. Which was her intention all along. "Wait till you see what I can really do with *a pole*! I took lessons in Las Vegas. Later, if you're good, I might, I say I might, give you a lap dance."

Malik looked at Trish, who shook her head violently.

The chase was on.

Rashid was all legs and arms as he did his best to capture his wife. Finally, when he did, Soraya looked up at him and said sweetly, "Sorry. Four more weeks to go before we can have sex. Did you forget that I just had a baby?"

Rashid sat down on the floor and dropped his head into his hands. Soraya gathered up her clothes and shoes and blew her husband a kiss.

Malik reached down for Trish's hand.

"Play along, okay? He's such a stiff some-times."

"Ah, Rashid, is there a reason you're sitting here on the floor? It doesn't look very emirish to me. Is something wrong?"

"You know damn well what's wrong. Go ahead. Torture me. See if I care. I suppose you watched it all."

"Well, not all of it. Just the last part. Sometimes, as you well know, the palace snitches are a little slow on the uptake. Is there anything Trish or I can do for you before we return to our quarters?" Malik's laughter and Trish's giggles did not go unnoticed by Rashid.

"Just shoot me and put me out of my misery," was Rashid's comeback.

Malik laughed again. "Look at it this way, my good, true, and loyal friend. You are the envy of every man in this palace." He turned to Trish and said, "Come along, dear. We've invaded my dear friend's privacy long enough."

Trish leaned over and whispered in Rashid's ear. "Be glad she cares enough for you to do such a thing. A love like that, my friend, is hard to find. Treasure it."

Rashid raised his eyes to Trish. "No, she did not learn that in Las Vegas. She was teasing you. You really need to pay more attention to your wife, Rashid. You truly do."

Rashid sat quietly for almost an hour as his thoughts took him everywhere and nowhere. Why was life so complicated? Why were women so much smarter than men? Why were men like him so stupid? When he received no answers to his agonizing thoughts, he got up and stomped his way into his apartments, where Soraya was waiting for him with a cup of tea and a plate of sweet cakes.

She smiled at him, stood on her toes, and kissed him gently. "Like the song says, Rashid, I will always love you."

"And I you." Rashid knew in his heart that no truer words had ever come out of his mouth.

CHAPTER 23

Winter gave way to spring; then spring sprinted into summer. It was autumn before Trish knew it. Her thoughts took her back to Princeton, where she'd grown up. This was football season, the leaves were changing, and there was wood smoke in the air from burning leaves as parents and youngsters decorated their porches with jack-o'-lanterns that some doting fathers had carved for the little ones. Stories of goblins and witches were the order of the day as children planned their costumes for the parties and parades that always took place on Halloween, a glorious, fun time when she and Emma were little kids. Then it would be Thanksgiving, and in the blink of an eye, the Christmas season would arrive. Surely, Emma would do it up royally for the first time in her new house. She'd always loved the holidays, just the way Trish had.

Emma's last call had been so upbeat.

She'd met a man, she said. The foreman of the construction company the girls had hired to renovate the building in which they had their new business. It had started out as a friendship and had developed into something more. Emma was what Trish called a happy camper these days. The last thing Emma had said before ending the call was, "Trish, I think I'm in love with Alex Thornton."

If there was any blight on her sister's new-found happiness, it was her daughter, Missy, who blamed her entirely for the misery her father was going through. To say they were estranged was to put it mildly. Emma, while sad at the estrangement, had said perhaps someday Missy would come around.

The Four *J*s were living together in a three-bedroom apartment in the same complex Emma and the girls had moved out of. Talk about payback. What Trish found incredibly amusing was that the Four *J*s, with not a day's worth of litigation experience and not even that much criminal-law experience, were representing themselves, which just went to show, as the old adage had it, that their lawyers had fools for clients. Prison was guaranteed, but if there was some way to delay the inevitable, the Four *J*s knew how to play it. The trophy wives were long gone. Emma had said she couldn't be sure, but she'd heard that the various kids were donating money to their fathers to ensure that they at least had enough to eat and pay the rent.

Clare was talking of marriage, Robin was fending off two suitors, and Alice was content to go out from time to time on a dinner date but wasn't ready for a commitment anytime soon. All in all, everyone on her side of the aisle was happy, according to Emma.

Trish tucked her cell phone into the pocket of her slacks. She was tired. No, she was numb. She could barely think these days. And she thought of these days, as she put it, as the last days. Time was reduced to hours. She wished she could cry, but there were no tears left to cry. She'd been banished from the sickroom, as she called it, because Malik was being bathed.

Hours. Minutes. Seconds. How many? She yanked at the cell phone in her pocket, scrolled down till she found Zack's cell phone number. She tried to calculate the time difference, but her mind refused to co-operate. She pressed in the digits and waited. Zack picked up on the fifth ring. She almost smiled when she heard, "It's your nickel. Talk to me."

"It's Trish, Zack. Is this a good time to talk?"

"Anytime is a good time to talk to you, Trish. What's up?"

Trish drew a deep breath. She could do this. She really could. She *had* to do this. "Malik is dying, Zack. We're down to . . . hours right now. I wanted to call you and the guys sooner, but Malik made me promise not to because he said you would all drop everything and hustle on over here. He . . . he said he didn't want you all to see him the way he is now. I tried to tell him it wouldn't matter, but he was adamant. Please say something, Zack. Maybe I should just hang up."

"No, no, don't hang up." The voice was so tortured, Trish bit down on her lip and tasted her own salty blood. "Is there *anything* I can do?"

"I wish there were, Zack. God, how I wish that. No, there is nothing. Well, you can pray for a miracle. That's what I've been doing. Before you ask, I found out only when I got back here. I have to go now, Zack. You'll tell the others?"

"Yes, of course. Will you call me when . . ."

"I will, Zack." Trish broke the connection and stuffed the phone back in her pocket. It was the first and only time she'd disobeyed her husband's wishes. She looked up to see Soraya standing over her.

"You called Zack?"

"Yes. Yes, I did. I had to do it."

"It was the right thing to do. Come along. Malik wants to talk to you. He said they prettied him up for you," Soraya said, her voice choked with emotion. "Rashid is almost catatonic. You and I have to hold things together, Trish."

"Did I tell you my sister is in love?" Trish said inanely. "Her daughter still refuses to talk to her and blames her entirely for the mess her father is in."

"That will change in time. Time heals all wounds. Do you believe that, Trish?" she asked fretfully.

"No."

"Me either."

"How are the children?"

"Fine. More or less. They sense something is awry. I guess Rashid and I give off vibes even the little ones can pick up on. Oh, Trish, I just want to go to sleep, wake up, and pretend this was all just a bad dream."

"Me too," Trish said softly. "Did the doctor say anything?"

"Not verbally. He didn't have to. His eyes said it all for him. You need to hurry. The doctor said Malik is fretting because you aren't there. He has something to tell you."

Trish sprinted down the corridors and ended up winded as she came to the door of Malik's sickroom. She took a moment to try to calm herself. She took a deep breath, smoothed down her hair, tried to relax her facial muscles so she could smile when she entered the room.

Malik's voice was so weak, Trish had to lean over to hear his tortured whisper. She listened, her eyes popping wide. She looked across at Rashid, who just stared at her. He gave a slight nod to indicate he knew and agreed with what Malik was saying. She sensed there was no time to argue, just time to agree, which she did.

Trish squeezed Malik's hand in both of hers, hoping she wasn't breaking the now-fragile bones. Trish leaned over again.

"Tell me. I want to hear you say the words, Trish."

Trish tried to swallow. Her tongue felt like it was three sizes too big for her mouth. Somewhere, somehow, she found the words. "I will do all you asked of me. I promise. I never broke a promise to you, Malik. Never."

Rashid stepped closer and reached for Malik's other hand and clasped it in his. Soraya stood at the foot of the bed, tears trailing down her cheeks. The doctor and the two nurses stood near the door, their eyes wet, their faces solemn.

Malik struggled to breathe. He needed to say something, wanted to say it, and he fought to get the words out. Only Trish could hear them.

And then he was gone.

The doctor raced over, his cheeks wet. He did what he had to do and pronounced Sheik Malik bin Al Mohammed dead.

Everyone in the room clamored to hear what the sheik's last words were.

Trish smiled. "He . . . said . . . he said that he always loved a good conspiracy."

And then everyone bustled. A gurney appeared like magic. Then everything moved at the speed of light, and before she knew it, Trish was in the back of a long white van, Rashid, Soraya, and the doctor alongside her. They all prayed over Malik's still body. The van raced away from the palace and through the streets, which were somehow free of traffic. Fourteen minutes later, the driver swung into a parking lot that was bare of vehicles and backed up to what looked like a loading platform. The gurney was unloaded. The occupants of the van scrambled out and walked around to the entrance of the crematorium.

They were served tea, which no one drank. They sat quietly, no words passing among them for four long, unbearable hours. When the huge mahogany doors opened, they all stood. A man in Western dress approached with a wooden box, which was sealed. He handed it to Trish.

As one, they turned to leave, Rashid in the lead. Outside, a long black car waited. They climbed in. Once again there was no traffic, and the long black car raced to its destination. The moment it stopped, Rashid literally flew out of the vehicle and held the door for Trish and his wife. The three of them sprinted across the tarmac to the waiting plane. Out of the corner of her eye, Trish saw one of the palace guards race up the portable stairs and her gold chest with the intricate lock and her purse disappear inside the plane.

"Go! They're burning fuel, and you know how Malik hated when that happened. Do not ask, little sister. We are doing what Malik wanted."

"But I am leaving you to face . . ."

"Go! Everything is in place."

Trish was blinded with tears. "I'll be back. I don't know when, but I'll be back."

Soraya clung to her. She bent over to kiss the box in Trish's hands. Rashid did the same thing before he gave her a swat on her rump. "Go already!" His voice was so tortured, all Trish could do was fly up the steps. She didn't look back.

That part of her life had ended.

The flight was long, but Trish didn't sleep. From time to time, she smelled tantalizing aromas coming from the galley, but she didn't partake of any of the food with which the stewards tried to entice her. She did drink cup after cup of the coffee that Malik so loved. Twice she got up during the long flight to use the lavatory, but she carried the sealed box with her.

In her seat, she talked in low whispers to the box in her lap. She didn't much care that the stewards were whispering about her. The truth was, she really didn't much care about anything but the box in her lap.

Hours and hours later, when the plane was ready to make its descent into Las Vegas's McCarran International Airport, a steward appeared holding a long white cashmere winter coat and a matching pair of white suede boots. Soraya had, indeed, thought of everything. It was winter again, almost Christmas again here in Nevada. She'd left the warm weather behind when she boarded the plane. She saw the gold chest and her purse at the front of the plane.

Forty-five minutes later, Trish was walking up the steps to her town house. She fished around inside her purse for her key, but before she could find it, the door opened, and Emma literally lifted her off her feet and swept her inside. One of the stewards was right behind her. He set the gold chest down, turned, and walked to the door. He reached inside his jacket for a white envelope.

"It's the information on the plane, where it will be hangared and the like," he said.

"I don't understand what that means," Trish said.

"The Gulfstream is yours now. It belonged to your husband, is what Rashid told me. I'm sorry we had to meet under these sad circumstances. Good-bye, Shaykhah." The man bowed low and backed out the door.

"Wait, wait, where are you going now?"

"Back to Dubai. It's a turnaround flight for us. We're flying commercial." He bowed low, and then the door closed.

Trish whirled around. "How did . . . Who?"

"Rashid called me. I also spoke to Soraya. All I had to do was go to the airport and the ticket was waiting for me. You have your own airplane! Amazing. Come, Trish. Let

369

me take your coat off. At some point, my dear, you have to let go of the box, even if it's just for a few minutes. Please, Trish, don't make this any harder than it is. Help me out here."

Trish walked into the living room and set the wooden box down on the coffee table, then slipped out of her coat. She was wearing a sundress with spaghetti straps. She looked down at the white suede boots and smiled.

"I made dinner, and yes, you are going to eat, even if I have to spoon-feed you. Go upstairs and take a shower and put on some warm clothes. We'll eat by the fire. I'm going to make us both one hell of a stiff drink. After that, we'll talk and . . . and whatever. The box is not going to go anywhere. Scoot now. This is your big sister telling you what to do, so will you just go already?"

"What did you cook?" Trish called over her shoulder.

Hands on her hips, Emma cocked her head to the side. "Now, what do you think I cooked? It's thirty-two degrees outside, and if you had been paying attention, you would have seen the snow flurries. The weatherman said possibly four inches of snow, but to answer your question, stew and apple pie."

"Sounds good. Actually, I am hungry. I can't remember when I ate last. Maybe yesterday or the day before. Whatever . . ."

It was almost midnight when the two sisters climbed the stairs to the second floor. They'd eaten the succulent stew, feasted on the apple pie, and each of them had consumed three double scotch and sodas. And they were now ready for bed.

"I don't know how to thank you, Emma. I was so dreading walking into a cold, empty house, carrying this box. You made it . . . all bearable. I don't want you to worry about me. I'm okay. I really am. I've had almost a year to prepare myself. That doesn't mean I'm . . . Oh, you know what I mean. What I wasn't prepared for was the cremation. Malik and Rashid arranged that and didn't tell me until . . . well, until the end. Malik didn't want to be buried in a hole in the desert. That was the bottom line. It's so sad, Emma. He was caught between two cultures, and in the end, he chose the one he wanted. Rashid and Soraya will make it right for those who have something to say. Malik replaced the council in the summer with more forward-thinking younger people. I'm still the shaykhah, but I handed over my power to Rashid and Soraya. It's sort of like power of attorney over here but a hell of a lot more complicated."

"What are you going to do with the ashes?"

"Keep them on the mantel in my bedroom so Malik is close to me when I sleep. He said" — Trish's voice broke — "he said I would know when the right time was to . . . to . . . The words he used were 'disperse them.' He said I wasn't to keep them forever, and I promised. I really am okay, Emma. Sad, bereaved, but okay. I'm also relieved that Malik is free of his pain and in a better place. Everyone says those words, but the listeners think them trite somehow. I don't."

"That's good. Breakfast is at seven. Don't even think about blowing me off. I shopped all day yesterday for food. We could survive in a storm for six months with what I bought. You know I love to cook, and you sure do need fattening up. Good night, little sister."

"Night, Emma. Thanks for coming. Thanks for being my sister, and thanks for just being you."

"Yeah, yeah, yeah," Emma grumbled good-naturedly as she walked through the door to her bedroom. "See ya at breakfast."

"Yeah, see you at breakfast."

Trish's last conscious thought before she fell asleep was, *And now this is my new life. I've come full circle. Good night, Malik. I will always love you, just like the song says. Always and forever, then into eternity, plus one more day.*

EPILOGUE

Three years later . . .

Trish squatted on her haunches and looked at the ground, defying a weed to poke through the freshly cultivated soil. She called this minuscule patch of a garden her own little paradise. From time to time, she likened it to the lush, almost tropical, gardens back at the Dubai palace. She'd planted each bloom herself, talking to the plant, and then, as she always did, talking to Malik. The fact that neither answered her made no difference.

Starting early in the spring, Trish had worked in her little paradise for three hours each morning, before the heat of the day took over. This year was no different. She looked over at her garden tools, which consisted of a pair of scissors, not shears, a big serving spoon, and a salad fork from her kitchen for turning over the rich soil she'd purchased at Home Depot. She didn't bother with gardening gloves, either, because she liked to feel the earth on her hands. The fact that her nails were a disgrace didn't bother her at all.

These days, as most days since she'd returned to Las Vegas, had been busy days. She didn't cry as much, and she didn't sleep all that well, but she knew she was progressing into what she called her boring world. She got up in the morning, made sure she cooked breakfast for herself, checked in with Emma and talked for at least half an hour. Then she did her gardening, which she actually looked forward to. By the time she finished her stint in the garden paradise, it was lunchtime. She made sure she ate, because she'd promised Emma, and a promise was a promise. Then she worked on her philanthropy, which consisted of giving away what she still insisted was Malik's money to worthy endeavors that she investigated thoroughly before handing over a check. It was hard giving away the money, whittling it down, because every month, more money appeared in the account. She called it magic money. Then, when she finished with that, she ran whatever errands she had to run and came home to cook a dinner for herself. Her evenings were spent reading, calling Soraya to check on the kids and gossip, and sometimes to cry. On very rare occasions, they laughed together.

Twice, she'd made plans to return to Dubai, and both times she'd canceled her plans at the last moment. She told herself she just wasn't ready to go back there. Maybe she would never be ready to go back. She simply didn't know. One day at a time was what had gotten her to this place in time, so she wasn't about to tamper with a work in progress.

Trish knew she wasn't happy, but she also knew she was content. She told herself it was a good thing that she knew the difference between the two emotions.

Ironically, since her return, her best friend had turned out to be Ernie. The girls, her old friends, had scattered, moved, gotten married, and relocated. One night a week, she had Ernie and his wife, Bella, for dinner, and one night, usually on the weekend, they invited her to their home for dinner. Ernie was now a full-time choreographer and much sought after, partly thanks to Trish's magic money. When her old boss Nathan retired shortly after her return to Vegas, she'd talked the owners of the casino into giving Ernie a chance, and it had paid off big for the young man. It went without saying that some of the magic money changed hands until Ernie proved himself. When he did, the casino even paid her back, which almost blew her socks off. And it was the best-kept secret in Vegas, so it really was true, that saying, "What happens in Vegas stays in Vegas."

Trish had just set a place for herself at the counter, cut her tuna sandwich, eyed the celery and carrot sticks, along with the peach, that were to be her lunch, when the doorbell rang. She frowned. No one visited her. No one but Ernie and Bella, and they always called before coming over. She wasn't expecting UPS or FedEx, and the mail had arrived earlier. The doorbell chimed again, a cheery five-note ditty.

She yelled, "Coming!" and raced to the door. She opened it wide and stood in shocked amazement at the man standing on her little stoop with a bouquet of sad-looking flowers in his hand.

"Zack!" she squealed.

He imitated her. "Trish!"

"What are you doing here? Come in! Come in! I was just going to have lunch. Can you stay? Did you eat?"

"I can stay, and I can eat. I'm in Vegas for a conference. It started yesterday, and we broke early today. I thought I'd come by and see how you were and maybe take you out to dinner this evening. What do you say?"

"I say yes! It is so good to see you. How have you been? How are all the guys? I can't wait to hear how everyone is."

"We're all fine. I can break it down later, but more importantly, how are *you* doing?"

Trish waved her hands about. "What you see is what you get. Pretty much the same old, same old. I'm sorry I wasn't a better e-mail pal. Sometimes, the days just seem to get away from me. Other times, they just drag. I try to keep busy giving away Malik's money, but as fast as I give it away, there's more to take its place. I gave up trying to figure it all out. I help my sister from time to time. I told you about the shop that she and her friends operate back in Princeton. If I see a one-of-a-kind something, I ship it up to her. They are doing fantastically well. What about you?"

"Like you, same old, same old. A little older, more gray hair, put on a few pounds. I try for the gym at least twice a week, but it doesn't always work out. There are days when I get fed up with teaching eager and not-so-eager minds and wish I were a plumber or a mailman. The feeling doesn't last long, though. By the way, great sandwich."

"I cook a lot. Emma made me promise. You know, one of those promises carved in stone, that I would cook and eat three meals a day. I'm pretty good at it." Trish suddenly burst out laughing. "Actually, I pretty much throw stuff in a Crock-Pot, and whatever comes out is what I eat. I already did that earlier, just chicken and vegetables. So if you'd like to eat here instead of going out, that would work for me. I have some good wine and also some good beer."

"Then I'm your guy. This really is a good sandwich."

Trish laughed again. This was so nice. She had company, and it was an old friend. What could be nicer?

"Have you gone back to Dubai? How is Rashid and his wife?"

"No, I haven't gone back. I had plans to go twice, but I changed my mind at the last moment. I don't know if I'll ever go back. They gave me a plane. Did I tell you that? The reason was, so all I had to do was call up, say, 'Fuel up,' and off we go. It's sitting in a hangar somewhere. Rashid is doing well. Malik would be so proud of him. Soraya is, first and foremost, a mother. The kids are growing and giving her a run for her money. She complains, but she loves it. She works a little for my sister, finding those one-of-a-kind treasures. She says it helps to do something besides chasing kids. We talk just about every evening. I miss them."

"Are you happy?"

"Not like I was happy with Malik. Let's just say I'm content these days. I try not to think about or dwell in the past, and Malik is the past. It was a different life and it's gone now and I can't get it back, so I have to move forward. At first I fought it, but things are better now. What about you? Why haven't you ever married?" Trish asked bluntly.

"I guess the right girl just hasn't found me yet." Zack laughed.

"What? You're waiting for her to knock on your front door?"

"I have to admit, that would be nice." Zack laughed again.

Trish joined in the laughter. "Come with me. I want to show you my garden. I work in it every day, right up until late fall."

"Wow! You need sunglasses out here. I never saw so many flowers in one spot in my whole life. This is beautiful. Ah, those flowers I brought you, they were the only ones left in the gift shop at the hotel. I am so ashamed after seeing these."

"Don't be. It's the thought that counts. How long are you going to be in town?"

"Until Monday. I can stay longer if you take me around sightseeing. As you know, us professors do not work in the summer. Well, some of us do, but I don't. I was going to go home to the farm, but my parents are going camping with some of the grandkids for weeks at a time, so I elected to stay home. I might take some road trips to see some of the guys. We're going to get together in New York over Thanksgiving, all of us. Each one of the guys committed. They're bringing their spouses. Can you join us as Malik's stand-in?"

Trish didn't think twice before she said, "I would love to."

"Great. That's settled, then. Now, what should we do?"

"How about I make us a pitcher of iced tea, and we sit on my tiny, as in 'tiny balcony,' and play catch-up? I can actually fit two canvas chairs on it. My sister calls it a platform with a fence, but it works for me."

"Then let's do it. I bet we can talk for hours and hours and hours, or until that stuff in your Crock-Pot is ready to eat."

And that was exactly what they did. Then, when dinner was over and the cleanup done, they talked till midnight, when Zack said he had to get back to the hotel because he had a six thirty breakfast date with several fellow professors he hadn't seen in a while, plus he was giving the opening address at the conference at eight.

"Can I come by later, around lunchtime? Think of something to do, and I'll drive."

"Okay."

No one was more surprised than Trish when Zack leaned over and kissed her cheek. "It is so damn good to see you, Trish. I mean that."

"I do know what you mean. You make me smile. Good night, Zack. See you in the morning. I'll figure out something to do."

Trish ran upstairs and over to the mantel in her room. She reached for the wooden box and started babbling. "And he's coming back tomorrow. He liked my stuff in the Crock-Pot. At least he said he did. He has gray hair now, Malik. Like me, he misses you. I'm going to go to New York in your place over Thanksgiving, as your stand-in for their reunion. I said yes. It seemed like the right answer. I know I'm not going to be one of the guys, but I'll do my best to represent you. Just once, Malik," Trish whispered, "I wish you could give me a sign that you hear me when I talk to you. Just once. Is that too much to ask?"

She sighed as she replaced the box on the

mantel. She bent down to adjust the sound on the surround-sound system she'd had installed. She liked to fall asleep to soothing music. She stood stock-still when she heard Whitney Houston singing "I Will Always Love You."

Trish smiled through her tears. "That's good enough for me," she said, singing along with Whitney until the song ended. Then she did what she always did before she settled herself under the covers. She opened her night-table drawer and reached for a small gold-colored velvet bag. Her hands trembled as she withdrew a small bundle of Malik's hair, which Soraya had given her. She said she had kept an identical bag for herself. She said it was Rashid's idea. Trish touched the ebony curl, and as always, a tear rolled down her cheek. She clutched the curl in her hand and fell asleep. In the morning, sometimes the curl was damp when she replaced it in the gold bag.

The following morning, Trish was up at the crack of dawn. She followed her normal routine, and when Zack arrived, she was ready, dressed in mint-green capris, sandals, and a white linen blouse.

The days passed quickly as Trish showed Zack Las Vegas. They ate on the fly, they gambled, they took in a show, and she introduced him to Ernie and Bella and the kids. They had a picnic on the patch of grass in her little garden. And then it was time for Zack to leave.

"I can't believe how fast these past few days have gone by. I so enjoyed your company, Zack. Don't be a stranger now, and I promise to be a better e-mail pal. Call when you're bored. I'm getting to the point where I'm tired of hearing my own voice. I'm thinking of getting a dog or a cat. What do you think?" Trish asked as she pulled to the curb at the airport.

"Go to the SPCA. They're always looking for people to adopt. Just stand there, and the animals will find you. I have a cat from the SPCA. I call her Tootsie because that's what they said her name was. She sleeps on my bed, on the other pillow."

"A cat, huh?"

"Go figure!" Zack laughed as he got out of the car. Trish popped the trunk, and he hefted his bag out. They stood for a moment before Zack hugged her and planted a big kiss on her cheek. "I had a really great weekend. Thanks, Trish."

"Call when you get home safe and sound," Trish said, clearly flustered.

"Yes, Mother," Zack drawled. He waved as he swept through the door someone was holding open for him. Trish waved back.

On the way back to her town house, Trish let her thoughts roam. She'd had such a good time this weekend. She realized what a recluse she'd become. It was time to do something about that. Even if it was just deviating from her pattern of living. Maybe she needed to start grilling instead of relying on the Crock-Pot every day. Maybe she should work in the garden late in the day instead of early in the morning.

Maybe she needed to *get a job.*

It hit her then, what Zack had said. She sat bolt upright behind the wheel and took the next turn off the highway, which would take her to the SPCA. She did exactly what Zack had told her to do. She stood still and looked around. When a mangy cat approached her, hissing and snarling, she dropped to her haunches and defied the animal to either bite or scratch her. It did neither. It simply lay down at her feet. Trish bellowed at the top of her lungs, "I'll take this one!" From there, she went to the dog kennel and did the exact same thing. When a skinny, big-eyed dog walked on wobbly legs over to her and looked up at her, she smiled. "Okay, fella, guess you're mine, too." She bellowed again, "I'll take this one!"

An hour later, she had both animals in

her car. They both stank to high heaven. She headed right for a vet who was three blocks from where she lived. She lugged both crates into the office, explained the situation, and said, "I'll wait."

To pass the time, she walked next door to a pet store that was attached to the veterinary office and loaded up her trunk with gear. Everything a dog or a cat would need forever. She eyed the dog food, bought a small amount, not liking the way it looked. "Looks like rabbit poop," she said to the salesgirl.

"Yes, but it's good for them," the young woman responded.

"My mother used to cook chicken livers for our dog," Trish said. The salesgirl winced.

Trish thought about her earlier promise to give up on the Crock-Pot. Not so fast. She could now put it to better use. She could cook for the two animals and make sure she got veggies into them, along with pure meat or chicken and no preservatives.

Damn if she wasn't on a roll.

Trish was back in the vet's office just as one of the aides was walking the dog and the cat out to her on leashes. "Here they are. Daisy put up a bit of a fuss, but she's superclean now, with all the fleas gone, and

Stanley didn't have any fleas. We gave them their shots, so they might sleep when you get them home."

"Is Daisy the cat?" Trish asked inanely.

"Yes, ma'am."

"That means you're Stanley," Trish said, scratching the dog behind the ears.

Trish paid the bill as the girl took both animals out to the car.

Trish made one more stop. She pulled into the driveway of Kickin' Stickin' Chicken and bought a whole chicken to go. Then she got six cod filets. Daisy and Stanley howled and hissed the rest of the way home as they fought to get to the boxes, which she'd put under her legs so they couldn't reach them.

The next several hours passed in a nightmare as Trish struggled with all the gear, feeding the animals, setting up the litter boxes, and putting down pee pads until the dog could get the hang of things. By five o'clock, she poured herself a giant glass of wine and sat down to try to enjoy it. She gobbled a chicken leg and wondered if she'd made a mistake in getting two animals. Especially two who didn't seem to like one another all that much.

Two hours later, owner and animals were sacked out on her couch. Daisy was purring, and Stanley was snoring gently. Trish was on her second glass of wine and feeling absolutely no pain.

The three of them slept on the couch that night. For the first time since returning from Dubai, Trish did not talk to the wooden box, nor did she weep over the dark curl of hair.

Hours later, Stanley licked her face to wake her. Trish bounded off the couch and raced to the kitchen door. Both animals barreled outside and beelined for her flower beds. She was about to yell at them to stop but stopped herself. They were just flowers, and the dog and cat needed to do what they needed to do. Her life was now changing, thanks to these new responsibilities. She'd lay down some rules soon, but for the nonce, the animals had to feel like they belonged. They were both back inside within minutes, looking at her with soulful eyes.

"Ah, yes, food. Okay, we have some chicken and fish left." The animals watched her as she prepared their food, never taking their eyes off her. "You don't ever have to worry about food, so just take your time." So much for her little speech. The two of them virtually inhaled the food, and Stanley even burped.

Trish talked to them as she pulled out her Crock-Pot and dumped in a frozen rump roast. Next went the carrots and some new potatoes and string beans. By six o'clock, there would be enough food to last the animals a few days.

Routine. She needed a routine. It would come, she was sure.

While she showered and dressed for the day, the two animals spread themselves across the doorway. Protective mode. That was what her mother used to say. She said, "When you're in the shower, you are the most vulnerable, and an animal knows it. That's why they guard the door." It made sense, because the moment she stepped out of the shower, the animals got up and went exploring.

And this, Trish Holiday Mohammed, this is your new life. She thought she could hear Malik laughing somewhere in the distance. Or maybe it was Zack who was laughing. She couldn't be sure; she just knew she liked the sound of it.

Back downstairs, the animals played and tussled with the toys she'd bought them while she called everyone she knew to tell them about her new roommates.

Zack laughed his head off as he offered pointers on cat care. "Cats are fiercely independent, so just let her do her thing until she settles into your routine."

Emma giggled, then laughed outright. "Did you buy a pooper scooper?" she asked.

Soraya and Rashid said, "Send me some pictures so I can show them to the kids."

Ernie whistled to show he approved of what she'd done, and said he and Bella would dog-sit if she ever needed a sitter. She said she would definitely need one come November, when she went to New York for the reunion.

And thus the routine began. Life moved forward, and before she knew it, life was pleasant, ordinary, and filled with laughter.

Before Trish knew it, summer was gone, her lovely flowers nothing but brown stalks. Her patch of grass was full of holes. Stanley was a digger. She didn't care. All she knew was that both Stanley and Daisy loved her, they were happy, and that made her happy.

Three days before it was time to leave for New York, Trish tried what she called "another dry run," which consisted of taking both Stanley and Daisy to Ernie's to see how they would do. The outcome was spot-on. The kids cuddled and loved them, and Bella walked Stanley three times a day. "You can leave with a light heart," she was told.

And then a surprise came by way of FedEx from Dubai, compliments of Soraya. It was a dress for the reunion.

The ladies still had your measurements, and I asked them to make you something that would blow everyone's socks off. I hope you like it.

"Wow!" was the word that escaped Trish's lips. The dress was plain, almost severe. It shrieked, "Designer label." It also bellowed, "High-end, pricey, one of a kind. You will be a knockout and the envy of everyone in the room." At the bottom of the extra-large box was a pair of shoes, nestled in tissue paper. A perfect match. But there was more — a matching beaded purse that was so exquisite, it made Trish's eyes water.

Trish raced upstairs and ripped off her clothes. All she could do was ooh and aah as she twirled this way and that way. It was all just perfect. The dress, while severe in style, was soft and clung to her slim frame. It fit her like a glove, and she absolutely loved the pumpkin-colored material. Perfect for fall.

And then a horrible thought hit her. She couldn't wear these things to a simple friendly reunion. The other women wouldn't be wearing things like this. They were all mothers with kids, who didn't spend money on themselves. How could they when they had to save for college, make mortgage and car payments? There was no way she could show up looking better than they did. She wasn't a show-off and never had been. If anything, she was a plain Jane, and who was she trying to impress, anyway? Zack?

Trish stripped down and packed everything back in the box and put it on the top shelf of her closet. Maybe someday she'd wear it. Someday far in the future.

Dressed in a dark brown suede skirt, the white suede boots Soraya had gotten her, and a white cashmere sweater, Trish walked into the room Zack had reserved at the Ritz-Carlton. She wore pearl earrings as her only jewelry. She fit right in with the other wives, whom she liked on sight. Within minutes, they were all comfortable with one another. Everyone but Zack and Trish was a couple. An hour was spent looking at all the kids' pictures, followed by comments on how this one looked older since last year. And then this was followed by what sports the kids played, what recitals everyone participated in. Trish basked in it all, glad to be a part of it.

Trish's eyes filled when Zack got up and clinked his glass for everyone's attention. He told a few stories about Malik, when they first met one another, he the rube from the farm, Malik with the dark skin in a strange land. There was laughter, some tears, and toasts to the greatest guy who had ever walked the face of the earth. Trish almost lost it right then, but Duke's wife squeezed her hand tight, and she was able to smile and nod in agreement that yes, Malik was the greatest guy ever to walk the face of the earth.

The evening ended on a high as one by one the other guys, Malik's dearest friends, shared their particular memory with her.

When it was over, Zack walked her out to the curb, where the doorman hailed a cab for her.

"I'll see you for breakfast. The others are all heading home for a day-late Thanksgiving with their parents and siblings. I was hoping we could take a drive to Princeton to see your sister."

"I'd like that. Yes, let's do that."

"Trish, you okay? Tonight wasn't too much for you, was it?"

"No, no, it wasn't too much. I'm okay. I'm really okay, Zack. I'm so glad you invited me."

"We should do this more often. You know, getting together."

"I'd like that, too. Let's plan on it, okay?"

Zack smiled. "Does that mean one of these days you're going to ring my doorbell and say, 'Here I am'? Meaning, of course, that the girl I've waited for all my life finally found me and knocked on my door."

Trish laughed. "Ya just never know." She stood on tiptoe and kissed Zack full on the lips. Zack thought he'd been kissed by a butterfly. He said so.

"See ya," Trish said, getting into the cab.

"You betcha," Zack said, grinning.

Trish turned to look out the window, then burst out laughing when she saw Zack pump his fist in the air.

"Nice going, honey."

"Yeah. You had a hand in this, didn't you, Malik?"

She heard the laughter, soft and gentle. She smiled.

"Be happy, Trish."

"Okay."

ABOUT THE AUTHOR

Fern Michaels is the *USA Today* and *New York Times* bestselling author of *Blindsided, Classified, Gotcha! Breaking News, Tuesday's Child, Late Edition, Betrayal,* and dozens of other novels and novellas. There are over seventy-five million copies of her books in print.

Fern Michaels has built and funded several large daycare centers in her hometown, and is a passionate animal lover who has outfitted police dogs across the country with special bulletproof vests. She shares her home in South Carolina with her five dogs and a resident ghost named Mary Margaret. Visit her website at www.fernmichaels.com.

The employees of Thorndike Press hope you have enjoyed this Large Print book. All our Thorndike, Wheeler, and Kennebec Large Print titles are designed for easy reading, and all our books are made to last. Other Thorndike Press Large Print books are available at your library, through selected bookstores, or directly from us.

For information about titles, please call:
  (800) 223-1244

or visit our Web site at:
  http://gale.cengage.com/thorndike

To share your comments, please write:
  Publisher
  Thorndike Press
  10 Water St., Suite 310
  Waterville, ME 04901